WHO WOULD SURVIVE?

He rode out of the central gate of the wall, lined with thousands of screaming Caths. In the great tower, surrounded by her officers, the Empress Lali watched from a royal chair.

The Mongs, across the way, were silent. They had formed a long, solid, dark line on the plain, before their camp of black tents. In front of the leading tent, on a high throne and surrounded by banners, sat a crooked figure that Blade knew must be the Khad Tambur, Shaker of the Universe.

As he waited for the man he meant to kill, he surveyed the plain about him. He saw nothing unusual.

A rider left the ranks of the Mongs and came dashing toward him. He began to circle around Blade, yelling and whooping constantly. He shook his lance at Blade. "Yieee—I am Cossa! Champion of all the Mongs. I come to slay you for my Khad."

They exchanged glances, each weighing the other. Blade said, finally: "Get on with it, then. Your Khad will be impatient." He too wanted only one thing, to kill this elusive Mong.

There was no fear in either man. No surrender. Death could be the only end . . .

THE RICHARD BLADE SERIES

HEROIC FANTASY SERIES

2

THE JADE WARRIOR

by
Jeffrey Lord

PARAMOUNT BOOKS

THE JADE WARRIOR

ISBN: 0-523-00202-5

PARAMOUNT BOOKS: distributed by David Gold & Son (Holdings) Ltd.,
15-17A Rich Industrial Estate
Crimscott Street
London SE1 5TE

THE JADE WARRIOR

J thought, privately, that if war was too serious a business to be entrusted to the generals, then the future of world civilization—and especially England's part in it—was much too important to be entrusted to scientists.

J kept his thoughts to himself.

He was an important man in his own right. As head man of M16A he was in charge of a very special branch of the Special Branch. But at the moment he was very much a third wheel at the party. He walked about the rose garden of the magnificent old mansion in Sussex and smoked his fine cigar—which he did not really care for—and sipped at the very expensive scotch—which he did like.

J was a pragmatic man, and he did not much like it when people talked above his head. Not that it was the fault of the other two men. It was his, J's, fault. He simply did not know anything about quarks and molecular reassembly. And he was worried about Richard Blade. They were getting ready to put his boy through the computer again. To send his best agent, and his good young friend, through the dimensional rift.

J did not like it. He had not liked it the first time, either, when Lord Leighton's giant computer had erred and sent Blade spinning into the X-Dimension of Alb. That had been an accident, a mistake, and they had very nearly lost Blade forever.

The three men reached the end of the rose garden and stood smoking and gazing over a box hedge at the river glinting in the moonlight. A swan slept nearby, its head tucked under its wing, and J thought of a glass swan he had had as a boy and had kept on a round mirror in his room in Dorset.

Dorset! J wished he had not thought of it. Dick Blade was in Dorset at this moment. Probably lying in the sweet smelling thyme near the Channel and making love to his Zoe.

And soon, very soon now, J would have to set the phone to shrilling in the little cottage nearby. He hated to make that phone call.

"J," said Lord Leighton, "are you moonstruck, man? I've spoken to you three times. Come, we're going back to the house for a brandy or two. Then I'll make that phone call to Downing Street for final confirmation and you can get on to Blade. Get him up to London first thing in the morning. No use wasting time now that everything is set up."

J nodded and dumped cigar ash on his dress shirt. "Yes, Lord L. Of course. We may as well as get on with it." Ordinarily he would have been a bit more tart with His Lordship and would have called him simply Leighton, not Lord L. But the presence of the third man was inhibiting. Mr. Newton Anthony was not only almost as big a boffin as Leighton himself—and Leighton was the greatest scientific brain in England—but Mr. Newton Anthony had some mysterious connection with one of the Treasury Commissions. He had procured the money that was going to propel Blade from the computer.

Mr. Newton Anthony had a very fat backside. As they went up the graveled path, J restrained an impulse to kick it. He sighed. After all it was for England. But why must it always be Blade, a boy who was so nearly like a son to him. Blade was actually thirty, but J always thought of him as a boy. J was himself sixty.

He knew very well why it must always be Blade. Because Richard Blade was the best, the most nearly perfect physical and mental specimen that they had been able to find. Out of a million files the personnel computers kicked

8

Blade's card out every time. There were times, J thought gloomily, when perfection was a curse. Not that Dick *was* perfect, of course. He was stubborn as hell and he had a murderous temper. And he liked the ladies just a little too well.

Ahead of him Mr. Newton Anthony was waxing philosophical.

"Solipsism, to me, has never seemed a tenable position. Tempting, yes. Oh, indeed yes. Very tempting. But the theory that the self is the only existent thing is not tenable. Why, it's very near to blasphemy. Rather like saying that the whole world, and God, dies when a single man dies."

J, following along, saw one of the security guards near a hedge. The man watched them, recognized them, then retreated into the shadows. J smiled to himself. Someone had to take care of the practical things. He had a hundred men around the place.

Leighton's unction, as he answered, made J a little ill. The old man was actually clinging to the fat fool's arm, as much as hanging on every word. J, who knew the old scientist well and liked him in spite of all their differences, knew what the effort must have cost him. Lord L had more brains in his poor wracked hump than Mr. Newton Anthony had in his whole fat head. Not that the man was really a fool, of course. He was one of the big boffins. But need he be such a pompous bastard?

But as they entered the house and made their way into a great high-ceilinged study where a discreet servant waited, Mr. Newton Anthony made rather a good point. J, who was a fair man, had to acknowledge it.

"And yet this Richard Blade, when you have altered the molecular structure of his brain with the computer, and sent him into the new dimension, will be a viable example of solipsism. He *will* contain an entire new world, or even a cosmos, in himself. In relation to ourselves back in this dimension, of course. It will be most interesting to see, Lord Leighton, just how your experiments with the chronos computer and the memory-expanding drug have worked out. And I will admit that I have not yet quite grasped the theory. You people are so damned secretive, you know."

J sighed and went to sit by a green phone at one end of the long center table. No help for it. Lord L was going to have to explain it again. Of course only *he* really understood it.

The servant gave them all brandy. Mr. Newton Anthony lit another fat cigar. J declined, as he was feeling more than a little ill. He watched the old man with compassion. Lord Leighton looked like the sick and overworked man he was. He was a hunchback and polio had struck him early in life, he scuttled like a crab rather than walked, and his evening clothes hung on him. His hair was snow white and thin enough to disclose a wrinkled pink scalp. It was his eyes that carried his spirit. They were large and yellow, lion-like, streaked with red, and at the moment they could barely conceal their loathing for Mr. Newton Anthony. Lord L knew that only *he* could understand his "memory stretching" theory. He was bone weary and wanted to get this over with and get to bed.

J took a deep breath and held it. Leighton was set to go off like a pneumatic fuse. J raised his glass of brandy to conceal his expression. If the old man blew now, there might not be any money for future experiments. This trip through the computer—and God help Blade—was pretty well set up. But Lord Leighton thought like a chess master—many moves ahead.

Lord Leighton took a sip of brandy. Very softly he said: "You will remember, Mr. Anthony, that Richard Blade had trouble with his memory his first time through the computer. I thought I had explained all that rather thoroughly?"

He was having difficulty keeping the old lion snarl from his voice. J took a hasty gulp of brandy.

Mr. Newton Anthony caught a hint of the snarl. Rather hastily he said, "Oh, that, of course I remember. I recall

10

our conversation distinctly. It is the precise technique that I do not recall. Just how you enlarge Blade's memory, how you 'stretched it,' as it were, and provided him with this memory reservoir?"

Lord Leighton lit a cigar with fingers that were like yellow claws, then continued. "Blade began to lose his memory almost as soon as he landed in the X-Dimension. We use that term for convenience. Actually it was in a land, or world if you will, called Alb. Blade did not, you understand, lose his memory totally either way. Going into Dimension X or coming out of it. But his memory was very bad. He could remember very little of our dimension while he was in Alb, and when he returned to us he could remember very little of Alb. Some things, of course, but not many. Obviously something had to be done."

"Obviously," said Mr. Newton Anthony, then looked as he wished he had not spoken.

"Since the whole purpose of these explorations through the computer is to acquire knowledge—treasure perhaps, but knowledge first, by which I mean the possible exploitation of civilizations that have acquired a vaster knowledge than our own. And I must admit that in this the journey to Alb was certainly a failure. Still, none of it is much good if our messenger cannot remember what he sees and learns and then bring it back. On Blade's first journey through the dimensional rift it did not make much difference. But I could not risk it again.

"I had to begin work on the memory molecule, Mr. Anthony. And I did, at once. I tried everything. I used known techniques and I invented my own. I tried any number of combinations of disciplines, even complex permutations of the portmanteau theory, in which Blade himself would have to consciously do the work. But this I really did not want—that Blade should have to consciously remember. I wanted to create an automatic memory and a storage well, so that Blade could be left free to fight for his existence in whatever new dimension he lands this time.

11

"I isolated the memory molecule, Mr. Anthony, and I borrowed a drug from the Americans, something called pentylenetetrazol—"

Here J winced and had a large drink of brandy.

"I also borrowed—some might say stole—a great deal of data on the famous 598 rat experiment." Lord Leighton chuckled a little evilly. "We scientists can be just as big thieves as any other profession, including burglars, and when I finally had what I wanted I invented the chronos computer—not to be confused with the dimensional computer—and I stuck it on poor Blade's head like a ladies hair dryer. For three months I subjected his molecular structure to moderate heat and intense pressure.

"And it worked. Now, when Blade's brain is addled by the computer, for that is as good a word as any, and he is enabled to see and experience a dimension that we cannot, even though it might be in this very room with us in a spatial sense, his memory molecules will stand firm. They will even be improved. And as a bonus there is the memory tank. Blade will make no conscious effort to remember anything, yet he will forget nothing. He will not even know that he has remembered it. And when he returns from Dimension X I shall simply tap that memory tank and pour the stuff out of him like wine out of a barrel!"

J smiled. For once Mr. Newton Anthony was looking more impressed than pompous. Before he could interrupt, Lord Leighton went on: "Now, sir, if we can make that call to Downing Street for final clearance! I am a very weary old man and I want to go to bed. I must be in London early tomorrow."

"I should certainly think we can," said Anthony, and picked up a phone in front of him.

The conversation was brief. Mr. Newton Anthony hung up and nodded to J. "It's on. You may call your man Blade now."

J picked up the green phone. The Treasury boffin said: "I should like to meet this Richard Blade before he goes through the computer. I cannot begin to imagine what sort of man he is."

J shook his head sternly. "Very few people can. For the simple reason that there *are* no others like him. But you can't meet him, sir. Strictly against security regulations. Sorry."

He dialed a single digit on the green phone.

2

Blade had slipped off Zoe's very brief panties and flung them to one side in the tall growing thyme and heather. By now they were dew sodden.

He put down an old mack, in a small depression along the cliff top that Zoe called "Blade's Snuggery," and after making love for the first time they lay close together and, by looking down a sort of winze, could see the Channel. It lay broad and flat, dead calm but for a fleck of lace here and there, and marred only by the lights of a freighter, far out, beating up to Thamesmouth. Just below them, on a ledge, gulls stirred and ruffled and dreamed their gull's dreams. The surf was only froth on shingle. The moon sailed away from them, a silver galleon showing its high stern in disdain.

Blade, his mouth against Zoe's ear—as small and soft and velvety as a pet mouse—said: "The moon is fair tonight along the Straits."

She had taken her mouth from his and turned away, and now she stirred but did not turn back to kiss him again. She muttered: "And idiot armies struggle on the darkling plain."

It was a game they often played, quoting and requoting from a favorite poem, and her reply was not exactly what Blade had expected. She had not used the word love. And she nearly always did, when she could. Love. For, of, about, to, Richard Blade. Not this night. Zoe had not, even in the last gasping throes of passion, murmured that she loved him.

13

Blade, dark-muscled giant that he was, was acute without being particularly intellectual. In many ways he was a sensitive man, an image belied by his rugged good looks and his outsize, Greek athlete's body. He was as tough as concrete, an efficient killer in England's service, and one of the best secret agents in the world.

Had been. Lord Leighton's computer had changed all that.

Now he kissed her ear and said, "What is it, Zoe? What's wrong? Something is wrong, I've known it all day."

She went tense for a moment, then relaxed.

"Who is Taleen?" she asked.

For a moment he really did not know. His memories of Alb were faint, tenuous, like smoke drifting and disappearing, faint beacons flashing for an instant and then doused in black. Lord L had explained it. His memory molecules could not restore the past.

Taleen? Taleen—the ghost came then, for a breath, a shimmer of golden girl flesh, a savage little mouth slashing at his, an imperious cry of passion somewhere in limbo.

Zoe said? "You don't answer me, Richard." She had been calling him Richard all day, not Dick.

He could not answer her. The brief carnal phantom vanished and he did not *know* who Taleen was. Had he ever known?

"I don't know anyone named Taleen," he said. "Should I? Why are you asking?"

When he touched her again she went rigid and pulled away, but her voice was calm. Zoe was always calm, except in passion.

"Really, Richard, I wish you wouldn't try to deceive me. I deserve better than that. So do you. We're neither of us fools, nor lying children. If you've found another woman for God's sake tell me, just simply tell me, and that will be that. I am not a clinger, you know. I don't make scenes. But after what we have had of each other I think I deserve honesty. That's why I am so puzzled and

14

hurt, really. I know you are honest, just as I know you are a gentleman—and that is why I cannot understand."

"Can't understand what, Zoe? For God's sake! What is this all about? You have been sulking underneath all day, and when I ask why, suddenly you come up with a name! Taleen? I suppose it's a name. And I don't know what in hell you're talking about!"

Did he know? What just now, faster than light, had pressed against his brain? A golden-orbed and blue-painted breast? Gone.

He pulled Zoe to him in an embrace that was nearly savage. She cried out. "Dick! Please—you're hurting me." For the first time today she had called him Dick.

"I'm sorry, honey." Yet he held her firmly, made her turn to face him so their eyes glinted close in the moonlight. "But you've got to tell me what this is all about, Zoe. It is all getting a little crazy, you know. Barmy as hell!"

Lord L would know, of course, and Lord L must be asked and made to tell. Was the giant computer, and the subsequent memory treatments, affecting his brain permanently? That could wait. Right now he was in deep trouble with the woman he loved.

"All right," said Zoe. Some of the hurt left her voice. "Maybe it was only a nightmare. Maybe I'm only a jealous fool. After all, Richard, I have never known you to lie to me."

She still called him Richard.

"Last night, Richard, after we had been in bed an hour or so, you began to make love to a woman named Taleen. You woke me up by threshing about and calling her name. You were going through the actual physical motions of love—sweating and groaning and crying. And you—you—" She broke off her words and looked at him.

Blade stared at her, stunned and a little afraid. "Why didn't you wake me, for God's sake?"

"I couldn't. I tried. Don't you think I tried! But I was afraid of you, afraid of being smashed. I know how pow-

15

erful you are, and how gentle you are, at least always with me, but last night you were a different man. I had never seen that man before and I did not like him. I hated him! You were a great ravening savage brute, Richard, and I was frightened to death. Finally I just slipped out of bed and watched from a corner until it was over."

"How long?"

"At least half an hour. When you had finally spent, actually spent, you sighed and rolled over and went back to sleep like a tired baby."

He had had time to think now and knew that this scene was only an entry into another—to others. This storm had been brewing for a long time and now it was going to break. He tried the light note.

"All it means, love, is that I had a particularly realistic nightmare, an erotic dream, and you had the bad luck to witness it."

He smiled at her, so close, their eyes mirroring. The smile that J, with his acerbic tongue, sometimes alluded to as the *coup de grâce*.

"It also means," said Blade, "that I am a lousy lover. A selfish pig that cares only for my own satisfaction. A pig that rolls over and snores without even a goodnight kiss. Now I ask you, darling, is that the Blade you know? Even if there were another woman, which there isn't—and I swear that on the Queen and my own sainted mother— would I treat *her* like that? Even in a dream? So you see it was only a nightmare. Someone else's nightmare. Not me at all. I think we had best just forget it. Come sweets, and give a kiss, and I'll pay you back threefold."

This time the quote did not work. The smile did not work. The famous Blade charm did not work. Zoe turned her face away from his.

"I think we had best *not* forget it, Richard. The nightmare, yes. You are probably right and it was only that. I am a little fool and there is no other woman named Taleen. It *is* an odd name, though. To imagine, dream up, even in a nightmare!"

16

Even the best, the sweetest, of them have nasty claws. Blade sighed and closed his eyes against the moonlight, plucked a stalk of heather and chewed on it, and silently goddamned Lord L and all the boffins, and computers, and J and M16A, and especially damned himself as far back as Oxford for having let himself be recruited there. He damned the concept of duty and knew he could never refute it. Most especially he damned, to the nethermost regions of the darkest pit, the Official Secrets Act. There was never any release from it. Not ever. Even if duty and country and decency did not deter—the Act did. They had you forever. You opened your mouth once, one faint whisper, and they hung you. Even J would do it. And J loved him like a son.

Zoe was speaking quietly. "Until a few months ago, Richard, you were asking me to marry you."

And so he had been. He had loved her then and he loved her now. He gritted his teeth and was silent. The gulls fluttered on their ledge. The moon sailed away to adventure. Blade waited. He might yet get out of this one, but it was going to be a near thing. Christ! He didn't want to lose this woman.

"I wouldn't at first," she went on, "because of a number of things. There was no rush, I didn't know very much about you, and I wasn't sure if I loved you enough for marriage. Then, when I was sure, and loved you desperately, you stopped asking. Just like that."

Blade groaned aloud.

Quickly she leaned to kiss his cheek. Her lips were chill and in her voice was a subtle note of change as she said: "Poor darling. Does it hurt so much?"

She was not, he knew, alluding to any physical pain. She had her lovely little sharp talons in him now and she was going to rend a little, just to even matters up.

"You disappear for long periods of time, Richard. You never give me any excuses, I'll say that for you. You just disappear and then come back with strange marks and scars on you, and an odd look in your eye, and you walk

17

in and expect me to pick right up where we left off. And I do. I always have, so far. I hop right into bed and I love it. But I can't love it forever, you know. I'm a woman. I want to get married and have children and have a husband I see every day. And every night. You won't even tell me what you really do for a living!"

Blade squinted up at her and made the effort. "Come off it, Zoe. You know what I—"

She put a cool hand over his lips. "Bureau of Economic Planning. Whitehall."

It was a new cover, one that J had dreamed up since the computer experiments began.

"I asked about your *real* job, Richard. That Bureau thing is only what they call a cover in the thrillers. I've looked into it. Father has friends, I have friends, and all our friends have friends. It wasn't so hard, really. You have got an office in Whitehall, and a pretty little thing as a secretary, and you spend about one hour a week there, signing papers that mean nothing."

Blade closed his eyes again. Somewhere a cuckoo sang a last sad parting note. Wait until J heard about this! The plumbing was leaking. It had, of course, been a hasty setup.

Zoe leaned to kiss him softly on the mouth. Her lips were warm again. "Dick. Sweetheart. If you are some sort of secret agent, doing some sort of dreadfully mysterious and dangerous work, why don't you just simply tell me? Just one word. I'll understand and never ask another question."

Hah!

"I can't tell you," he said. "I can't tell you anything at all."

"Not even yes or no?"

"Not anything."

There was silence. The cuckoo cried a last time. Zoe was leaning over him, her marvelous taut breasts touching his face.

"All right," Zoe said at last. "Will you marry me, then?

18

Right away. I love you so much that I'll settle for just that. Marry me and I'll try my best not to be a hindrance to you in whatever it is you do."

"I can't marry you."

When the computer thing began they voided his old Official Secrets Act and had made him sign a new one—with a special codicil. No marriage. J was the best security man in all Europe and he did not trust bedsprings, even connubial ones.

Zoe drew away from him. "You can't marry me? Or won't marry me?"

"Can't. I—"

They heard the phone ringing in the cottage then, a hundred yards back from the cliff, shrill and angry in the quietness.

Zoe stood up abruptly and starting brushing off her skirt. "I'm not expecting a call."

"I am. Come on. I'll carry you."

Blade snatched her up and ran down the path, carrying her as effortlessly as a man carries a kitten. There was a four-step stile just at the turnoff to the cottage and he took it in stride, vaulting the high stone like a thoroughbred at the National.

Zoe cried out. "You fool. You'll cripple both of us!"

Ordinarily she would have loved it.

There was no particular hurry. Blade knew the phone would keep ringing. It did.

The phone was in the bedroom. Blade flung Zoe on the bed in a flurry of skirts and long bare legs and went to answer it. It was an ordinary black phone with no scrambler attachment.

"Hello."

"Hello, dear boy. How are things?" J's tone was bland and calm as the Channel a hundred yards away. He sounded as if he were about to invite Blade to tea the next day.

"Things might be a little better," Blade said. He glanced at Zoe on the bed. She had arranged her skirt and

19

was regarding him with an odd little smile, her chin cupped in her hand. A reclining Mona Lisa.

"My dear fellow," said J, "I hope I haven't interrupted anything." J sounded as though he actually meant it.

"Only a blazing quarrel, sir. Nothing to worry about. What is it? Is the deal going through?"

"It is," said J. "First thing in the morning. Can you be at your office in Whitehall to sign the necessary papers? Quite early?"

"Right, sir. I'll be there." He hung up.

Blade went to a closet to get his light suitcase, very conscious of Zoe's dark eyes on him.

"Off again, darling?"

He nodded, still without looking at her, and began to toss things into the suitcase. He hadn't brought much down from London this time.

"When shall I see you again?"

At last he could be honest. "I don't know. And I'm not being evasive, Zoe. I just have no way of knowing when I will see you again."

He was about to add—perhaps not ever, but cut it off in time. That would be cruel. She loved him. She was going to imagaine things anyway, but at least they would be in the realm of ordinary human fears. Bad enough. Tell her he was going into a new dimension, with only a fifty-fifty chance of ever getting back, and she would go mad. Or think he was. And anyway there was the ACT.

Blade said: "I have to do a little job. I can't say when it will be finished."

"Dick!"

He turned and she was holding out her arms to him, her eyes moist and her mouth trembling. He went to her. It was like one of those beautifully done scenes in the silent movies when no word is spoken and no shred of meaning lost.

She pulled him down on top of her. He took her tenderly, then with a rising lust and ardent savagery,

20

matched by her own, until the peak was reached and they could be tender again.

Blade did not tarry. He left her crumpled and pale and completed, weeping a little, and went away.

3

He entered London with the dawn. He drove straight to the Tower—J had meant him to read Tower for Whitehall—and found J waiting for him by the site of the old Water Gate. J was wearing a Burberry against the morning chill and smoking his pipe. The harsh morning light made him look older than sixty, and the sacs under his eyes were a flaccid purple.

Two burly Special Branch types were waiting for them near a postern. As they headed for it Blade looked at the head of M16A and asked, "There is no possible way out of the Official Secrets Act, sir? Ever?"

J's eyes were compassionate above their fleshy bags. In a tired voice he said, "But of course there is, my dear boy. Death."

The Special Branch men took them down a long ramp and into a tunnel that emerged in a maze of subbasements and, finally, to the bronze elevator door that Blade remembered so well. Even J was not permitted beyond this point when an X-Dimension experiment was GO.

They shook hands briefly. J looked as weary, and worried, as Blade had ever seen him. He had little to say.

"Good luck, my boy. Seems strange to say this—where you're going—but don't worry about things here. You've signed all the proper papers and your affairs are in order. I'll take care of everything in the event—"

They were standing a little aside from the armed guards, waiting for the elevator to come up. Blade smiled at his boss and half whispered, "I've been thinking about that, sir. In the event—I'll just be a non-person, won't I? That should cause a sweat over at Somerset House."

It was an effort, more than anything, to cheer the old

21

chap up a bit. Blade had never seen him looking so miserable.

J took him seriously. "It will be arranged, my boy. It will be taken care of. Here's your lift. Good-bye."

Ten minutes later Richard Blade, wearing only the usual loincloth, followed Lord Leighton into the master computer room. The hunchbacked old scientist, in a soiled white smock, hobbled on polio-ruined legs through a maze of lesser computers. Blade, with a feeling of some revulsion, listened to the song of the future: *One-oh—one—oh—one-oh-one-oh—*. Binary logic. *Be-bop-be-bop-be-bop-be-bop—*. Milliseconds that would soon be nanoseconds. One billionth of a second. Spinning magnetic drums and tiny bulbs flashing GO-GO-GO-GO.

It was most certainly GO. They entered the small room where the dimensional computer waited like a gray crackled Moloch. Blade had not been in this room since his first trip through the computer. It had not changed. There were the thousands of multicolored wires running through portholes into the penetrailia of the vast machine. There was the small square of floor covered with rubberized fabric. There was the glass booth and the chair that always reminded Blade of an electric chair.

And yet everything had changed. Lord L, as he applied tar-smelling ointment to Blade's huge body, waved a fragile hand at the monster.

"Completely rebuilt. Radical changes. The old one was only sixth generation—this one is at least eight. Skipped one, you see."

Blade, who knew that conventional computers were only in the third generation, was impressed. This crippled old genius was already five generations ahead of the rest of the world in cybernetics. That in itself, with all its implications, should get England back in the race. Was this trip really necessary?

He was in the chair now and the old man was carefully

taping the shiny electrodes to Blade's flesh. They were the size of a shilling and shaped like a cobra's head.

Lord Leighton finished the job and flashed his tawny eyes at Blade. "You're nervous. Much more so than the first time out. Afraid?"

Blade was not a liar. "Yes sir. A bit. The first trip was an error. It happened so fast I had no time to anticipate. I hadn't had time to tense up and I didn't know where I was going."

Lord Leighton patted his shoulder and said, with perfect logic, "You don't know where you're going this time, either. Do you now? But don't let it worry you, my boy. I have made the most complex calculations and the matter is now quite proved out. I'll have you back all in good time. In the meantime you must remember—make no conscious *effort* to remember! The memory molecule will take care of all that. Ready?"

"As ever I'll be," said Blade grimly. "Get on with it, then."

Lord Leighton closed a switch.

The first time there had been pain. Great slashing scarlet pain. This time there was no pain, only a huge and relentless hand pressing him beneath tons of water. He could not breathe and it did not matter. He did not need to breathe. He was hurtling through a vacuum filled with thunder. Silent thunder that he felt but could not hear.

Richard Blade began to disintegrate. He watched the process with a cold part of his brain that did not care. He felt nothing. He was not interested. He was bored with it all. He saw his hands fall off and his feet detach. His head left his body, which by now was impaled on an icicle the size of the Empire State building. His head circled the body, which was still coming apart, like the planes after King Kong. His belly had split now and his viscera were coming out like pink and blue ribbons and getting tangled in the buzzing planes.

He saw the fist coming. A fist the size of the world.

23

Blade's floating head could not duck. It could only wait. He smiled. What did it matter? It was only a fist. The size of the world.

The fist slammed into him and at last there was pain.

Chapter 2

Richard Blade lay for a time, face down, on rocks that were still hot. Hot from a sun that had passed its zenith so long ago that now dark shadows lapped his naked body. He lay unmoving, without a tremor, scarcely breathing. He was in X-Dimension once more and there would be danger. Wherever he was, whatever *it* was, there was danger. He must begin the slow and difficult process of orientation. He was allowed no mistakes.

Without moving his head he examined the terrain immediately before him, and to both sides. Blade had tremendous peripheral vision—one of the many reasons he had survived so long in the murderous game of espionage—and he saw that he was in a cup-shaped depression. Lying on sun-heated rock and surrounded by a ring of tall jagged boulders.

The rock beneath him was lightly dusted with sand. He gathered some in his fingers and brought it close to his eyes. Black. Fine and black.

Wind gusted through the rocky bowl, sandblasting his eyes and face and enormous rugged body. Borne on the wind was sound—a rising and ferocious din of battle. It could be nothing else. Blade had known battle and he recognized the cries and curses of men trying to kill each other. And yet another sound! He put his ear to the rock and listened intently. Horses. Many hundreds, or thousands, of horses careening across the earth not far away.

Now trumpets, brazen and haunting on the wind that scoured him. Trumpets and a new high screaming of frenzied men. Men in pain. Men dying. Men defeated. Men victorious.

WHOOMPP! A new sound. A gun. By the sound of it a giant cannon of some sort. It had a deep, hollow, bell-like sound that Blade had never heard before.

For the moment he judged himself safe. It was time to see as well as hear. He crawled on hands and knees to the barricade of tall rearing boulders, going against the wind that still howled in his little shelter. He found a crevice in the rocks and peered cautiously out.

Blade had marvelous sense of direction and he placed himself immediately in relation to the battle raging beneath him on a broad and far-flung plain. He was a mile to the rear of the fighting and he reckoned his elevation at about two hundred feet. For a man with Blade's eyesight every detail was plain. He began to study the frenetic bloody scene that unrolled beneath him like some vast panoramic painting.

A mile beyond his vantage point a great wall undulated along the horizon like a yellow snake. Blade drew in his breath and shrugged his big shoulders in admiration. He was impressed. That wall must be fifty feet high, broad enough for four horsemen to ride abreast, and it had no end. It stretched away to either side as far as Blade's keen eyes could see. It simply vanished into distance.

Before a sector of the wall nearest Blade the fighting raged more fiercely. Hordes of horsemen raced back and forth before the wall, firing arrows from peculiarly short bows, all the time screaming in a high savagery that set Blade's teeth on edge. Bad tactics, though. What could horsemen hope to achieve against the wall?

"Like trying to kill an elephant with an air gun," he muttered to himself. What could they hope to gain.

A moment later he saw. The attackers were trying to taunt the defenders into a sortie. Blade smiled. Surely they would not be fools enough to—

They were. He watched, incredulous, as a huge gate in the wall swung open. Horsemen and men on foot rushed out. The attackers screamed in triumph and charged in. The two forces met with a clangorous shock that made Blade wince, even at his distance.

The melee was brief and bloody. Men and horses went down in scarlet heaps. Spears and arrows arced and glinted in the fading light—there was a nacreous tint to the air now—and there was no quarter given. Men killed and were killed in the act of killing.

A gutted horse, riderless, broke away and galloped within bowshot of the hidden Blade. It was a small sturdy beast with a wild mane and very long hair. Just beyond Blade's vantage the horse stopped, and began to graze on sparse grass growing from the black earth.

Farther down the wall a new horde of attackers were trying to raise scaling ladders. They were on foot, hundreds of them, rushing in with long narrow ladders and covered by the fire of bowmen. The defenders on the wall greeted them with spears and arrows and heavy stones. Great cauldrons of boiling oil were poured down on the few ladders that went up. The attack broke and retreated.

The party that had sortied out was now also retreating. It was continually attacked by the charging horsemen. The defenders fought their way back into the gate, covered by murderous spear and arrow fire, and boiling oil, and at last the ponderous gate swung shut.

Blade saw the gun. His eyes widened. It was enormous. He had never seen anything like this gun. He guessed the muzzle to be six feet across. It must be fifty feet long. Hundreds of men were tugging it up a ramp behind the wall.

Blade watched with something akin to awe. It was one hell of an impressive gun, yes, but how did they expect to hit anything with it? It was tilted at an impossible angle and it was not even aimed at the attackers' camp, a vast cluster of black tents off to Blade's right.

A moment later he understood. They were firing the huge gun for effect.

Whoommph—Boinggg—

The muzzle flash was tremendous. Great clouds of black smoke billowed up and cloaked the wall and the defenders. Blade, a little amused now, saw the projectile leave the huge maw of the cannon and begin to sail. Toward him.

The trajectory was so high, and the muzzle velocity so slow, that he had ample time to observe the effect of the gun on the attackers. They broke and ran, on horse and foot, screaming defiance and shaking their weapons at the wall and the gun, but running nevertheless.

Blade grinned. The gun worked in a fashion.

He watched the projectile coming his way. It reached apogee and began the swift fall to nadir. It was going to strike very near him. Blade moved a bit uneasily. The thing was damned big. It looked like a good-sized meteorite coming to slash at the earth's hide. In the last minisecond Blade noticed something very strange about it. It was transparent. It was green and he could see through it.

The great ball smashed into a boulder fifty yards from Blade with tremendous sound. He flattened himself and cringed in the shelter of lesser rocks. No one had ever called him a coward—or a fool.

The thing exploded in a shower of cruel green shards that sang about Blade's head. One great jagged fragment missed him by inches, a long glittering sword of green that would have decapitated him.

It was over. Blade reached for one of the small bits that had landed near him. He stared in utter disbelief. Jade! Jade such as he had never seen in his life, and he knew much of jade. His father had had a fabulous collection.

But this jade was beyond belief. A stone that was so transparent he could see his hand beyond it, a green that outshone all the seas, that could not be imagined and must be seen.

Jade cannon balls.

It was dark!

Just like that it was dark. As though someone had switched off a light.

28

Of all things, Blade had not been prepared for this. He had noticed the graying of the day, the pearling, without giving it much thought. There would be twilight and then darkness and then he meant to venture out onto the plain and find himself some clothes and a weapon.

So it was dark. Blade shrugged and stood erect. He dropped the bit of jade. It couldn't be very valuable if they used it to make cannon balls. But this was X-Dimension where the sun just dropped out of sight and—

And the moon came up! Just as speedily. Someone had turned on the light again.

It was a half moon lying on its back high over the black tents of the attackers. Fires, hundreds of them, were springing into life on the plain now. Dark silhouettes moved to and fro before the fires and he heard a faint sound of singing. He glanced toward the wall. Torches were moving along the broad roadway atop it.

No need to ponder. It was all going into the memory tank for Lord L to siphon out when he wished. When— or if—Blade got back.

That was the prime objective. Explore, observe, survive. Become a habitué of this particular X-Dimension, wherever and whatever, and wait until Lord L snatched him back. That was his duty. His job. And he might as well get on with it.

Richard Blade, as naked as the day he came wailing from the womb, cautiously stepped from his sheltering rocks and began to descend to the battlefield below him. He made his way in the direction of the great wall, allowing instinct to guide him. Something in his brain whispered that his best chance for survival lay beyond that wall.

Chapter 3

As Blade drew near the wall he began to encounter the corpses of men and horses. Here they were piled thick atop each other, there scattered thinly, and one thing he noted above all. There were no wounded. They were all dead. If the defenders had left wounded behind them when they withdrew behind their wall the attackers had killed them before being scattered by the giant cannon. Already a sickly stench was beginning to rise from the hundreds of corpses, a nostril-wrinkling miasma rising like mist.

Yet life other than himself moved among the dead. He heard them at first, a stealthy retreat before him, and the gobbling sound of feeding. Jackals? Hyenas?

The moon shone out of cloud rack and he saw they were neither. Eyes flashed red at him and white fangs snarled and there was a scampering. Apes! Small flesh-eating apes.

He was looking for clothes, and armor and a weapon, and he may as well have the best. He began to examine the dead in the intervals of bright moonlight, keeping low and skulking like one of the strange apes. He saw at once that the enemies were of two contrasting physical types. Two of them, a little apart from the others, made a perfect paradigm. They lay close in death, each with a sword in the other's heart, each grinning at the moon they could not see. Blade bent to inspect them closely.

One, of the party that had sallied from the wall, was tall and well formed and even in death had a certain dignity. His skin, as best Blade could see in the uncertain light, was a light yellow. Lemon colored. His armor glinted in the moonlight, and Blade thought it bronze until he touched it. Wood! Very hard and finely carved wood. He scraped it with a nail. It was paint that made it appear bronze.

The companion in death was a swarthy man with thick dark hair, very coarse in texture. He was short and bow-legged and powerfully muscled. He wore leather chest armor and on his head was a pointed leather cap. His breeches were of skin, and he wore knee-high boots fashioned from the same animal hide. Blade stared down at him for a moment. The legs told the story. Bowed and powerful. Horseman.

One of the carrion apes, bolder than the others, glowered at Blade and began to feed on a body not ten feet away. An arrow lay nearby. Blade picked it up and flung it at the beast, which retreated with a snarl and a flash of defiant fangs. As Blade stared after it, a glint of gold caught his eye. Something about the corpse the ape had been about to devour. Blade went to see.

This man, one of the wall defenders, was wearing gold-painted armor. On his chest plate was painted a golden orb of some sort, possibly a moon, and on his shoulders he wore what Blade recognized as epaulets. But it was the thick golden chain around the dead man's throat that convinced Blade. He tugged at it, found a catch, and loosened it. It was of woven gold, many plaited, and of exquisite workmanship. This had been a man of consequence.

Why not? Blade smiled grimly as he began to strip the body. As long as he was going to be a ghoul he might as well travel first-class. The dead man had obviously been one of rank and prestige—and that same rank just might help Blade get behind the wall.

The man was wearing a short silken tunic beneath his armor. Blade covered his own nakedness and began to don the armor. Here he ran into trouble. The dead man

31

was as tall as Blade, but with none of his brawn. Blade could not get the corselet to fasten around his massive chest. To hell with it then. He found a helmet nearby, also with the golden orb painted on it, and placed it on his head. It fitted well enough and reminded him of ancient Greek helmets. There were nasal and ear plates and a high arching panache of the same silken stuff as the underrobe. Blade nodded. His face was well enough concealed. As an afterthought he scooped blood from a gaping wound in the dead man's chest and smeared it on the visible part of his face.

He was searching for a weapon to match the splendor of the armor when he saw the lights bobbing toward him. Blade sank to the ground with a muttered curse at his own carelessness. He had been so intent on his new guise that he had been caught off guard. And yet—they had come very silently!

He turned on his face and reduced his breathing to the barest minimum. Play dead and they would soon pass him by.

It was with an eerie feeling that he heard the voices. They were the first distinct and individual voices he had heard since coming into this new land. Other than the hubbub of battle he had heard only his own voice.

A voice of command said: "Look farther over there. To the right of the pile of Mongs. And do not look for a face, fools, but rather for his armor. You all know what manner of armor the Emperor wore!"

The voice was light, high pitched, with a silky cultured quality and an odd singsong effect, like spoken music.

Blade was not interested in tonal effects. He had just gotten himself into a jam. Or had he? It might be an easy way of getting beyond the wall, though what happened then might not be so pleasant.

Another man said, "I do not think we will find the Emperor tonight, sir. We are not even sure where he fell. And if the Mongs see the lights they will come to investigate and I, for one, have had enough of fighting Mongs for one day."

The command voice: "Do as you are bid or your head will join those of the captured Mongs tomorrow. I promise you this."

Another voice: "Why is the Empress Mei so insistent that we find her husband?"

"To do his body honor, of course. What else?"

A man laughed. Blade winced.

Another man said, "And who is afraid of the Mongs? They will not fight at night. We all know this. They are afraid of the corpse spirits, the barbarians."

Command voice: "All of this chatter convinces me that you do not value your heads at all. So be it. We shall return behind the wall and I will have the Empress sign the order for your executions."

Muttering. Grumbling. Blade held his breath. Someone kicked him in the chest. Blade closed his eyes and played dead as he never had before.

No use. Light fluttered over him, a man bent to look at him, then called out softly. "Here he is. Over here. I have found the Emperor Mei."

If they take off the helmet, Blade thought, and examine me carefully, I've had it. He had no weapon and there must be at least six of them. Maybe he would have time to start talking—maybe—

Command voice was just over him now. "Yes. That is the Emperor. See the chain of office. Put him on the litter and let us go. Hurry. I do not fear Mongs but those corpse-eating apes make me nervous."

Richard Blade could be, when the occasion called for it, a superb actor. It had stood him in good stead many times and it did now. He now gave a terrific performance as the corpse of one Emperor Mei, deceased, whose widow, the Empress Mei, wanted him back to honor him. And this occasioned laughter? His brain, even as they carried his big body off the field of battle on a litter, began to click over like one of Lord L's lesser computers. He was getting into something. But what?

It was a long ride. One of the litter bearers grumbled: "I do not remember the Emperor as being so heavy. Or do the dead weigh more than the living?"

"You are a fool," said the command voice. "Desist. The sooner this task is over the sooner we can all get to our beds."

"And our women." Laughter.

Blade dared not risk even a peep. He attuned all his senses, and was aware of being taken through a postern gate in the great wall. Then through a long, echoing tunnel where torches flared and smelled of a pungent incense that Blade could not identify.

Out of the tunnel and into open air again. Into semi-darkness. Only four litter bearers and the command voice behind at some distance. Blade risked a look.

He was being carried across a vast formal garden. There were flowering shrubs and trees shaped into the forms of men and beasts and a long, shimmering black pool that cast back the reflection of the torches. They were skirting the pool, on a paved path. Blade glanced down and would have sworn the path was made of jade blocks.

Behind them the command voice said: "Hurry, you idiots. I want my dinner and bed, and the Empress wants her dead husband."

One of the bearers laughed. "Why?" More laughter.

Blade began to wonder again about this Empress Mei to whom he was soon to be introduced—as a corpse.

Command voice said: "That is none of your affair. And long noses have been cut off. Heed."

Blade restrained a grimace. They seemed to do an awful lot of cutting off of one thing or another.

A man said: "I have never seen the Empress, sir. Do you think?"

"No! The Jade Empress is not for your eyes, you fool.

34

She will not enter the Temple of the Dead until we leave. Now *will* you get on!"

They marched between a long line of flaring torches and Blade closed his eyes again. Not before he had seen a tier of gracefully ascending steps that led to a tomblike structure. Both stairs and tomb cast back glittering emerald sparks as the torchlight laved them. Everything behind this wall seemed to be made of jade.

The Jade Empress! Blade was in peril and knew it. He could very well be dead within a minute, yet he confessed to a growing desire to see what this lady was like.

He was carried into the large room and placed on a jade altar at one end. The only light came from a single torch in a sconce high up on the wall. They left him there and tramped out.

Silence. The torch guttered in a draft that wafted across the long room, bringing with it the same cloying fragrance Blade had noted before. The torch leaped and sputtered and cast its long flame sideways, tossing shadows over the altar. A door had been opened.

Blade lay on his back, his head turned just enough to allow him to survey the long room. There was nothing behind him but the blank cold wall. She must come from the opposite direction.

Movement in the clotted shadows. A small section of the wall moved and swung, noiseless, a marvel of counterbalancing, then swung back. Silence. He was no longer alone in the Temple of Death.

Through slitted eyes Blade watched the shadows. She was there, watching him, amorphous and wraithlike, yet very much a presence. He waited, trying to control his breathing. The effort was painful and his heart was thudding like a drum in his big chest. Why? This was merely a woman come to see a corpse. Why did he feel this tremendous bursting sense of excitement? It made no sense, yet there it was. He had experienced it often before, just prior to combat—or entering a woman.

Feet moved and rustled on stone and she stepped into

the light and slowly approached the altar. In one hand she carried a long curved dagger. Blade tensed. What did widows do to their husband's corpse in this strange place?

She stopped six feet from him. She gazed at the bier, her face impassive, breathing lightly, her breasts moving only slightly beneath the single garment of silken stuff that clung to her like a second skin. If there was imperfection in that body, he could not see it. In that instant he named her, in his own mind and in the context of his own dimension. Venus. Jade Venus.

She raised the dagger and pointed it at the man she thought was dead. "So, Mei Saka, it has come to this at last. They bring you to me, in this Temple of Death, and I must honor you and pretend that you were honorable. Such lies! And whom do we deceive? The common folk of no account. All others, our own kind, knew you for what you were."

Blade watched her face intently. A face men dream of when they would conjure the impossible woman.

A master craftsman had drawn that oval in one sure stroke. Blade was a connoisseur of women and he knew perfect art when he saw it. *Symmetry*. Every feature in absolute balance. The brow high and imperious, the nose fragile and patrician, the mouth finely chiseled and yet sensuous. Wet now, moist and scarlet as a little tongue flicked out like a pink snake. He felt his loins stir and respond. God! What a woman. And what a corpse *he* was!

She took a gliding step nearer to him and brandished the dagger again.

"I have come to kill you again, Mei Saka. For my own honor, not for yours. The wise say that this cannot be done, that a man can only be killed once, but I do not care for this. I *must* kill you again, Mei Saka, so that I can rest. When I have had revenge I can find content in the arms of new lovers and forget you lived."

Another step toward him. She was breathing harder now and Blade could smell the fragrance of her. The body sheath she wore was so nearly transparent that he saw her

36

breasts tautly outlined, sharp and hard, the nipples erected by her excitement and hate.

"I hope you can hear me, Mei Saka, wherever your dark soul dwells. I would have you know this—I had you killed! I knew of your plot to betray Cath and I sent one to kill you from behind. I then had that one killed so he could never betray me."

She held the dagger aloft. "It is clean now, you see, but it has been bloody. Not an hour ago I slew the second man and had his body destroyed."

Blade watched the dagger. Beautiful she was, and as dangerous as a cornered tigress. He must move soon to take control of the situation. Correctly handled it could be much to his advantage. She was high born and of station and authority—such a hostage could gain him breathing space. Time. But careful. Very careful. No mistakes.

Another long step toward him. The dagger flamed in the torchlight. For the first time he saw her eyes. Really saw them. And in them saw both heaven and hell.

Long almonds of green, narrowed but with no slantiness, wherein chrysolite seas moved and washed. Depthless pools of jasper where hate sparked and spun. Wide set, fringed by dark lashes, timeless and deathless and with promise of the Secret, they were of a purity beyond knowing. Blade, bold and bloody adventurer that he was, shivered. His body moved slightly in an involuntary movement he could not control.

She smiled. Her teeth flashed white in the dim light.

"So, Mei Saka, you do hear me? Your muscles relax in death, or so the wise would say, but I know better. You *hear* me! Then feel this, Mei Saka! You have been killed once, to save Cath. I, the Empress Mei, kill you again. For revenge!"

She was so fast that Blade nearly took the dagger in his heart after all. She came in a rush as fast as a heartbeat. Blade moved sideways and caught at her descending wrist and pulled her close to him and their faces were an inch apart.

"Don't scream," Blade said softly. "Make no sound. I will not harm you."

Those incredible eyes stared into his. Her mouth opened slowly, a pink cavern of shock and fear. She made no sound. She fell against him, lax and supple, and he felt the glow of her body on his own.

They stared, one at the other. A caught second of time that had no ending. Eternity in a single breath.

Blade moved a big hand toward her mouth and whispered, "No sound. Let me speak."

Those wondrous eyes closed and she fell slowly into his arms.

Chapter 4

She was out cold. Fainted dead away. Blade deftly swung off the bier-altar and lifted her onto it in his stead. The long eyes were closed now and it was a relief, as if someone had switched off the current, unwound the charm. He picked up the dagger and examined it. No wood here. Or jade. Good steel. Another second and she would have had his guts out.

He stood quietly, watching her, until he was sure she was not feigning. He doubted it. His grin was dry and twisted. He must have been quite a shock, coming alive like that, a stranger with a blood-smeared face.

When he was sure she was not feigning, he ran lightly to the temple door and cautiously peered out. He could see no guards. What need to guard the dead?

The gardens stretched away dark and silent. A torch sparked here and there. The air was soft and warm and filled with the unidentifiable fragrance. Blade studied it all with the supreme animal sensitivity that had kept him alive so long. He was a shadow among shadows, watching and listening, and saw nothing that spelled danger. He went back to the bier.

She appeared to have absolute authority, this Empress Mei. That was better than he could have hoped for. Now it was up to him to exploit the situation. Just how this could be done he did not know at the moment. At least he had made a beginning. So far he had made no mistakes—except the cardinal one of getting mixed up with Lord L—and no use worrying about that! His future was uncertain, he must grope for it step by step, and at the moment everything depended on how he handled this woman. And how she reacted to him. Therein, of course, was the rub.

He had removed the helmet. He ruffled his thick dark hair and rubbed a chin on which black stubble was beginning to sprout. In no time at all he would have a beard. He frowned down at the unconscious woman. He picked up a fold of her body sheath and fingered it. Silk and yet not silk. Velvet. Like flesh itself to the touch.

Blade watched the even rise and fall of her breasts. He had felt sexual excitement at first sight of her, but now that was gone and he did not know quite what he felt. He frowned again. His first concern was with himself and with the job he must do here in—Cath? That had been the name mentioned by her. A country, a state, a world? All these things, and much more, he must find out.

The garment did little to conceal her body. She was tall, with a tiny waist and long slim legs. Her skin was the color of ancient ivory. Just that. Not yellow, not white. Old ivory.

Her eyes fluttered. Blade put his hand gently over her mouth. He had used his tunic to wipe some of the blood from his face, but he supposed he was still a fearsome sight. She was coming awake now. A lot depended on the next few moments.

The green eyes opened and stared up at him in wonder. Blade bent over her, his hand on her mouth, the other pinning her easily to the altar-bier. He whispered. "You are awake now? You hear me? You understand? Nod if you do."

Comprehension grew slowly in the eyes so near his. She moved under his hand. Blade tightened his grip just a bit. "I am not going to harm you, Empress Mei. You must understand that. I come as a friend. And I need *your* help. I must have it. You will listen to me and make no sound?"

She stopped struggling and nodded up at him. He eased his grip, yet kept a hand over her soft mouth.

"My name is Richard Blade. I am a stranger in Cath. An utter stranger without friends and without knowledge of your country. I have nothing but these clothes I stand in, this armor, and this weapon." He let her see the dagger she had dropped.

Blade said: "I will serve you, Empress Mei, and be a friend to you. If you will be a friend to me. Will you?"

She did not nod. The green eyes were wary, waiting, watching the dagger in his hand. He thrust it into his belt.

"I will take my hand from your mouth now," said Blade, "if you will promise to make no sound. Nod if you agree."

She nodded.

He removed his hand from her lips, though keeping a firm grip on her. She rubbed her mouth with slender fingers and widened her eyes at him.

"Whisper," said Blade. "Keep your voice low."

She smiled in derision. "You are indeed a stranger in Cath. No one will dare come here unless I summon. I am the Empress Mei!"

Her voice, now that hate had left it, had the same sweet, singsongy, musical effect that Blade had noted in the others.

The red mouth curled now in disdain. "You have already forfeited your life, stranger, by touching me. But that can wait. I have never seen anyone like you before and I will listen. So speak."

"You are not afraid of me now?" He watched her carefully. A frightened woman could not be trusted.

She shrugged and her flesh was sinuous beneath the scant garment. "I am not afraid of you, stranger. I fainted because I thought Mei Saka had been feigning all along, was not killed in battle, and meant to kill me in this place. I thought it was a trick."

"Your husband is dead. I took his armor and was brought to this place. I had nowhere else to go and it seemed safe for the time. I cannot explain more than that now. Later I will tell you everything. Now I must have

41

your help—shelter and food and clothing and a manner of life so I will not be suspect and killed."

The emerald eyes narrowed at him and she said a surprising thing. "The armor suits you. You look more of a man in it than Mei Saka ever did."

Blade nodded his thanks. "That is kind of you, Empress, but hardly to the point. Will you help me? And trust me in all things—especially trust me when I say that I mean neither you nor Cath any harm?"

"I will trust you. I will help you. Let me up now, stranger, and never dare to touch me again!"

She very nearly got away with it. Blade's ears were sharp and yet he had not heard the patrol approach. She had. She sat up and swung her feet off the altar and gave him an odd little smile. It was only because Blade had developed an extra sense in these matters, and because he saw her throat muscles tense, that he caught her in time.

He lunged for her and covered the scream in time. She pulled away from him, struggling with surprising strength, and drew breath for another scream. Blade had fallen off balance, pinning her to the altar, and he covered this second scream the fastest way he could. With his mouth.

The moment his lips touched hers she ceased to struggle. She went limp and and boneless, her arms dangling, her head to one side and her mouth lax beneath his. Blade, who had only meant to silence her, began to kiss her. He could not stop. Had the patrol actually entered the temple and put lances in his back he could not have stopped.

At first it was like falling endlessly into a sweet-scented scarlet well. A red moist well that sucked at his own mouth and drew him down and down. He had kissed a thousand women and never any like this. Strangers met and lightning flared.

For a long time she did not respond. Nor did she evade. She let him kiss her and in passivity her own desire grew. She put her arms around him. With their mouths still glued together Blade lifted her back on the altar. Her

42

mouth was coming to life now and her tongue was a demon that enticed. Then no longer did it entice, but attacked. Her sharp little tongue stormed into his mouth, striking and sucking and biting and trying, with real intent, to devour him.

Blade did not think. He could not and did not want to think. He was engulfed. The cosmos was this pink red moist whorl of mouth beneath his own.

They did not speak. They did not look at each other. They were two beautiful animals come together, bent on coupling, and there was no love nor tenderness here. Each fought desperately for his own ultimate pleasure.

She ripped off her garment and flung it away. Blade, without knowing he did it, stripped himself and lowered himself. The enormous brawny man, hirsute and dark tanned and rippling with muscle, bore her down on the cold stone of the altar-bier and was merciless.

She made one sound then, the only sound she made during the encounter. She screamed, small and shrill, as he violated her. After that she fought him silently, clinging with her legs and arms, her ivory pelt a part of his own, the sweat of both beginning and mingling and streaming in the crevices of their straining bodies.

For long minutes they fought, both wanting to end and neither wanting to end. There was no end. No beginning. This was moment of birth and moment of death. This was *all* there was.

But there was an end, and it came for both in the same millionth of a second. Silence could no longer be endured and she screamed once and Blade gave a grunting cry that was not human and yet had all of humanity in it.

By then the patrol was at the far end of the gardens and did not hear. It was just as well, for Blade was helpless as any infant for a few seconds. It was dangerous, what he had just done.

He was the first to regain his senses. She lay inert and unmoving beneath his weight, and for a moment he thought she did not breathe. Then her breasts moved,

43

slightly, and she opened her eyes and peered up at him and smiled and stroked his face.

Blade whispered. "You will help me now, Empress Mei?"

She closed her eyes and smiled again and kept stroking his rough cheek. "I will help you, stranger. And you tell me truth, for you are indeed a stranger. You are like no man of Cath. I swear to that!"

Blade swung himself off the altar and began to pull on his tunic. The armor he would leave, or hide. It was too small anyway. He picked up her dagger and thrust it into his belt.

"We had better go then, Empress. At once. This is not a safe place. For me, at least."

She extended a hand to him and her smile said all there was to say. She was a subdued and contented woman, this Empress Mei, and neither of them thought to question it.

"We will go, Blade. But you must not worry now. You are safe with me. I rule Cath and my word is law. As your word shall be."

So, thought Blade, are complex matters made simple. For now. He was a man very aware of time and the snares it puts down every passing second.

"You will not call me Empress," she said. "Never again call me that."

He picked up her garment and handed it to her. "What do I call you, then?"

She thought a moment, then laughed softly. "You will call me Lali. Just that. It was a name my father had for me when I was very young and innocent. He was killed by Mongs when I was only a child and no one has ever called me that since."

Blade regarded her with affection. Now that the storm was over he felt an odd tenderness for her—and knew he must never drop his vigilance.

"Lali? All right. But I am not a father."

She was fastening the sheath of silken cloth about her

splendid body. "Indeed you are not! Yet you must call me Lali."

"I will call you anything you like, but let's get out of this place. Think, Lali! How would you explain me to that patrol if they should come in here?"

Her aquamarine eyes were shrewd. "How am I going to explain you to anyone? To my people and my wise men and my chiefs? Even to myself. Ah—that is going to require much thinking. And perhaps a few lies. I am very good at lying, Blade."

"So am I," he said, "and I will help you. But I lie better on a full stomach and after I have had a bath and some sleep. Do we go, Lali, or do I carry you?"

She touched his face and kissed him lightly. "We go."

She led him to the far wall of the Temple of Death and pressed against one of the pillars with a finger. The wall slid open without a sound. Beyond was a narrow tunnel, well lighted, sloping downward.

"Come. This leads to my private apartments. We shall have a bath together, and talk."

"And eat?" asked Blade hopefully. He was ravenous.

She brushed her fingers over his flat, hard-muscled stomach. "And eat. And then you will make love to me again."

Blade could see nothing wrong in that program.

She led the way. Without turning she said, "You are sure that Mei Saka is dead? My husband? If he is not, everything could be spoiled. I will not give you up now and there would be fighting in Cath, which must not be. We have enough trouble withstanding the Mongs."

"I cannot be positive," he told her. "I am a stranger. But I took the armor from a body that was very dead indeed. And the searching party thought I was your husband. I think it is certain enough."

She tripped along lightly before him. He watched the play of muscles in that marvelous body and wondered that this Emperor, this Mei Saka, could have been fool enough to endanger a relationship with her.

45

"That is good," said Lali. "My assassin did a good job. It is too bad that I had to have him killed."

A thought struck Blade. "Suppose that tomorrow, in daylight, your husband's body is found? Even naked, someone may recognize him."

Her trim buttocks flirted before him and the lovely shoulders shrugged.

"There is no danger. The carrion apes will leave nothing. And I will think of a story to explain why there is no body in the Temple. That will be easy. The difficult thing will be to explain your *living* body, and why you look as you do. Any fool, with one look, can see that you are not of Cath. But do not worry. I said I would think of a lie and I will."

Blade somehow thought she would.

A few minutes later he was in the midst of luxury that staggered him. And Blade had known luxury in his day as well as privation.

They bathed in a great pool of warm scented water. There was no soap, as Blade knew soap, but rather a fragrant soft powder which they rubbed on their bodies. And each other. Lali scrubbed him intimately and asked that he do the same for her. They talked.

They were waited on by a score of pretty bare-breasted girls, wearing only what he thought of as a bikini bottom. Lali paid absolutely no attention to the girls except to give orders.

Blade, when he was in H-Dimension—J and Lord L had come to call it that, Home Dimension—lived in a world of intrigue where no servant could ever be trusted. When he confessed his uneasiness she merely laughed and said: "They will not speak of you. They dare not. All I have to do is snap my fingers and they lose their heads."

He believed her.

After they had eaten she took him to a great chamber with a thick circular pad of silken material on the floor. It was her bed. In Cath, she explained, everyone slept on the floor. She thought it was strange that he should think it strange.

They made love again. Then talked. Then made love again. Then talked. By the time the sun shot up with the same blinding suddenness with which it had disappeared—it was going to take Blade a while to get used to that—she had, as she had promised, concocted a marvelous lie. She was very quick, very clever. And at the moment very much subdued and in love with him.

The servants brought shades to black out the room and as he fell asleep Blade thought that he had done very well indeed so far. He thought of an old American joke. He was living the life of Reilly.

He just hoped that Reilly didn't come home!

Chapter 5

Thuck—Thuck—Thuck—the executioner's sword flamed in sunlight and descended. The heads fell into a ditch and were immediately covered over with loose black earth. The next Mong, who had been waiting patiently, squatting with his hands bound behind him, spat in contempt and moved into place at the edge of the ditch. *Thuck*—the head rolled down to join the others, the mouth still contorted in a grimace of defiance.

These Mongs died well, Blade thought as he watched from a high tower on the great wall. He waited for Lali to join him. They then would mount horses and ride along the top of the wall to inspect the Cath forces and survey the Mong camp out on the plain where the black sand never stopped swirling. Blade had now been three weeks in Cath. Already he was restless, and dared not show it.

Queko, Chief Captain of the Caths under the Empress Mei, stood beside Blade on the tower. As tall as Blade, but very slim, he had the lemon-colored skin and the handsome straight features that distinguished the Caths. A fine soft fuzz covered his upper lip and chin. Caths had very little facial hair.

Blade, on the other hand, had by this time a luxuriant black beard which he kept trimmed short.

Blade had voiced his thought aloud. Queko, who so far had shown neither hostility nor friendliness to Blade, said: "They are savages. Barbarians. They have no imagination and therefore they have no fear. Why shouldn't they die well? They have been taught that they will prevail in the

48

end, so one Mong more or less does not matter. They may be right. There are millions of Mongs. The more we kill the more they come."

Queko spoke in the high-pitched musical tones of the Caths. His eyes glittered sideways at Blade. "Perhaps, Sir Blade, you have by now found a solution to this problem. I hope so, because the Mongs are bleeding us like leeches."

Blade concealed a smile. J and Lord L would be a little surprised to know that he had promoted himself to a Sir. But it had been necessary. Back in H-Dimension it meant little, here in Cath it was most important.

He said nothing more. Queko excused himself on plea of military affairs and left him. Blade watched the long lines of captive Mongs, squatting patiently on the plain behind the city, move toward the executioner. Something of a paradox here. The Mongs took no captives. The Caths took them, treated them well, then cut off their heads.

Blade turned away. He was beginning to feel uneasy. He was also aware that he was not doing his job very well. He was in X-Dimension to explore, investigate, probe. Yet he had been three weeks in the same place.

The fact was that he was as much a captive as any of the Mongs.

He descended the tower and stood on the broad roadway atop the wall. Here came his captor now. Lali. She who bound him with chains of silk and flesh.

She came riding toward him, sitting well in the high wooden saddle. She wore a little peaked cap atop high piled hair, a small corselet of painted wood, and flowing breeches stuffed into tiny boots. Underneath she would be wearing the diaphanous body sheath with which he was now so familiar.

Lali pulled her horse up and saluted him with her whip. "Good morning, Sir Blade."

"Good morning, Lali." They exchanged a secret smile.

49

The *Sir* was Blade's sole contribution to the tremendous lie they were living.

A horse was brought for Blade and he swung easily into the saddle. "Come, Lali, let's ride down to the cannon."

They rode together down the wall, past groups of Cath soldiery and officers preparing for the day's fighting. Hearts were touched with fingertips as Lali rode by, and the brawny, bearded Blade was the object of curious stares. It was the same day after day. They did not understand Blade, nor did they question. Lali was an absolute ruler—compared to her Catherine the Great had been a democrat—and if their Empress wanted Blade, who was to question it?

Lali touched his knee with her whip. "You left me early this morning, Sir Blade. I awoke to an empty bed. I do not like that." The deep green eyes were narrowed on him.

Blade did not apologize. He knew better, and in any case apology was foreign to his nature.

"I had business," he said brusquely. "I made an early tour of inspection. I am trying to think of a plan to rid us of these Mongs, Lali. I cannot do it in bed."

Lali expected love-making every morning before rising. She explained it in direct speech. "Mei Saka, may he rot in the bellies of the carrion apes, had not touched me for two years before you came, Blade. I am a woman of great passion and demand."

They came now to the great canon and dismounted. "I will forgive you this time," she said. "Not again."

The silken leash.

Blade inspected the huge gun with his usual awe and amusement. Lali could never understand why he was so fascinated by it. It had always been there, ever since she was a child, and the explosions frightened her almost as much as they did the Mongs.

She watched, a trifle impatiently, as Blade walked around the cannon. He had been very nearly right in his first estimates. The muzzle was five feet across, not six, but the gun was sixty feet long. The wheels of its eight-wheeled carriage were twelve feet high. It took ten barrels of crude powder to charge it and five hundred men to move it up and down the ramp. What puzzled Blade was why the damned thing had never blown up. The barrel was of wood, thick and ornately carven, and reinforced with wide steel rings. Steel was hard to come by in this province of Cath. It all had to come from the south, from the Imperial City of Pukka.

Blade shrugged, as he always did, and went back to Lali. Those old gunsmiths must have known something about wood, something that had been lost with the years.

Together they watched the Mongs moving about out on the plain. The sturdy little horses, long haired and with bushy manes and tails, wheeled and swooped amid the blowing clouds of black sand. Soon the attacks would begin. Day after day.

Year after year, as Lali explained later that night.

"Khad Tambur, the Lord of the Mongs, wants the big gun. If we let him have it he will make peace and go away."

They had been in Lali's bed. Blade, yawning, said: "Then why not give him the gun? What use is it? You never kill any Mongs with it—you just scare them and then they come right back."

For the first time he saw her horrified—and angry. The lovely eyes darted green sparks at him.

"Give them the gun? Give Khad Tambur our gun! You are mad, Blade. No! Not mad. I forget you are a stranger. But the gun is the symbol of Cath. There is a legend. When the gun is captured Cath is doomed. He who possesses the cannon rules the world. That is why Khad Tambur is so determined to have it. For the power it brings. Why he keeps trying year after year, and why he sacrifices so many hundreds of thousands of his men. Give up the gun! Never breathe that again, Blade. Even I could not save you. The people would tear you apart."

Blade had pressed her back on the bed and forgotten it.

This morning there was a sense of something different in the air. The Mongs did not attack as usual. There was the usual scurry and bustle in the great village of black tents and the cooking fire smoke hung in clouds above the plain and mingled with the blowing black sand. But the usual forays did not come. The milling horsemen stayed out of range, making no effort to entice the defenders out for battle, and the foot soldiers did not come forward with their scaling ladders.

Blade wondered if the Khad Tambur had suddenly found wisdom? Until now he had been a singularly obtuse commander, wasting men against the wall day after day.

Lali, shielding her eyes with a hand, stared over at the Mong camp. She wrinkled her beautiful nose. "Something is wrong, Sir Blade. They do not come to fight as usual."

Blade smiled. "Maybe the Khad is getting smart at last. He is going to fold his tents and steal away. I know I would have, long ago. He can't win this way."

Lali chewed her lip with small perfect teeth. "That is not good, Sir Blade. We must kill Mongs. Every day we must kill more and more Mongs. How can we do that if they go away?"

Blade pointed. "Look! Maybe your answer is coming now. He's not very big, is he?"

A single horseman had left the Mong camp and was riding toward the wall. As he drew near Blade could not repress a smile. The rider was a dwarf, or midget, dressed as a Mong warrior. Over his head, on a small lance, he waved a single horse tail.

Blade looked at the girl. "He wants a parley. But why send a dwarf, a stunted man? He can't really be a warrior."

Her face was pale, the emerald eyes blazing with rage. "It is Khad Tambur's idea of a joke. An insulting joke. No—it must be the idea of that bitch whore! Sadda, Khad's sister. It is like her to think of an insult like this."

The little man, riding a little pony, stopped near a postern in the great wall. He waved his horse tail all the while he shouted in a voice that was amazingly gruff and deep. The Cath soldiers, obedient to orders, did not fire. Blade quickly mounted and rode up the wall road until he was directly over the tiny rider. Queko was there, a tolerant smile on his handsome face, along with a little group of Cath officers.

The little warrior was sturdily built in perfect proportion. Off the pony, Blade judged, the man would be less than three feet tall. Yet his legs were heavily muscled and his biceps bulged.

The Mongs used no stirrups. The messenger sprang lightly to stand on the saddle, perfectly balanced, and cupped his hands as he shouted up at the towering wall.

"Caths! Soldiers of the province of Serendip, of the land of Cath, and most especially to the Empress Mei and all her high officers—the Khad Tambur sends you this offer. Listen well, for it is Khad Tambur who speaks through me, Khad Tambur who is the Scourge of the World and Shaker of the Universe."

One of the common soldiers laughed and shouted back. "Get on with it. minikin. Stop blowing through your mouth and say what you have come to say! Then go before we put a little arrow through your little carcass."

A Cath officer struck the man and he fell back, muttering.

The messenger shouted on: "The great Khad Tambur has many ears within your wall—"

Lali, who had come spurring up to join Blade, scowled and said, "That is true enough! Spies."

Blade winked at her and patted her knee. "Be quiet, Lali. Please. I want to hear what the rascal has to say."

She favored him with a scowl. She had not liked the way he had ridden away and left her.

"The great Khad has heard that a stranger is among you. A man called Sir Blade, who is a courier-captain from the capital of Pukka, sent by Pukka to determine why you Caths cannot defeat the Mongs. This Sir Blade

53

arrived three weeks ago, coming in secret at night. Is all this not true, Caths?"

Blade and Lali exchanged glances. The exact lie they had concocted to explain his presence. The Khad Tambur *did* have a good spy system.

Richard Blade acted on impulse, but it was an inevitable impulse. Had he kept silent he would not have been Richard Blade. Lali, sensing what he was about to do, clutched his arm. Blade shook her off and spurred to the edge of the wall.

"That is true," he shouted. "I am Sir Blade. What of it?"

The dwarf warrior stared up at him with a friendly grin on his wide mouth. He had a snub nose and close-set eyes, dark and twinkling. His skin was swarthy and unlike most Mongs he was smooth shaven.

He waved the horse tail at Blade. "I give you greeting from the great Khad Tambur, Sir Blade. I see that you are all that our spies have said. You are a giant and will therefore no doubt accept the offer of the Khad—"

Blade found himself liking the little Mong. He put his hands on his hips and laughed down. "What offer, little man? Get on with it."

Behind him he could hear the hurried, whispered consultations of Lali and her officers. They did not like what he was doing.

The dwarf danced nimbly on his saddle. "If you will fight the Khad's champion in single combat, before this wall in a place that shall be chosen, the Khad will abide by the results. If you, Sir Blade, defeat his champion the Khad promises to depart this place and never return. If you lose, Sir Blade, the great cannon is to be surrendered to the Khad."

There was a murmur of outrage behind Blade. He waved a hand at the dwarf. "A moment—you shall have an answer." He spurred away from the wall's edge and dismounted.

Lali was surrounded by a silent circle of Cath officers.

54

Only Queko dared to speak. "Why not, Empress? Something must be done and it may be that this is the answer. Surely Sir Blade can slay any Mong that might be sent against him. He is a giant and they are all small men. And he has great skill with arms. We have all seen that."

Lali was in such a fury that she struck at Queko with her whip. "I will not have it! I will not consent! Sir Blade is too valuable to risk in such foolishness. I must have him by my side. I must have his advice. He has come all the way from Pukka for just that reason. No—no—no!"

Blade pushed his way through the circle of cringing officers. Here, before witnesses, was the time to stand up to Lali. Yet it must be done with skill. He had a plan.

"I say yes, Lali! It is a chance to get rid of the Mongs at last. Queko is right—I can defeat any of them." In fair combat he never doubted that he could. He knew tricks that the Mongs did not dream of. Or the Caths, for that matter.

She turned on him sullenly. "You do not understand, Sir Blade. Khad Tambur will not keep his word, even if you win. Nothing will be changed. And if you lose—"

One of the officers, more daring than the others, laughed and said: "If Sir Blade loses we will not keep our word, either. We will not give them the gun."

Nervous laughter. Lali glared around and there was silence. She touched Blade's arm. "So what is gained? Except that you might die? I would not have that, Sir Blade."

The marvelous green eyes pleaded with him. Blade understood perfectly. She *didn't* want to lose him—from her life, from her bed.

From below the wall there came a whinnying cry. It sounded like a horse speaking. A great cry went up from the assembled Caths. A horse speaking!

The horse said: "These Caths must be very stupid, or great cowards. I have a half-brother, called an ass, that could have made up his mind in half the time."

The Caths were half amused, more than a little frightened. But it served to break the tension. Blade touched Lali's shoulder and said: "I know what I do. Trust me. Listen to my terms and then see if you do not agree."

He mounted again and rode to the edge of the wall. The horse, or the pony, was still speaking.

"Hurry, Sir Blade, hurry. I am hungry. I have not been fed yet this morning because I am on the Khad's business. My back is breaking, too, because of this huge man that dances atop me. Hurry, Sir Blade!"

Blade grinned down at the little man. The rascal was dancing nimbly on his saddle, pulling the pony's bridle to make its head bob, and pretending to be outraged at the animal's words. Most of the Caths were staring in awe by this time. As civilized and advanced as they were, in some matters, they had never heard of ventriloquism.

"Bid your pony keep his mouth shut," Blade shouted. "I will answer you now and I have no mind to compete with a horse."

The pony stopped speaking and its head drooped as the reins were loosed. The little warrior smiled up at Blade.

"It is a good trick," said Blade, "but I have seen better in lands you will never know. Now no more of this clowning—listen well."

The dwarf touched his cap. "I listen, Sir Blade."

"Take this message back to your Khad. I will fight his champion. To the death! If I am defeated he is to have the cannon. But if I win he is to surrender to me his sister—the woman called Sadda. I do not care if you Mongs stay or go—but if I win I must have Sadda. Take that message to your Khad, dwarf, and bring me back an answer. Speedily."

The dwarf was smiling, his little eyes twinkling, but there was shock and astonishment on his face. And something else—fear and a new respect. The man touched his cap with his lance and dropped into the saddle. "As you say, Sir Blade. With speed." He sent the pony scurrying across the plain at a gallop, riding with dash and grace as did all the Mongs.

There was silence behind Blade. He ignored the others and rode to where Lali stood biting her lips and, Blade hoped, already wavering. He knew how much she hated Sadda, sister to the Khad Tambur.

That night, though Lali was as frantic as ever in her love-making, there was a reserve about her that troubled Blade. Yet there was nothing he could do. He had taken out as much insurance as he could.

While Lali was bathed and anointed by her maidens, Blade had a chance to do some deep thinking. They usually bathed together and it was evidence of her mood that this night she chose to make her preparations alone.

The sun had dropped away as suddenly as ever. The eternal scent of the *banyo* trees filled the chamber. The *banyos* bloomed night and day, in all seasons, great pom-poms of red and yellow fragrance that gave the air of Cath its softness and incense.

Blade stood at the window, watching the torches flare in the palace gardens. Khad Tambur had agreed to the bargain. Whether he would keep it, if his man lost, was another matter. Blade thought it was just possible. For three weeks he had been keeping his eyes and ears open and he was an expert at weighing and evaluating information. Rumor had it that the Khad and his infamous and lovely sister did not get along well. Rumor also had it that they were lovers.

Blade shrugged his big shoulders and dropped his robe and twisted a wisp of silk about his waist. He did not care about Sadda's corrupt sex life, even if all the rumors were true. It was amazing how much the Mongs and Caths had come to know about each other after so many years of fighting. If one knew how to do it, and cared, you could learn that the Khad was mad for a certain type of melon which he preserved in snow brought from the high mountains at great cost of life.

Yes, the Khad just might keep the bargain if his champion lost. At least he would be rid of Sadda, and he could pose as an honorable man who kept his word. And Lali

57

would have Sadda to torture and dispose of as she pleased. It was a great temptation to her. It was because of Sadda that her late husband, Mei Saka, had plotted to open the wall and betray Cath. Blade had heard it all, many times in three weeks, and the venom in Lali's voice and eyes sent shivers up his back.

Blade was counting on that hate. Without it, without the promise of getting Sadda in her grasp, Lali would never let him go through with the fight. She would have him arrested first, even killed. She was capable of both.

Lali was late tonight. Blade watched a lightning storm play over the Jade Mountains far to the south. An entire range of the precious stuff. It was quarried much the same as marble was back in H-dimension. Blade frowned. He doubted that jade was the sort of treasure Lord L and J were looking for. And that was another thing—he was not accomplishing anything! He must somehow stop this eternal war between the Mongs and the Caths so he would have freedom of movement. No way of telling how much time he had left before Lord L snatched him back through the computer.

Still no Lali. Was she plotting something even now? He went to the circular pad bed and lifted a corner. The dagger was still there. The only weapon he had. If Lali sent a company of guards for him he could—but of what use? He might kill a few Caths, but in the end he would be killed or imprisoned.

An incident two weeks before had put Blade very much on his guard. He was normally alert and watchful, suspicious, but a week of luxury, of food and sex, and royal treatment had lulled him. He had made a perfectly normal and human mistake. One of Lali's maidens, bolder than the rest, had smiled at him. Only that. A smile. Blade had smiled back.

Lali had not even been there at the time. And yet, the next day, the head of the maiden had been placed where he could not fail to see it. Lali never spoke of it. Blade never forgot it.

58

Lali came into the bed chamber wearing only her body sheath. Fresh from the bath, her hair down around her shoulders and caught behind her head in a jade ring, she watched him from those depthless green pools. She came to him and kissed him on the cheek, then turned in his arms so he could unfasten her garment.

"I have decided to let you fight the Khad's champion, Blade. I have been speaking with my wise men and they agree that it is best."

He unfastened her garment and let it slither down around her feet. He kissed her ear and caressed her breasts from behind, as she liked, stroking the nipples softly with his fingertips.

"You are as wise as your wise men, Lali. I will kill this Mong they send against me and there will at least be a chance to break this stalemate. The Khad may keep his word, or he may not, but there is a chance."

She writhed a bit in his arms, a sensuous movement that began his own arousal. He kept stroking her breasts. She liked that above all things except the ultimate act. At times he could drive her into frenzy by breast play alone. He wanted her in a frenzy tonight. He would give her no time to think, to have second thoughts.

She leaned her head back on his shoulder and nuzzled him with moist red lips. "I have been talking to my spies. I have as many in Khad Tambur's camp as he has in Cath, you know."

Blade gently squeezed her breasts. "And?"

"The Khad has imprisoned his sister. That whore Sadda. She has been placed in her tent under guard. And the guards under threat of death if she escapes. My spies say that she is in a towering rage."

Lali half turned to look at him. "You have better win tomorrow, Blade. But if you lose and we refuse to give up the great cannon, as we will do, you had better be dead! Do not let them make you prisoner. I have loved you too much to enjoy seeing the pieces of your body paraded before the wall. You can expect no mercy from the Mongs.

59

You would find little enough from the Khad, but *if* you lose, and are taken prisoner, *and* he releases Sadda, she will undoubtedly ask for you as a slave. She will blame you for her humiliation. And she will treat you as I would have treated *her*. No, Blade. Do not lose. But if you must lose—be sure you die in the doing of it."

She came into his arms then and kissed him and her tongue was like a flame in his mouth. At their first encounter in the temple he had been too stunned by desire, too overcome by animal passion, to think at all. Now the edge of that desire had been blunted and a part of his mind was clear. He thought, not for the first time, how closely related were sex and death.

Lali led him to the circular bed, having first stripped the silken cloth from his loins. She was eager and insatiable. Their passion flamed until they could stand the tension no longer, and Lali moaned for release. When it came, she cried out in pleasure.

After the first tumultuous bout, as they lay replete and lax, Lali said: "I am sure you will win tomorrow, Blade. So sure that I have prepared a cage for Sadda. Quite a nice cage—full of sharp spikes. And next to her cage is also a cage of the carrion apes we have caught. They will be starved. I want Sadda to see them—and I want them to see Sadda. When I am finished with her they shall have what is left."

Blade kept his eyes closed. "I shouldn't imagine there would be much left for the apes."

He was not as appalled as, perhaps, he should have been. He understood why. He adapted to a new environment with great speed. It had been so in Alb, the first X-Dimension he had explored. So it was now. He was already speaking in the sweet high musical tones of the Caths and, in many ways, thinking like a Cath. Lord L had explained it in terms that Blade had not totally understood. The organism, in any and all circumstances, will adjust itself to survival. Simple enough in the essence.

Isolated civilizations, Blade had read somewhere, will

develop along parallel lines. There will be time lags, but the ultimate goals will always be the same and will ultimately be reached.

It would seem to apply to X-Dimension as well. He wondered what the anthropologists back in H-Dimension would make of that? If they ever came to know of it. If he, Richard Blade, ever got back so they *could* come to know of it.

"There will be enough left for the apes," Lali said. "I will make sure of that."

She rolled over on top of him.

Chapter 6

Black sand clustered across the sunny plain as Blade rode out the central gate of the wall. The wall was lined with Caths, thousands of them. In the great tower, surrounded by her officers, Lali watched from a royal chair. The Caths were noisy.

The Mongs across the way were silent. They had formed a long, solid, dark line across the plain, before the camp of black tents. One of the tents had been moved forward. Before this tent, on a high throne and surrounded by banners, sat a crooked figure that Blade knew must be the Khad Tambur, Shaker of the Universe. Spies reported that he had a crooked back and lewd tastes, though impotent.

Blade rode his big gray horse to where a lance had been planted. A horsetail fluttered from it. He waited. Where was the Khad's champion?

As soon as the sun shot up there had been a brief conference with Homunculus, the same little warrior who had brought the challenge the day before. Details had been arranged. Blade found himself liking the little rascal again.

Just before he rode away the dwarf gave Blade a strange look, his dark eyes intent and serious above the grin, and said a strange thing.

"Beware the ground, Sir Blade."

Just that. Beware the ground. Blade puzzled briefly and then forgot it. It had been a warning, perhaps well meant, but a warning against what?

As he waited for the man he meant to kill, he surveyed

the plain about him carefully. He saw nothing unusual. Just flat barren earth studded with small rocks here and there, patches of gravel, and the ever present black sand. He could see no hazard in the ground itself.

A rider left the ranks of the Mongs and came dashing toward him. Blade soothed the gray and pulled his head around as the rider began to veer off at an angle. Blade spun the mace over his head to loosen his shoulder muscles. The weapon had been made for him by Cath armorers as he supervised. It had a short wooden handle to which was attached a length of chain. At the end of the chain was an iron ball studded with razor sharp bits of jade. A fearsome weapon, and Blade knew how to use it.

He carried a square shield and a short sword. In his belt was the same dagger he had taken from Lali that first night. He had selected the gray horse from all the enormous stables behind the wall and had the animal amored with thick silken quilting.

The rider, yelling and whooping constantly, began to circle behind Blade. He quietly pulled the gray around to face the danger. If he could, he meant to make the Mong come to him.

The Mong warrior was in no hurry. He dashed within twenty yards of Blade and pulled his shaggy little horse into a rearing halt. He shook his lance at Blade.

"Yieeee— I am Cossa! Champion of all the Mongs. I come to slay you for my Khad." He had really come to study Blade and he did so now, the dark eyes missing nothing. He was a small man, but compact and muscular, with bushy hair and an enormous moustache. He wore a pointed leather cap and leather chest armor. Below the waist he was bare except for short breeches, and his thick legs were thrust into high boots of skin.

For a few breaths they exchanged glances, each weighing the other. Blade said, "Get on with it, then. Your Khad will be impatient."

The Mong set his horse to prancing. He reached for a short bow on his shoulder and fitted an arrow to it. Blade moved his shield into position and nudged the gray lightly with his spurs. Let the man get off his first shot, then charge him. The gray was big and powerful, the Mong horse a pigmy by comparison. At the first opportunity he meant to ride down the Mong and his horse, send them crashing to the earth. Once he had the Mong on foot the mace would do the rest.

The Mong yelled and loosed an arrow with a careless motion. Blade's shield was ready but the arrow came in low and zipped into the gray's quilted armor where it dangled harmlessly.

That was it. Trying to bring the gray down! Blade twitched the bridle and the gray began to move about a bit.

The Mong, still yelling threats, began to circle Blade. The man was a superb horseman. As he dashed past he leaned far over, so he was nearly invisible, and fired arrows from beneath the belly of his horse. One of the arrows nipped the gray just above a fetlock and the animal reared and whinnied. Blade calmed him and waited.

The Mong came back, riding upright, now between Blade and the Mong camp. He appeared puzzled as just how to come to grips with this big man who sat and watched him with such calm and contempt.

Blade rose in his stirrups and swung the mace over his head. He taunted the man. "You say your name is Cossa? What does that mean in Mong? Coward?"

The Mong wheeled his horse abruptly and rode away, back toward his own lines. Blade waited patiently.

The Mong came back at a gallop, now carrying a shield and brandishing a long lance. Beneath his helmet Blade smiled. This was more like it.

The Mong came straight at him, the lance poised. Blade moved the gray a little sideways, took the lance on his shield and swung the mace at the man's head. It was not there. The deadly iron ball whistled harmlessly just where the man's head had been. Then the Mong was away, his lance still intact, and circling to come back at Blade again.

Blade wheeled to face this new attack, comforting the gray. This time his tactic would be a little different.

The Mong came driving in with a scream of defiance. The lance splintered on Blade's shield. Instead of trying to mace the man, he forced the gray directly into the smaller horse. There was a tremendous shock as both horses screamed and pawed at each other. The Mong horse was shaken; it stumbled but did not go down. Blade cursed softly.

The Mong fooled Blade. Instead of retreating he came in again, fast, thrusting at Blade with the splintered end of his lance. Blade shielded himself and before he could swing the mace, the man leaned over to slash at Blade with a curved sword. Blade missed with his mace again and warded off the sword stroke with his shield. He reached for the man with one big hand, trying to grab him and drag him off the little horse, but once again the Mong was not there. He broke clear and dashed away, sending back whoops of defiance. Blade was now covered with sweat beneath his wooden armor. Elusive was the word. The man and his horse were like quicksilver.

He decided to anticipate the next charge. He had been letting the Mong take the initiative and that was not working. He waited until the Mong swung around, near his own lines, and selected a new spear from a number jabbed into the ground. He took his time about it and Blade knew the man was thinking and catching his breath.

Blade talked to the gray and began to move him just a bit, slowly, picking up momentum. Then the Mong wheeled and came charging back.

Now! The Mong pulled his horse around, reared, yelled, and came at Blade again. Blade put the spurs to the gray and thundered forward straight at his attacker. With this much momentum, and squarely met, the little horse would have to go down.

The Mong realized the situation too late. Blade put the gray into a thundering gallop and met the enemy head on.

The shock was terrible and Blade lurched in the saddle, but the gray rode the little horse down and sent it sprawling and kicking. There was a roar of joy from the wall. The long line of Mongs was silent.

Cossa the Mong was out of the saddle even before the horses met. He landed on his feet, running. Blade went after him, swinging the deadly mace. The man ran back toward his own lines, veered sharply to the left, and kept running. Blade, to cut him off, spurred very near the Mong lines and then cut back. No spear was thrown by the watching Mongs, no arrow loosed. They watched in silence.

Blade was unaware of them. His heart was thudding, he was bathed in sweat and the battle fever was on him. He wanted one thing and one thing only—to kill this elusive Mong. He tossed away his helmet so he could see better.

The Mong had run back toward the wall. Fifty yards from Blade he stopped, jabbed his lance in the ground, and fell to one knee. He whipped the crooked little bow off his shoulder, notched an arrow and waited for Blade to attack. His horse, with a broken leg, was dragging itself off to one side.

The gray was trembling under him. Blade soothed the beast and considered. No longer was it so easy to ride the Mong down and mace him. The man had been fast enough to consolidate his position. If Blade charged him now the gray would almost certainly be killed by arrows.

Blade stroked the horse and the animal calmed somewhat. A fine beast, but that was not Blade's prime consideration. If the gray went down while charging, Blade would take a terrible fall and might well brain himself on any of the stones about. Even if he didn't he would be at a moment's disadvantage and he had seen how fast this Cossa was.

Blade rode nearer to where the Mong waited. There was no fear in the man, no surrender. He spat at Blade and called out.

"Why do you hesitate, Sir Blade. You have a horse and I have none. Why don't you come and kill me?"

"I will. I am only considering how best to do it."

Cossa laughed gutterally. Here was no sweet musical tone of the Caths. Harshly the man said, "Take your time, then. I am in no hurry to die."

Blade was close enough now to count the arrows in the Mong's quiver. Three left. It was worth the chance and it would look far better if he killed the man on foot instead of riding him down. Prestige might count in later dealings with the Khad. Blade swung down off the gray. He patted the animal on the rump and the gray went skittering away, to stop after a few feet and begin tugging at some sparse grass that thrust out of gravel.

Blade swung the mace and advanced on the Mong. They were down to the bone of it now.

Cossa waited until Blade was within twenty feet before he shot his first arrow. The aim was deadly—at the man's throat just above the armor. *Zzzzz—thuck.*

Blade pulled the arrow from his shield and tossed it to one side. "Two arrows left, Cossa."

"One will be enough, Sir Blade."

Blade moved in cautiously, lightly, the shield held ready for sudden defense, the cruel mace swinging at his side.

"At least you are a man," said Cossa the Mong. "You give up your advantage and fight me on foot. No true Cath would have done that."

Blade moved closer.

"You do not *look* like a Cath," said the Mong. "You are dark and you have a beard. What are you doing with those overcivilized fools? You should be with us, stranger. With the Mongs! You even have the look of a Mong about you, though I have never seen one so huge."

The bow movement was so rapid that Blade could not follow it. There was a streak in the air, a keening *twang.* The arrow took Blade in the fleshy part of his left leg just above the knee. It was painful. Blade did not so much as glance down.

"One arrow, Cossa."

The Mong spat again and laughed wildly. "Who knows, Sir Blade? One may be enough—or it may be my time to follow the black sand to my destiny."

Ten feet separated them now. Cossa ran at Blade, at the same time releasing his last arrow straight at Blade's groin where the armor joined. Blade got his shield down just in time.

Cossa came in screaming. Blade dropped the shield, leaped sideways to avoid the first rush, and drew his sword. He held it in his left hand, the mace in the right, and moved in on the man.

The Mong rushed to meet him, his curved sword flaming in the brilliant sunlight. Blade fended the first blow with his own sword and swung the mace. Cossa ducked under the deadly iron ball and danced away.

Blade waited. He had seen how the captured Mongs died beneath the executioner's sword and he knew that Cossa would not run. The man had to die or win, as did Blade himself.

The Mong came in again, slashing furiously, so furiously that Blade had to fall back a few steps. He had no chance to swing the mace as he fended off the clanging blows. Sparks whirled and hissed and sweat ran into his eyes. For a moment it was cut and slash and parry and hack. Blade was on the defensive. Their swords locked and their faces were so close Blade could smell the Mong's sour breath.

Blade put a foot in the man's chest and kicked him away. Cossa nearly went sprawling, and Blade spun the mace and sprang forward for the kill. But the Mong kept his feet and, ducking under the blow, aimed a blow at Blade's head which he barely parried in time.

Cossa was gasping for breath now and Blade himself was tiring. The mace was begining to feel twice its weight. Blade let it drop to his side and made a long lunge with his sword. The Mong danced away.

Blade recovered and stood his ground. He twirled the mace again. Cossa could hardly breathe now, yet he found wind to laugh and taunt.

"You are a giant, Sir Blade, but I have slain bigger men in the high lands where the snow apes live. Now!"

Cossa came in to the attack again, silent now. The curved sword hummed in the air. The Mong's flat, bearded face gleamed with sweat. Blade sensed that it was the man's last effort, that the Mong would gladly die if he could take Blade with him. As Cossa charged he plucked a short dagger from his belt with his left hand. If he could get close enough he could dagger Blade even as the bigger man was killing him.

Blade hurled the mace with all his force. It struck the Mong at the knees, a bone crushing blow, and the chain whipped around the shattered knees. Cossa went down with a strangled cry of pain and rage. Blade leaped forward.

Cossa, on his back, both legs broken, still tried to defend himself. He slashed up at Blade with his sword. Blade brushed it aside and put his own steel through the man's throat, just at the collarbone, a terrible downward thrust that carried through flesh and bone and arteries and embedded the point six inches in the earth.

The Mong screamed once, a sound drowned in the burble of gushing blood. He arched and clutched at the sword transfixing him and looked up at Blade with a baleful dying stare. He tried to speak but only blood came from his gaping mouth.

Blade whistled at the gray, which was croping grass nearby. He was mindful of Queko's advice that, should he win, he must take every advantage of his triumph. As he swung into the saddle he glanced at the Mong lines. Closer than he had thought. He was less than a hundred yards from the throne where Khad Tambur sat, surrounded by his banners and his guard, glowering over the plain at his dead champion.

Blade coaxed the gray around. He had recovered his mace and sheathed his sword. There was no sign of overt hostility from the Mongs, only silence and dark looks. Perhaps Queko was right. The Mongs worshiped courage and prowess in battle. Force was the only thing they understood. There was a chance, if he displayed enough contempt, enough confidence and courage, that he could browbeat the Khad into keeping his bargain. Blade put the gray into an arrogant canter and headed straight for the Mong lines and the waiting Khad. As he went, he swung the mace around his head so the cruel jade spikes made a sparkling blur.

He prepared his speech. It had best be short, and he away in a hurry. No sense in pressing things too far. The words formed in his mind.

"Now, Khad Tambur, O Shaker of the Universe! I am victor. I demand my rightful spoils. I will have your sister, Sadda, as my captive. And you, and all your Mongs, had best be gone before another day or—"

In that moment, flushed with battle and victory, Richard Blade was an arrogant man. Too late, just a minisecond too late, he saw the trap. The big gray never saw it.

The rawhide cords had been cunningly laid in trenches and covered over. Tensioned sticks of bow wood awaited a releasing trigger. Somewhere in the crowd of sullen Mongs a man pulled a cord. The web of trip lines sprung into view.

The gray was caught at the knees and went down in a long plunging fall. It whinnied high in distress. Blade went over the gray's head, headlong and helpless, and even as he saw the rock and knew he would strike it, he saw again the grinning dwarf and heard the words:

"Beware the ground, Sir Blade."

He had discarded his helmet. He sought to shield his head with his arm but the heavy mace encumbered him. His head struck the rock, and the plain and the silent Mongs vanished in a scarlet flash.

Chapter 7

Blade awoke in darkness. He was naked except for breeches. His wrists and ankles were weighted with heavy chains and manacles. His head pained him and above his right eye was a great mass of spongy congealed blood. There was a dull ache in his left leg where Cossa's arrow had taken him.

He lay staring at a ceiling he could not see. He was in a tent, for he could hear the slither of wind and sense the rippling of the thick feltlike material. A black tent. A Mong tent.

Richard Blade was not a man for self-recrimination. So he had played the fool and walked, or cantered, into the trap. Now to get himself out of it—if that were possible. If not—but he would face that when it came.

He was still alive.

He tested his chains and knew he was not going to break them. He lay quiet again and stared into the darkness and listened to the sounds of the camp around him. He began to adjust and react, all his senses attuned now, and he realized that he was deep in the Mong encampment. He heard song and the complaint of harsh voices: yells, screams, children in uproar as they played at some savage game. Horsemen went thundering past not far away.

He was lying on something soft—soft but scratchy. Blade put his face to it. Woven horsehair.

There was movement near him and for a moment moonlight shafted into the tent. Then darkness again.

Someone had entered the tent. Someone who stood there in the dark and breathed softly and watched him.

Blade sat up, his chains jangling. "Who is it?"

There was a scratching in the gloom and a light flared. A twist of wick burning in oil in a handled bowl. The shadow behind the flame was grotesquely small. The dwarf.

Blade managed to summon a wry grin. "Hello, little man. You see I did not heed your warning. Next time do not speak in riddles, I—"

A mistake. The dwarf moved close to him, one finger to his grinning mouth, a look of panic in the dark eyes. Blade hushed. He *was* a fool.

The dwarf put the lamp down and scuttled away into the shadows again. Blade heard the tent opening rustle. The dwarf came back and squatted a discreet distance from Blade. He spoke in a harsh whisper.

"No harm this time, Sir Blade, but guard your tongue. No more mention of that or I will share your fate and I would not like that. I come from Sadda, who trusts me as much as she trusts anyone, and I would keep it that way. I cannot help you, Sir Blade, even if I would. But you can help *me*, who did give you warning, by forgetting I ever gave it."

Blade nodded. "It is forgotten."

For a long minute the dwarf was silent as he studied Blade from head to toe. Blade returned the scrutiny.

Here was no warrior. The dwarf wore a little pointed cap with a bell on the peak. Around his neck was a small iron collar. Below that he wore a jerkin of leather, with yellow stripes, and tight-fitting leather breeches. On his tiny feet were shoes of some sort of skin, with the fur inward and the toes very long and curled up and held in place by stiffeners.

Blade got it then. A fool. The Khad's fool! But he had sounded like Sadda's man—

He badly needed a friend. Blade whispered, "Does the

73

Khad know you're here? Or his sister, the one called Sadda?"

The dwarf, without apparent effort, turned a backward flip and landed in exactly the same position. From the darkness behind Blade a mocking voice spoke. "No to the first, yes to the last. And who are you, Sir Blade, to question me? I am sent to question *you*.

For a moment Blade was startled. He had forgotten the dwarf was a ventriloquist. And better at it than Blade had known. The grinning mouth had not twitched a muscle.

"To question me? Who sent you to do that? What is your name, little man?"

The grin was fixed. "They call me Morpho. That is enough for you. And it was Sadda who sent me to look at you, to question you, and to report back to her."

Blade stretched his huge body and the chains jingled. He smiled at the dwarf. There was much here he did not understand. He sensed that beyond all this mystery there might be a chance for his life.

"Then look," said Blade, "and question. And take back a report that will keep me alive. I will reward you for it one day."

Morpho put a finger to his mouth and shook his head. Behind Blade the voice spoke again. "Not all fools dress like fools."

Blade accepted the rebuke. He waited.

The dwarf walked on his hands around the tent, always careful to stay out of Blade's reach. Even upside down the grin was there. The silence got on Blade's nerves.

"Must you always grin, little man? Always? This is not a time for grinning."

Morpho dropped to his feet and came back to squat. "I must always grin, Sir Blade. I am a fool, from a family of fools. When I was a baby the doctors cut my mouth—look near and you can see the scars—so that I must wear a fool's grin from birth to death."

The dwarf leaned closer in the smoking lamplight. Blade saw the faint scars at the corners of the grinning

74

lips. He kept silent. The man would get on with it when he was ready.

Morpho put a finger alongside his nose in thought, frowned, then began to whisper.

"I am honest with you, Sir Blade. What else with a man who is so near to torture and death? You are not a Cath and you are not a Mong. Just what you *are* I do not know. Our spies behind the wall could not find out, other than you pleasured the Empress Mei greatly. It is said that you are an envoy from Pukka, come with great powers. This may be. It is strange all the same that the Emperor Mei Saka has disappeared and the Empress, instead of putting on the yellow cloth of mourning, welcomes you. You would speak, Sir Blade?"

He might as well carry the lie through, for what it was worth. Blade was thinking fast now, and he had heard that the Khad was a greedy man. He was grateful for all he had learned in his three weeks behind the wall.

"The Emperor Mei Saka is dead, eaten by carrion apes and his bones forgotten. It *is* true that I come from Pukka, sent as special envoy by the High Emperor of all the Caths, to replace the Low Emperor, Mei Saka, and find out why you Mongs cannot be defeated. They are very impatient in Pukka and do not understand why this fighting must go on year after year."

Morpho grinned and watched Blade with alert dark eyes in which there was no belief. But he nodded and said, "As you say it, Sir Blade. I will tell Sadda all these things."

The dwarf's eyes roamed up and down Blade's powerful frame. "I will also tell her what she most wants to know—that you will make a magnificent slave in more ways than one. It may be that she will save you from the Khad yet."

Blade was getting out of his depth again. "How can Sadda save me, little man? *Our* spies reported that she was a prisoner and was to be bound and turned over to me if I

75

won. How can Sadda do anything for me? Or for herself? There must be much hate between the Khad and she."

"Hate?" Morpho's head nodded vigorously. "There is. There was. There will be. Yet they are still brother and sister and, until one of them is dead, they must rule the Mongs together. Each has his faction and the spies are thicker than flies on pony dung. They quarrel constantly and make up constantly. Each always on guard against the other. And now that you have lost, after having won and thrown the victory away, the Khad has released Sadda from her tent and they are friends again and tonight that will be celebrated. You will be judged and disposed of, Sir Blade. That is why I am here on Sadda's errand—to see if you are worth saving as a slave.

"She is subtle, is Sadda, and knows that for just now she has the advantage over the Khad. He would have handed her over to the Caths, I think, if things had gone otherwise today. So he would have been rid of her and no real blame to him. But things did *not* go otherwise, because you are something of a arrogant fool, Sir Blade, if a brave one, and now the Khad must put a good face on it. Sadda knows this. She knows that if she asks him for something soon, before his temper changes, that she is likely to get it."

Blade nodded. "And she will ask him for me? As a slave?"

Morpho turned one of his amazing flips and stared at Blade, his mouth grotesque in the wavering light of the lamp.

"If you are fortunate she will, Sir Blade. If not you will die at dawn on the plain before the wall. Plans are made. All the Caths to be summoned to watch. A parley in which the Khad will ask once again for the giant cannon. Which, of course, the Caths will not part with. Not even for you."

Blade had to agree. They would not part with the great cannon. Lali would be distressed, but Lali would have to let him die on the plain.

"The Khad," said Morpho, watching Blade's face closely, "has planned a special death for you. Would you know of it?"

Blade shrugged. "Why not? Words do not hurt me." He was suddenly aware that this was some sort of test and had nothing to do with Sadda or the dwarf's errand. Morpho was trying to find out something for *himself*.

"You will be tied to a stake and your guts cut out," said Morpho. "Then you will be strangled. You see what a genius the Khad is?"

No mistaking the hate and scorn in those last words. Blade knew that if he had not found a friend he had at least found an enemy of the Khad. It was not much, yet more than he had had a few minutes before.

A vast shiny black face poked itself into the tent. Blade stared in surprise. He had not known there was anyone on guard outside.

The black wore a peaked turban and a colored sash wound about his loins. He waved a heavy sword at the dwarf in a peculiar motion. Morpho signed back and the black disappeared. Blade blinked and watched the tent entrance. Had he really seen it? Or had a genie swirled like dark smoke in and out of the tent?

Morpho saw his expression and chuckled. "Eunuchs. Sadda's men. The Khad gave leave that they might guard you, instead of his own men, which is a reason to believe that you may live a time yet, Sir Blade. But that will be as the black sands write. And my time is up."

He turned a double back flip toward the entrance. "I will do my best for you, Sir Blade. I promise nothing. But I will extol your virtues as a slave. You understand me, Sir Blade?"

Blade nodded sourly. "If what I have heard of Sadda is true I understand you. You mean bed slave?"

The mouth moved in the bad light. "That is what I mean. Now I go, after one last warning. Do not show fear. Be bold, but not too bold. I would have you live, Sir Blade."

77

The dwarf was gone.

Soon afterward they came for him. The blacks first three of them with flaring torches, and he saw why Morpho had not feared their eavesdropping. They mad throaty animal sounds. Their tongues had been torn ou and he guessed they had also been deafened by the way they stared and motioned with the thick-bladed swords.

The larger of the blacks hauled Blade to his feet and examined his chains. They threw a twist of cloth at him and signed that he wrap it around him. His chains were enormously heavy and cumbersome, and Blade had barely completed the task when the tent entrance parted and a warrior came in. He approached Blade and gave him a fierce stare.

"I am Rahstum," he announced proudly. "Chief Captain of all the Mongs and high servant to Khad Tambur Scourge of the World and Shaker of the Universe. You are wanted in audience, stranger, by the Khad and his sister, the Most Magnificent Sadda. Are you ready, stranger?"

Blade did not doubt that he was high rank. His leather armor was new and burnished to a high luster and there was a silver chain about his neck. From each of his shoulders dangled a horsetail. His high peaked cap was worked with silver. He was taller than any Mong Blade had seen before, and his eyes were a piercing light gray instead of the usual dark brown and did not have the Mong slant about them. They stared at Blade now, above a thick sprouting beard, with a mingle of curiosity and contempt.

It was time, Blade thought, to assert himself a bit. I could do no harm. He glared back at the splendid Captain.

"You will not call me stranger," he said coldly. "I am Sir Blade, come from Pukka, great city of all the Caths, and there will be a great ransom paid for me."

Blade plunged on. "You will treat me with respect, Captain—" He let more ice creep into his voice— "with the respect due my rank, or you will be sorry for it."

The gray eyes widened and for a moment there was

doubt in them. Then white teeth flashed through the beard in a derisive smile. The man made a mocking little bow.

"I am sorry, Sir Blade. But I am also curious. I have roamed the world much and I have never before heard a title such as this Sir. You would enlighten me, perhaps?" His tone was that of an intelligent and educated man, and Blade did not think he was a Mong.

With great dignity, considering that he was in chains and loin cloth, Blade explained: "Sir is a high rank in a great secret society in the south of Cath. Few have heard of it, but I am next to the High Emperor in rank. I am not a Cath, as you can see, and it is part of the society's mystery that I cannot tell any man who and what I am—except that I come from a far-off place beyond the edge of the world. Where the waters of life fall away in a great stream to the place of death. Thence I come. Thence I will return when the black sands have written it."

His voice was deep and bell toned. Blade was rather proud of himself. It was a nice bit of mumbo-jumbo.

It had no effect on the Captain, but the file of Mong soldiers behind him muttered and looked uneasy. The man called Rahstum laughed curtly and said, "Tell that to the Khad, Sir Blade. *He* may believe you."

He gestured to his men. "Bring him along, you stupid animals. And do not talk to him, nor let him talk to you. He might cast a spell on you." He spun on his heel and stalked from the tent.

As he was conducted through the tent village, Blade kept his eyes and ears open. He was flanked on either side by the Mong guards and there was no hope for escape, though the great wall lay less than a mile away to the south. It was as tight a spot as he had ever been in, in any dimension and what he saw was not encouraging.

They crossed an open space where a long gallows stood. A dozen naked Mongs dangled from it, some by the heels, some by the neck. All were dead. Nearby another Mong had been impaled on a sharpened pole.

Rahstum glanced back at Blade with a cold smile. "The

79

Khad's justice. Thieves, deserters, murderers and some who spoke against the Khad. How great a ransom will your friends pay for you, Sir Blade?" And the man Rahstum laughed.

The laugh, and the gallows, sent a grating chill along Blade's spine. For the first time he felt real fear. He knew the symptoms and took immediate steps to banish them. Fear was a progressive and corrosive weakness and could not be tolerated. Blade took a deep breath and began the fierce concentration of which he was capable. Survival. Think only of survival.

They plunged into another maze of tents from which came cooking smells and the sounds of women and children. They were skirting the edge of the village now, and on the bleak plain Blade saw thousands of horses and ponies grazing, or sleeping, or moving restlessly about. Horsemen were patrolling the herd on all sides.

They passed a long row of wagons, high sided and with felt-covered tops, with huge wooden wheels. Several of the wagons were off to one side and were guarded by mounted warriors. These wagons had slatted sides and were dimly lit and a sound of voices came from them—groans, curses, screams, a snatch of a song.

Rahstum had drawn his sword and now he pointed with it to the wagons. "Slave wagons, Sir Blade. You may come to know the inside of them—if you are fortunate."

The huge black tent of Khad Tambur was set well away from the village itself. It blazed with light, and as they approached Blade heard a weird and plangent music that raised gooseflesh on him. Strident deep horn tones mixed with plucked strings and a high jangle of bells and muted, irregular tympany.

They halted at the tent entrance. Two Mongs stood guard, flanking a fascia of lances thrust into the earth. Horsetails fluttered from the lances. On the tallest lance was a skull. It grinned at Blade.

The Captain sent one of his Mongs into the tent. As the tent flap parted Blade caught a glimpse of a girl dancing n a cleared space before a dais. But for a loin cloth she was naked, sweating and whirling and undulating in pale yellow light while the wild music swirled behind her. Her belly was like a thing apart from her, with a life of its own, shimmering and shaking, the sleek muscles writhing like a basketful of snakes. The tent flap closed.

One of the guards spoke to Rahstum. "Minga dances well tonight."

Another guard laughed. "That is not all she does well."

"I know, I know. I'm saving my pay. One of these days I will be able to afford her."

There was general laughter among the other guards. "Fool! Afford Minga on *your* pay? You will be an old man first, and then what good will it do you? Or Minga!"

There was a roar of harsh laughter. Rahstum broke it up with a gruff command. The tent opened again and a man beckoned.

The Captain took Blade's arm and thrust him roughly forward through the tent entrance. They took six paces forward, Blade's chains clanking and galling his wrists and ankles. Rahstum loosed his arm and fell back. Blade gazed about him, his face impassive, his spine straight and his massive shoulders squared back. They all stared. Blade gave back look for look.

The music ceased, trembling away in a dying fall. For the space of several breaths there was a silence in the great tent, a silence filled by garish yellow light and an oppressive heat of close-packed bodies. Every flat Mong face swiveled toward Blade, judging him, hating him.

Blade, in that sibilance of breathing, impaled by those hostile eyes, had never felt so alone.

From his throne Khad Tambur spoke: "Bring him forward. I would know what manner of man can kill a champion of mine."

Rahstum the Captain gave Blade a little push. His voice was not unkind as he muttered: "Go to the throne and fall on your knees. Keep silent and keep your head down."

81

Blade was silent but he did not keep his head down. He walked as proudly as though he wore silks and a crown instead of chains. As he approached the throne he saw Morpho, the dwarf, seated on a pillow to one side. Their eyes met. The dwarf's glance was dark and blank, speaking only idle curiosity.

Blade halted three paces from the throne and gazed at Khad Tambur. The Khad, thin and narrow shouldered, was bent forward at an absurd and painful angle. Arthritis of the spine, thought Blade. He stared back at the single dark eye that fixed him so malevolently. Only the right eye functioned. The left was covered by a drooping lid.

The Khad twisted on his throne and there was mingled rage and amazement in his tone. "You *dare* to stand before me?"

Blade now was playing it by intuition. "I stand," he said calmly. "Sir Blade bows to no man."

A whimpering sigh blew through the big tent like a minor chord. Someone laughed nervously. Then silence again.

The Khad's single eye blinked and he twisted his racked back once more to look at the woman at his side. She also sat on a throne, but lower on the dais.

"Well, sister? You thought to have this one as a slave? What of it now? This is no slave."

Two brown eyes studied Blade over a veil. He met the glance squarely and did not look away. So this was Sadda, sister of Khad Tambur. Sadda of the sinister reputation. Sadda for whom Lali, whose hatred was as pure as black crystal, had prepared a cage.

The woman did not speak. The Khad nodded and motioned to the guards nearby. "Very well, sister. I think we must teach this Sir Blade some manners." To the guards he said: "Beat him to his knees."

The guards leaped in with reversed lances to club Blade down. He tensed for the blows.

The woman held up a hand. Her fingers were long and delicate, the nails painted a blood red.

82

"Hold," she commanded. "An ox is beaten, or a slave, and that is good for them. But this man is not an ox, and not yet a slave—though he may be. I say hold. Do not touch him."

The Khad was scowling. The woman leaned to whisper to him. The Khad shook his head, still scowling. She tapped his arm and whispered on, intent and serious, her mouth moving rapidly beneath the veil. Blade stood calmly, watching the woman from the corner of his eye, giving no hint of his inner turmoil. The heavy chains jangled as he crossed his superbly muscled arms across his chest.

He could tell little about her face beneath the veil. Her hair was dark and lustrous, well oiled and piled in a heavy coronet atop a well-shaped head. She wore a little jacket that left her breasts bare, as was the custom with some Mong women. Her breasts were small, taut and compact and firm, with large reddish-pink aureoles surrounding small nipples. Her waist was tiny, flaring into well-developed hips and legs that appeared slim beneath filmy pantaloons. Her feet were bare, the nails painted the same bloody red as her fingernails, and she wore a golden bangle on each ankle.

The Khad was still shaking his head. Sadda argued on. The tension expanded like gas in a balloon. Blade risked a glance at Morpho. The dwarf did not meet his eye. He was idly juggling four small balls, his carven grin fixed on his task.

The Khad twisted away from his sister. "So be it," he said in loud disgust. "He is yours until the ransom comes—if there be a ransom."

He fixed his good eye on Blade. "You heard the word, you who call yourself Sir Blade? Your friends in Cath, in Pukka, will go ransom for you?"

Blade began to hope. He nodded gravely. "They will pay ransom, Khad Tambur. But you must send a messenger to Pukka for it—they of Serendip, behind the wall here, will not have enough of treasure." It would take a

83

horseman a long time to get to Pukka and back, even under safe conduct. He wondered if Lali had already been approached.

Khad Tambur answered that in the next breath. "I know all of that. After you were taken I parleyed with the Empress Mei. To no avail. She would not surrender the gun for you. And if I cannot have the cannon I *will* have half the wealth of Cath!"

He sounded like a small boy cheated of his favorite toy and demanding the world to placate him.

There was bustle and murmur in the tent now and the Khad held up a hand for silence. "Hear this, all of you. I, Khad Tambur, give this man Sir Blade to my sister as her slave. To do with as she desires—so long as he is kept alive for ransom." He moved painfully on the throne to glare at Sadda. "See that you do keep him alive, sister! I care not how, nor what else you do to him, but he must be breathing when the ransom comes. I will not be cheated of everything!"

He made a washing gesture with his hands and raised a finger to Morpho the dwarf. The little man plucked a large round melon from a box filled with melting snow, cut it in half, and hastened to the throne. The Khad munched on his melon and glared at Blade. Through a mouthful of melon, without turning, he snapped at Sadda.

"Well—get on with it then! You have your wish. See if he is slave or not—or if you can make him one. Only be sure he does not bleed to death!"

Blade understood then that while he might be out of the frying pan he was still very much in the fire.

The brown eyes were watching Blade over the veil again. The scrutiny was long and deliberate and missed not an inch of his lean, brawny, hard-muscled frame. Somewhere back in those brown eyes a cold spark glowed.

When she spoke to him her voice was husky and soft. She crooked a finger. "Come and stand before me, slave. You are no longer Sir Blade. You are slave. Later, if you please me, I will think of a new name for you."

Blade moved toward her. Their glances met and locked and she was the first to look away. She pointed a finger at the thick rug before her throne.

"You who would not kneel to the Khad must kneel to me. You were not slave then. You are *now*. Kneel!"

Blade was tempted. His nerves were raw, screaming, and for the first time he admitted that now, just now, would be an excellent time for Lord L to pluck him back to H-Dimension. If that was cowardly, then he was a coward.

Yet he dared not be cowardly! These Mongs worshiped and understood only courage. Instinct warned him that at the first sign of weakness on his part he was lost. They would forget the ransom and tear him to bits. Cruelty was a way of life with these Mongs.

Blade said: "If I will not kneel to a man is it likely that I will kneel to a woman?" He smiled at her. It was his very best smile and it took every ounce of guts he had. The Khad was dangerous. Sadda carried murder in those brown eyes.

Khad Tambur, laughing, choked on the melon he was eating. To his sister he said: "You do not make a good beginning, sister. This is going to be amusing after all—making a slave of this one."

Blade saw her lips move beneath the veil. She too was smiling. She pointed to the rug again. "Kneel. I give you one last chance."

Blade shook his head. "I will not kneel." He hoped she could not hear the thudding of his heart. He had chosen his way and now he must stick to it.

Sadda made a sign and a minute later an enormous black entered the tent from a side entrance. He carried a wooden block, rather tall and narrow and with a peculiar notch scalloped into one side. He was followed by another black who carried what looked to Blade to be a long butcher knife.

Sadda gestured to the blacks. "Arrange it."

They set the block on end near Blade. He saw, with

sickness growing in him, that the notch was so contrived that a man stepping into it would have his genitals just level with the top of the block.

Sadda watched him over the veil. "You will not kneel?"

"I will not."

She turned to one of the blacks. "Show him what he will be if he does not kneel."

The black unwound a cloth from around his waist and groin and in a moment stood naked before Blade. It was the first time had had seen an eunuch and he did not like the sight.

The Khad said: "Be only sure that he does not bleed to death. I warn you, sister!"

"He will not bleed to death." She pointed to a fire pan that a third slave had brought in and placed on a tripod. A cauterizing iron glowed white hot in the pan.

Sadda pointed to the eunuch who displayed himself, then at Blade. "You would be like that one?"

He was sweating heavily now. It ran into his eyes and he blinked against the salty sting. He was frightened, as badly frightened as he had ever been in a lifetime of adventure and danger. He could face death well enough— but this!

And yet he must gamble. He had come too far to turn back. Turn coward now and he lost everything. He knew that. He *felt* it. He *must* gamble.

He stared at Sadda. "I would *not* be like that one. I admit it. But I will not kneel."

Sadda snapped her fingers. Guards rushed forward and seized Blade and pushed him to the block. One of the blacks, muddy eyes gleaming, tore away Blade's loin cloth and seized his genitals and stretched them on the block. Another black moved forward with the long knife and raised it, poised, over the block.

Blade stared straight ahead. At all costs he must not weaken. The next few seconds would decide whether he had won or lost his gamble.

The silence in the tent was like a living thing. The knife gleamed cruel and keen in the tawny light.

Sadda spoke so softly that it was almost a whisper. "You will not kneel to me?"

Somehow Blade managed to get the words out. Firm, controlled, with out a quaver in his voice. "I will not."

The moment stretched into eternity. Sadda made a sign with her upraised hand.

Chapter 8

They put Richard Blade into a prison wagon and placed him on public view. He did not mind. At least a dozen times a day he glanced down to reassure himself that he was still a whole man. He was, and that, for the moment, was enough for him. He had won his gamble and defeated Sadda. At the last second she had signaled the blacks away and ordered that Blade be taken from the tent. He had seen her since, but only at a distance. Sometimes she would ride to within fifty yards of his cage, never closer, and sit there on her small horse and watch him for a long time. Blade ignored her. In the end she would spur away, riding as wildly and as well as any Mong Warrior.

His wagon was placed apart from the other slave wagons, on the windy black-dusted plain near the circle of rocks where he had first entered X-Dimension. The wooden slats of his prison were strong and well set, but even so he might have escaped but for the guards posted every night. In the daytime, when the sun blinked to life like a lightbulb, he had no chance. As soon as dark was near his cage was patrolled by six Mong warriors. There was nothing to do but bide his time and wonder.

He had expected that Sadda would make a household slave of him, for very personal reasons of her own, but in this she fooled him. Every day she came and watched, but only that.

The dwarf did not come near.

But he was not neglected. Crowds of Mongs came every day to jeer and jabber at him and poke sharp sticks into the cage. For a time he endured this patiently, merely grabbing the sticks and snapping them in two. One day he lost his temper and snatched away a sharp stick, reversed it, and jammed it halfway through his tormentor's chest. The Mong ran screaming into the crowd, which only laughed at him. After that Blade was left pretty much alone. They still came to stare and gibe, but they kept a respectful distance.

He was fed twice a day on crude black bread, horse-meat, and a large bowl of potent Mong drink called *bross*. This was made of mare's milk and blood, mixed half and half, with some fermented grain added. At first the *bross* sickened him, smelling as it did of faint decay, but in time he came to like it. And respect it. It was as potent as whiskey.

Every day the Mongs attacked the long yellow wall and every day they came back defeated. Now and again the huge cannon would boom and a jade ball would go whistling harmlessly overhead to smash itself on the rocks. At first he entertained hopes that the Caths would mount an attack, or a sortie at night, and fight through to rescue him. This he soon discarded as unrealistic. The Caths were hard pressed, even behind their wall, and he could not expect that Lali could influence her chiefs to waste men. To his own surprise he did not think much about Lali, except to wonder if she had taken a new man into her bed.

Rahstum, the Khad's captain, occasionally rode by the cage to speak with the guard officers. He would glance at Blade, the pale gray eyes narrowed in some private speculation, but he never spoke.

After a week of this Blade began to fret and plan escape, no matter how impossible or chancy it seemed. He was filthy and his beard a knotted tangle. He had been given a pair of ragged breeches, but otherwise had to endure sun and cold, wind and storm, and the eternally blowing black sand as best he could. Straw was tossed into the wagon, but by now it was filthy. He began, at night, to test the bars as best he could without the patrol becoming suspicious. This was not easy, for the guards continually circled the wagon, riding close every now and then to peer at him. But none would speak to him, not so much as a word, and Blade, though well aware of the irony, had to admit that he was lonely.

During the day, when they were not attacking the wall, the Mong cavalry drilled on the plain near Blade's cage. He knew something of horses, and horsemanship, and he had never seen skill like this before. They wheeled and formed and charged and reformed with clocklike precision. In open warfare he knew that nothing could stand against them. It was the great wall that baffled them, and against the wall the Khad sent them daily to die by the hundreds.

Did the Khad never think of flanking the wall? It must end somewhere. Either the Shaker of the World was singularly stupid or so obsessed with the great cannon that he could think of nothing else.

He watched the Mongs play a game in which they charged at a ring which was suspended from a post by a cord and set to swinging. The ring was no bigger than those brass ones that Blade, as a small child, had plucked from a carousel in Brighton to gain a free ride. The Mongs had to pick up the ring on their lance points at full gallop. Very few missed. Those who did were forced to ride between the lines of their companions and were well beaten.

On the ninth day Captain Rahstum rode up to Blade's cage and dismounted. Two Mongs were with him, one carrying a large square block of wood.

Rahstum surveyed the captive through the stout bars, hands on hips, as immaculately dressed as ever in leather armor that sparkled in the sun. Blade thought again that this man was not a true Mong. He was too tall, and his skin too fair beneath the heavy beard.

"So, Sir Blade, you survive well enough. Your cage agrees with you, I see. Though I will admit there is something of an odor about you!" And he wrinkled his nose.

Blade was silent, staring back at the Captain. Something had changed. He could smell it. But he was not to be provoked.

At last Rahstum said, "You are well fed? There is enough of food?"

Blade nodded. "Of what it is, there is enough. But a man of my station should not be made to exist on horsemeat and black bread. I wish you would speak to the Khad about this. And I could use some clean straw as well."

Rahstum stared at him for a moment, his gray eyes puzzled, then to Blade's surprise he broke into a roar of laughter. He pounded his knee. The two Mong soldiers who had accompanied him allowed themselves uneasy grins.

When the Captain finally stopped laughing he said: "I begin to believe, Sir Blade, that you really are a Sir. Whatever that is. You faced down Sadda and the Khad both, and there has been no cry or complaint from you. Now you complain of the food and bid me carry a message to the Khad for you."

He went off into another gale of laughter while Blade watched in patience. The wooden block, he saw now, was really a collar. There was a neck hole cut in it and a crude iron lock.

Rahstum abruptly stopped laughing. He drew his sword and pointed to the cage door. "Get him out of there and put on the collar. No—hold. We will need more than the three of us."

After Rahstum summoned another half-dozen Mongs the door of the cage was opened. The Captain beckoned Blade out.

"A step up in your slave's life," he said. "You are to wear a collar and serve as one of Sadda's house slaves. Make no trouble for me, Sir Blade, Sadda does not want you dead—else you would be—and I do not want to bear blame for killing you. So I advise you to submit. You will sleep warmer, have better food, and who knows—before long you may have a little golden collar."

At this the Mongs all tittered and grinned at each other until Rahstum frowned at them.

There was no point in resistance. Blade came out of the cage and allowed them to affix the wooden collar around his neck. It was large, clumsy and awkward, but not too heavy for a man of his physique. In time it would wear skin from his neck and he would develop sores, but he did not intend to wear it that long.

It was not the collar that galled him so much as the way he was led back to the main encampment. A rawhide line was tied to the collar and Blade was pulled along behind one of the horsemen. His leg, though healing well, was still stiff and sore, causing him to limp, and when he tripped over a rock and was dragged ingloriously through the dust, there was a great roar of scornful laughter from the Mongs. Rahstum at last halted the party until Blade could regain his feet, saying that Sadda's slave must not be damaged.

They left the main camp and approached a lesser scatter of black tents surrounded by a high withe fence. The fence was sectioned so it could be transported from place to place in the wagons. It was patrolled by mounted guards wearing armor slightly different from any Blade had seen before. This would be Sadda's private camp and headquarters.

Blade was unleashed while Rahstum conferred briefly with a guard at the gate. When Rahstum came back he glanced at Blade with his cold gray eyes and a dry smile moved beneath the heavy beard.

"Fare you well, Sir Blade. Be a good slave and earn your golden collar."

The Mongs tittered.

When Rahstum and his men had ridden away, Blade was herded into the enclosure at lance point. A clone of smaller tents surrounded one large one from which scarlet horsetails fluttered. As Blade was marched past the large tent he heard women speaking and laughing and there was a palpable odor of female flesh and perfume in the air. The tent had round openings in the sides, similar to portholes and covered by drop cloths. As he passed, Blade saw a veiled face peering at him from one of the apertures. Sadda?

In one corner of the enclosure was a smaller square, a stockade of heavy pointed logs set deep into the earth and bound by withes. Along the tops of the logs ran an ingenious arrangement of rawhide cords and little bells that would sound an alarm when touched.

This stockade was guarded by regular Mongs, older men who all bore the scars of grievous wounds. Some lacked an ear, or a nose, and many were without one arm. One had no left leg and made do with a crude crutch. Blade, missing nothing, saw that little love was lost between the two groups. Sadda's men were all young and handsome and laughed a lot. The stockade guards were Khad Tambur's men, worn out in battle.

He was shoved rudely into the stockade and the gate closed behind him. Blade shrugged and looked about him. At least he was not in chains. He shifted the wooden collar on his neck, easing it as best he could and went to explore. The stockade did not seem very well populated.

Two sides of the stockade were lined with small roofed carrels, narrow and deep and with the roof so low that a man must stoop to enter. As Blade stared around him a voice said, "Come talk to me, Sir Blade. I cannot come to you."

The voice was deep and gruff, with a coarse tinge of humor in it. Blade, startled, glanced about for the source.

It came from a carrel to his left, near a corner of the stockade. Blade stalked to the alcove and stooped to peer in. A man lay in the dirty straw. Both legs were missing just above the knees. He raised himself on heavily muscled arms to grin at Blade. "Welcome, Sir Blade. I invite you to share my palace." He balanced himself dexterously on one arm as he waved a hand around the little sty.

"All my servants have run off and there is no food nor drink. I hope you can forgive, for I am ordinarily an hospitable man."

Blade squatted in the entrance. "You know my name. How is that?"

The legless man laughed and let himself fall into the straw. "No magic, Sir Blade. Everyone in Cath and Mongland knows your name by now. We heard of you even before you were taken prisoner. And when you stood up to Sadda and the knife, your fame grew. That is bad, of course, for you will have to pay for it in the end."

Instinct told Blade to like and trust this legless man, at least to some degree, and there was something contagious about the coarse humor. Blade chuckled wryly as he made himself comfortable in the dirty straw.

"For a famous man," Blade said, "I am not as well fed and lodged as I would like."

The legless man laughed again and raised himself to a sitting position. "Be thankful, Sir Blade. You are alive. That is a miracle in itself. And I hear that you have caught Sadda's eye and that will lead to more good fortune, at least for a time—if you are man enough in bed!"

Blade scratched at his tangle of beard, which was one great itch, and considered this strange prisonmate. There was something familiar about the hawkish face, the tone of skin, and after a moment he recognized it. This man looked vaguely like Rahstum, the Captain! One thing was certain—he was no Mong.

The cripple had been subjecting Blade to the same intense scrutiny. His eyes, like those of Rahstum, were a pale gray. Suddenly he extended a hand to Blade. "I am called Baber. As you have guessed I am not a Mong. I am of the Cauca tribe. And you are thinking that I look like Rahstum, the Captain?"

Blade admitted it.

"That is because Rahstum is also a Cauca. Believe me or not, Sir Blade, but we were once soldiers together and I his commander. Who would think it to see me now."

Blade, who had been lonely in his wagon cage, welcomed this new companionship. He set out to learn all he could, especially about his own probable fate.

Baber, laughing coarsely, pointed at the wooden collar around Blade's neck and said, "You will exchange that for a golden one if you are humble and careful and submit yourself. And make no great mistakes. That is why you have been moved from your cage to this place, to serve your apprenticeship, and so that your spirit may be broken. I have been prisoner for many years and I have seen it happen a dozen times. Sadda must always have a new favorite to replace the old. You will be the new one someday. When she has humiliated you enough."

Blade frowned. "I am not very good at being humble. I had my chance at that and just between us, Baber, I was in a sweat of fright. But I did not think it good policy to grovel or show fear. I gambled with the knife and I won. So I am still alive. Must I be humble now?"

Baber, who had a tonsure of baldness and was gray at the temples, squinted at Blade. In a serious tone he said: "I know. I know all of it. News travels fast among the Mongs. But you were not a slave then, Sir Blade, and also what you did once cannot always be done again. There is a limit to Sadda's patience. What little wisdom I have tells me that it is better to stay alive as long as possible. Let me tell you a story that is known to my tribe, the Cauca."

In the old times, Baber said, there was a certain wizard who fell out of favor with the king. All of his prophecies turned out to be false and the king ordered the wizard's head to be struck off. The wizard begged a year of grace in which he promised to teach the king's dog to talk. The king was intrigued, though skeptical, granted the time with the proviso that if th wizard failed to teach the dog to talk he would be boiled in oil instead of merely beheaded.

A friend of the wizard asked him why he had made such a bargain.

"Because a year of life is precious," the wizard replied.

"Anything can happen. I might die a natural and painless death. The king may die. And I might even teach the dog to talk in a year."

Baber laughed and rolled over in the straw. "So you see, Sir Blade, that it might be well to play the humble part for a time. Stay alive! Anything can happen."

That was true. Blade knew that the Khad had sent a messenger to Pukka, in the south of Cath, to demand a great ransom for him. He had no notion of what Lali could do, or would do, about this. All he knew was that Lali had agreed to safe conduct for the messenger and had provided him with an escort. It would be two or three months before the man could return—with news that no one in Pukka had ever heard of Blade! He did not like to think of that. The Khad would certainly snatch him back from Sadda and have him executed in the cruelest possible manner.

Baber had been watching Blade with a peculiar glint in his eyes. Now, in a near whisper, he said: "You see the wisdom? Be humble and play the fool if you must. Stay alive and wait. I do not say that I know, because I would be a liar, but I can guess at changes that are coming. There is hate and bad blood between Sadda and the Khad. When they were younger they were lovers, so breaking a taboo of their black god, Obi. And now that they are no longer lovers, they are haters. But they share power and at the moment neither can rule without the other. They are fearful and uneasy and all the Mongs know this and feel it. A stone thrown into a pond disturbs the bottom as well as the surface. There is unrest among the Mongs, and dissatisfaction, but the Tamburs have ruled them for a thousand years and no one yet has courage to go against them. And this war, these endless wars against the great wall, sorely try the patience of the ordinary people. Thousands of the best Mong warriors die every month because the Khad is a madman and thinks he must have the great cannon of Cath. So heed a poor legless fool who was once a warrior, Sir Blade and—"

Baber had been looking over Blade's shoulder. He broke off abruptly and lowered himself into the straw so that only his head showed.

"Here comes Aplonius! He wears the golden collar now and is in charge of us. Patience, Sir Blade! Bear it. He is nothing but be careful."

Blade remained where he was, squatting, watching the approach of the man called Aplonius. He knew at once that he was in for a bad time.

The man who came toward him, swinging a long whip, was a Mong. But like none Blade had seen before. He was taller, his skin lighter, and instead of the flat, nearly concave Mong features, he had a jutting nose and narrow-set eyes. His hair was bright and thick with pomade and curled atop his narrow head like miniature waves. He wore gaily colored breeches thrust into high boots and a tight fitting leathern jacket. His mustache was dark and neatly trimmed and a few dark hairs straggled from a weak chin.

Around his skinny neck was a golden collar, light and of exquisite workmanship. When he was close enough Blade saw that raised letters encircled the collar. *S S S S S*

This was Sadda's current favorite. Blade could not believe it. This was a man?

The slim dandy stopped before Blade and sneered. "So you are Sir Blade? Come to work as house slave for the Lady Sadda?"

The narrow-set eyes blinked down at him and Blade saw rage and fear in them. More than fear—terror, that the man was trying to conceal.

Blade stared back, trying to hide his contempt. "I am Sir Blade."

Whap! The whip caught him a stinging blow across the face.

"Rise when you speak to me," said the dandy. "Rise and bow as low as you can. Lower than you can."

Whap—whap! The whip slashed across his face, back and forth, biting like an adder.

It was a near thing. Back in H-Dimension even J would

not risk Blade's temper. Now the blood pounded in his head and his heart was bursting and he was instantly bathed in sweat. Every muscle in his great body tensed and his bearded lips parted in a snarl. He could have torn this Alponius in half and he very nearly did. Sheer discipline and will power restrained him. Blade battled with himself—and won.

He stumbled to his feet and bowed, the heavy wooden collar pulling over in ludicrous subservience. The action served to mask the rage in his face.

Aplonius, who had skipped back in alarm, sneered again and gave Blade a dozen blows about the head and shoulders. Each blow raised a long red welt. Blade gritted his teeth and took it. Baber was right. Stay alive. Take it. His turn would come. Carefully he counted each blow.

When Aplonius was breathless from whipping Blade, he stepped back again, panting and switching the whip against his leg. He pointed to the carrel next to that of Baber and pointed with the whip.

That is your hole. You will remain in it until I say otherwise. You will not speak with that old fool again!" He pointed the whip at Baber's head, just visible in the filthy straw. "You understand, swine? No talking. I will have you watched and if you are caught talking, you will wish you were dead. Understand that well! I cannot kill you, because the Lady Sadda does not wish it, but I can make you wish that I *would* kill you. Now get over there and be silent." He slashed at Blade with the whip again.

Blade did not look at the man. He did not trust himself. He was sick and trembling with rage. He went into the carrel next to Barber's and sat down in the straw.

Aplonius' voice followed him. "Slaves do not have titles. You are no longer a Sir, whatever it means. I would call you swine if I had my way, but that is too indelicate for the Lady Sadda's ears. So you are now called Blade until the lady finds a better name. Tomorrow, Blade, you will go to work. You will labor and you will learn. You will walk humbly and you will wear your collar and you

98

will never raise your eyes unless I give permission. That is understood, swine?"

Blade somehow managed to get the words out. "That is understood."

Aplonius went in to the carrel where Baber lay in his straw. Blade could not see—the wall between the carrels was solid—but he could hear well enough.

"You are an old fool with a long tongue," said Aplonius. There was the sound of blows being rained on the legless man. "I do not understand," Aplonius continued, "why I am not allowed to kill you and have done with it. Why, old man? Why? You have no friends or you would not be here. Why am I not allowed to kill you?" His tone was a querulous whine and he seemed genuinely puzzled.

Blade kept his eyes down, staring at the straw between his legs, welding mental chains on himself so he would not go and kill that perfumed obscenity.

Finally Aplonius stalked away with a final sneer at Blade. "I will see you tomorrow! Mind what I have told you."

Blade watched him out the gate, where the Mong guards bowed low to him. When Aplonius mounted a pony and rode away, his back to them, the guards made contemptuous gestures. Blade's grin was hard. Aplonius was not loved.

"Psst." It was Baber whispering through the wall. "Sit with your back to the wall and speak without moving your lips. The guards know we speak, but they do not care so long as our lips do not betray us. They hate Aplonius as much as we."

"That," Blade said, "is a lot of hate!"

He heard Baber sigh. "I know. I have often wondered if there is anything but hate in the world. In my country, two years' march to the north over the Hima mountains, it is the same. But enough of that, Sir Blade. We cannot change the world. You bore yourself with that—*thing* just now. I was afraid you would lose your temper and kill him."

"So was I."

"That might have spoiled everything," said Baber. "And to no point, because he will be dead soon enough. Sadda tires of him, I hear. Did you see the terror in his eyes?"

Blade said he had. He was watching the sun hovering low over the stockade wall. Any second now it would plummet out of sight.

Baber laughed, a cruel sound now. "He is already dead and he knows it. Sadda tires of his peculiar brand of lovemaking, though it has pleasured her for some months. And now you come. Aplonius knows you will replace him when Sadda is ready, and as he is a coward he suffers greatly. He is helpless. He is as much a slave as we are, golden collar or not, and there is no escape for him. But let us talk of other things."

Blade had been thinking hard. He said, "I agree to that, Baber. And I am very ignorant yet, though I keep my eyes and ears open. Let us talk of what you meant when you said there would be changes."

Silence. He could imagine Baber squinting and scratching his balding head.

"I said there *might* be changes, Sir Blade. I said I did not know for sure. I am not a liar. And if there are to be changes they will come in their own time and cannot be hurried. You must understand this and promise me, if I tell you what I can only guess at, that you will do nothing to hasten matters and will not act alone. I think I trust you, Sir Blade, but I must have that promise. I am a legless old man and I will die soon, but I do not want to die in this place."

Blade promised. And added, "Do not call me Sir Blade. You heard what our friend Aplonius said! Call me Blade if you will. Or friend. I am both."

"As you will," said Baber. "Listen, then. And remember that nothing of this has been told to me. I speak only from my own head. But I watch and I listen and I see what is coming.

"The Captain Rahstum is a countryman of mine, as I said. He is a great soldier, but he is a mercenary and fights for gain, as I did once, as do all the Cauca. But Rahstum prospered and I did not. But when I fought for another tribe against the Mongs and was taken prisoner, it was Rahstum who saved my life. That was some years ago, and it was Rahstum who persuaded the Khad to cut off my legs instead of my head."

To Blade it seemed a doubtful act of mercy, but he said nothing.

"It was all one to the Khad," Baber continued. "I was rendered useless as a warrior and it was a favor for his Captain. Ever since then Rahstum, by his influence, has kept me alive. Barely so, and in this filth, but still alive. I do not really understand why, for I cannot be of use to him. A legless man! I tell you all this to show that I know something of Rahstum, of how he thinks. After all he is a Cauca.

"Now, in this blood hate between the Khad and his whorish sister, Rahstum walks a careful path. He is a great captain and the Khad has much need of him. The Mong soldiers respect him. And of late Sadda has been wooing him, because she will need him when she moves against the Khad. You begin to see a little?"

Blade saw that Rahstum was walking a tightrope with his head finely balanced on his body. He said as much.

Baber chuckled. "That is so. Rahstum waits and watches and must have nerves like an ox. Meaning none at all. He cannot be too friendly to one, nor can he show enmity to either. He must wait until the boil bursts."

"But what," asked Blade, "has all this to do with me?"

"You killed Cossa, did you not? Not even Rahstum could have done that. And I have seen you and now I understand more. It is possible that Sadda, when the time comes, has other use for you than just to warm her bed."

"And if she had me she would not need Rahstum?"

"That is part of it, Blade. Not all. Sadda, if my guess is right, will test you well before opening her mind to you. Maybe she will never open it. But no matter, because if Sadda was to win out, we, you and I and the Mongs, would be no better off than if the Khad won. Both are mad. Both are bloody. And there can be no peace, with the Caths or anyone else, until both are dead. Rahstum knows this. That is why I think, Blade, that when the time is ripe Rahstum will also want you on *his* side."

Blade thought for a moment, then: "You say Khad is mad? I do not understand. When I saw him he looked sane enough."

"He is mad, Blade. He has the falling sickness from time to time, and in some way it seems to relieve his madness. He had a long sickness just before you were taken, so now appears not to be mad. But it will come back. And when his madness is fully upon him no one is safe—no man, woman, or child, especially girl children. The Khad's is a very nasty madness, Blade."

Blade felt a chill trace through him. What talk was this of children? He asked Baber what he meant.

"Sadda's madness is a cunning madness, Blade. She is sly and bloodthirsty and treacherous. But the Khad's madness is a demon that not all of Obi's blessings could wash clean. He is impotent, as is well known. Except with little girls. Children and young girls not yet old enough to be married. So when the madness is on him the Khad takes whatever child pleases him and has his will of her. Then another and another until the madness passes for the time."

"And the people do nothing? The Mongs, the fathers, they do nothing to halt this?"

Barber's chuckle was grim. "They do nothing. Yet. They hide their children as best they can and they mutter and complain, being careful not to be heard. Did you pass the gallows place when you were brought in?"

"As I was being taken to the Khad's tent I passed it."

"You saw a man impaled?"

102

"I saw him. He was still alive."

"Poor fellow. He was a sub-captain, a fine warrior and faithful to the Khad until, in his last fit of madness, the Khad took his daughter and had his way with her and killed her in the doing. And then, for such is the way of the Khad's madness, he gave the child a great funeral and bestowed much treasure on the father. At the funeral the Khad betrayed great remorse and beat his breast and called on Obi to forgive him. For this is the Khad's way— when his madness passes he cries in his tent at night and begs forgiveness for his deeds. But this time the father would not forgive and, after the funeral, tried to slay the Khad. You saw what happened."

"I saw."

"He did not await his time," said Baber. "He struck too soon. We Caucas have a saying—revenge which is longest in coming is the sweetest. Do not forget that, Blade."

After a moment Blade said: "There is a dwarf by name of Morpho. Do you know him?"

For a long time Baber did not answer. When he did his tone was curt and the friendliness had gone. "I know of him. I have seen him. What of it?"

It was clear enough that Baber did not wish to speak of the dwarf, yet Blade plunged ahead. "He is a strange little man. He came to me, when I was first taken, and hinted that he would like me to live. He said he came from Sadda, as perhaps he did, but I think there was something else. I have not seen him since, except for the night I faced the knife, and then he did not know me. I have been wondering if he is friend or enemy, or neither? And if he is Sadda's man, or the Khad's? After hearing you speak I wonder even more."

The sun dropped out of the sky. From the wall the giant cannon boomed, the muzzle flash a huge blossom of red flame in the sudden darkness. The jade ball keened far over them to splinter itself harmlessly into shards that, and Blade smiled grimly, would be priceless back in H-Dimension.

103

"We will not speak of the dwarf," said Baber at last. "I know of nothing to his credit, nor anything against him. He may even be his own man, a rare thing."

Blade took the hint and did not mention Morpho again. Presently guards came with their evening meal in wooden bowls. It was still horsemeat and coarse bread and a great tankard of the powerful *bross*. After drinking it all Blade felt sleepy. He closed his eyes as Baber talked on. Torches had been lit in the stockade, one at each corner, and when the night wind came it tinkled the warning bells along the top of the stockade. As sleepy as he was, Blade noted this, and stored it away for use in the future.

The *bross* had no effect on Baber, except to keep him wide-awake and talking. Blade drowsed and listened and was not surprised to learn that Baber had once been a great poet among his own people, as well as a warrior. Poets were highly regarded among the Cauca. It account-ed for the man's fluency and gift of imagery, which Blade had wondered at, and also for his laughter and sonorous voices, even though—and here Baber's laughter was rue-ful—it had been many years since he had stroked a *jadar,* which, Blade judged, was some sort of lyre.

Presently Blade was half between sleep and waking. Baber's voice was a lulling drone in the torch haunted gloom, with the words slurring now and making no dis-tinct sense. Blade posed himself a question.

Would he be glad or unhappy if Lord L were to snatch him back to H-Dimension now. At this moment? Before he had seen his adventure through. He could not really answer himself. At best he was ambivalent. He knew his peril. Death and torture were as real in this dimension as in his own natural one. Yet to seek out, to know, to perse-vere and above all to conquer, was in his nature as cruelty was in the Mongs. The adventure, the search and solving, beckoned like a lantern on a mountain. Besides, he was an Englishman to whom a task had been entrusted. That it was a shocking and weird and unbelievable task, so fantastic that only five men in the world knew about it, made little difference. It must be done.

Strangely, for Blade was not an intellectual, he found himself thinking of hope. In his mind he capitalized it. HOPE. He had seen the superficial and cynical splendor of the Caths; he understood the mindless cruelty of the Mongs. There was no hope in either.

Yet how often had he thought the same back in H-Dimension, when you only had to read a paper to feel disgust! Blade began to see *here* what he had not seen *there*. There *was* hope! Things did change. Six steps forward and five back left a net total of one step gained.

With a strange sense of personal enrichment, and oddly comforted, Richard Blade fell asleep.

Chapter 9

A week passed. Blade, the great collar dragging at his neck, worked like the slave he was. He worked in the women's quarters, empting night soil and scrubbing the pots afterward, and was taunted by dark eyes flashing over veils. Not once did he see Sadda or the dwarf, though once he thought he heard Morpho's voice coming from her quarters.

Rumor had it that the Khad was approaching a new season of madness. Every day the Mongs attacked the wall, sometimes luring the defenders to sally out, sometimes not, but always losing men and retiring in defeat.

When there was no work in the women's quarters Blade was put into the field to labor. He dug latrines and carried great timbers and repaired the high sided wagons, discovering that the Mongs had no clue to using grease on the wheels. No one had thought of it yet. He helped corral and tend the enormous herds of shaggy little horses on which the Mongs depended.

In all this he was guarded like the image of the God, Obi, which sat in a wagon apart. A huge black-painted wagon that only the Khad could enter. Not even Sadda was permitted to gaze on Obi.

In a perverse way Blade enjoyed the work away from the women's quarters. He was free of Aplonius' whip and did not have to struggle to keep him from killing the man, For Aplonius whipped him well, many times a day, and always in front of the women.

At night, when he was taken back to the stockade, he

and Baber talked. Or rather Baber talked and Blade listened and questioned. And grew wiser and wiser.

As the second week began, and as Blade sat in the dirt eating leavings which Aplonius had thrown him, Sadda left her great tent and approached them. Aplonius, as pomaded and perfumed as ever, brave in his gaily colored clothes, immediately began to fawn. Blade was sickened and, in that moment could almost feel pity for the man.

Aplonius saw Blade glance at the woman as she drew near and slashed him across the face. "Eyes down, swine!"

Blade cast his eyes down, but contrived to watch just the same.

Sadda was bare breasted and veiled, as always. Aplonius bowed low and saluted with the whip. "Good day, my lady Sadda. How lovely you are. You enhance the day. You perfume the air. What can I, who wear your golden collar with gratitude, do for my lady Sadda?"

"You can have him bathed, Aplonius. He stinks! He smells like a corpse left too long uneaten by the carrion apes. Have him well scrubbed—and give him suitable clothes. My women will give them to you."

She turned and walked away without another word.

When Aplonius turned back to Blade his eyes were swimming with terror and he was wet with sweat. Blade stared at the man and said, "Your time ends, Aplonius. Mine soon begins."

Aplonius lashed him in a frenzy, lashed him until he could no longer raise his whip arm. Blade endured it stoically, knowing with a fierce certitude that this was an ending and beginning.

He was put into a great tub of near boiling water and scrubbed by the same women who had been taunting him. Their attitude had changed, and there was much laughter, many sly glances and crude jokes. They, as well as Blade, knew what was coming. They were marvelously impressed by his muscles and, though none dared touch him, he knew the wish was there.

Blade was perfumed and his hair and beard trimmed.

He was dressed in a leather jacket and loose leather breeches that ended at the knee, and given a pair of horsehide boots that came to mid-calf.

During all this he adroitly managed to steal a short-bladed knife.

That night, when he was taken back to the stockade, the cumbersome wooden collar was removed at the gate.

As the guard pried the lock away with his sword point he winked at Blade. "Orders from the lady herself. You climb in the world, Blade. I do not care for that, for you will not last forever, but I am glad to see that Aplonius is cast out. I only hope I have a chance at him."

Blade, who always planned ahead, stooped to pick up the wooden collar. "I would keep this if I can."

The guard shrugged. "Keep your collar? You have grown so fond of it, then? Keep it. Wear it in your sleep if you will. You are a strange one, Blade."

The guards did apparently received new orders, for that night they did nothing to prevent Blade and Baber from talking in Baber's sty.

Baber, when he saw the new finery and smelled Blade, laughed and nodded his bald head. "I told you. It comes. But why do you carry your collar about? I would have thought—"

Blade passed him the stolen knife beneath the straw. Baber, keeping the knife hidden, felt it and glanced at Blade in awe and admiration. "You are a fool, my friend. You risked everything when you stole this. And to what purpose? What am I, without legs, supposed to do with a knife?"

Blade pushed the wooden collar toward him. "You use it, Baber, to carve wheels from this wood—four small wheels. I will somehow find you more wood for a plat-form and axles. We will make you a little cart which you can use for legs."

Baber nodded. "That is good. I would not have thought of it. But even when I have a cart for legs, then what?"

Blade regarded him steadily. "Did we not speak, once,

of things that might come to pass? Changes. Perhaps they come sooner than you think. You must be ready."

The older man's glance sharpened, "You have heard something?"

"I have heard nothing. But now I am to have a little freedom and I will know what to do with it."

Baber frowned. "Not too soon, Blade. Not too soon! The golden collar does not mean that you are free. It makes you even more a slave! Sadda is like wind, and as unpredictable. She may use you one night and have you killed."

Blade, who knew his own sexual prowess, smiled and said, "I think not. I shall teach her what a real man is like. So will I gain time. You could help me, Baber, if you would tell me what you know of Morpho the dwarf. Do not lie to me or turn close mouthed. We are not friends? I *know* that there is something about Morpho that you do not tell me."

Barber's face closed like a blank door and he would not look Blade in the eye.

Blade waited a moment, then said: "We walk a dangerous path, you and I. And the Captain Rahstum. And, I think, the dwarf also. I *must* know everything I can, Baber. Is the dwarf friend or foe?"

The old man scratched his scalp and frowned. At last he said, "I cannot tell you that in truth. But this I can tell—the dwarf is his own man. As is Rahstum, and you and me. I say only this, and then no more, that if Morpho comes with a message for you, trust him! I may be wrong, and that mistake mean our deaths, but sometimes a chance must be taken. Trust the dwarf if he comes to you. But do not go to him. Never!"

An hour later the guards came for Blade. Baber saw them coming and whispered in the dark. "They come to take you to Sadda. It is your time. Spend it wisely so there will be more of it for both of us."

Blade stood up and brushed the straw from his fine new clothes.

"Carve your wheels, old man, four of them. I will not forget you."

They took him to a small tent near the women's quarters. At a table a guard sat polishing a gold collar with a bit of cloth. The cloth was blood stained and Blade knew he would never have his revenge on Aplonius.

The guard held up the collar and squinted at it. Torch light glinted on the golden esses. S S S S S

The guard tossed the collar to another man. "Put it on him. He is now bed slave to the lady Sadda."

There was muffled laughter among the guards. One of them cursed and said, "That creature Aplonius lasted longer than I had wagered. He cost me two good ponies."

More rough laughter. The man who had been polishing the collar began to count on his fingers, frowning as he did so. "Eight—nine—ten! As many as my fingers exactly." He stared at Blade. "You are the tenth bed slave in two years. If you believe in Obi you had better start praying now."

Blade stood silent as the little gold collar was clasped around his brawny neck. It was too tight and one of the guards plucked at it with a finger.

"He has a neck like an ox. Sadda will have to get a new collar."

"Or a new slave," laughed another guard. "But come. His mistress will be getting impatient."

He was taken to the great black tent where Sadda had her quarters. A single guard ushered him in through a maze of carpeted corridors, for the big tent was subdivided into many apartments. The guard sniffed at the perfume and prodded Blade with his lance butt. He grinned. "If I were not such a coward I would like to break loose in here one day. But I *am* a coward and so must go to the whores—or get married. Which is the worst not even Obi knows."

They came to an entrance covered by a golden cloth. Before the entrance was a thick rug. Blade pulled aside the golden cloth and entered the domain of Lady Sadda.

110

A single tall candlestick stood in the exact center of the apartment. It was six feet high, of carven wood and with a flat base. Atop it one long taper cast a wavering light.

Blade stood for a moment adjusting his eyes and senses. The room was carpeted and the wall hangings glimmered gold and scarlet. Off to one side was a thick floor mat, not unlike the bed he had shared with Lali except that this one was square instead of circular. The whole apartment reeked of musky perfume, and incense that had a sweetish charred wood odor to it.

For a long time he did not see her. Then he heard her breathing and saw her sitting on a small chair in a corner, near the entrance to an inner apartment. She was naked except for the veil. The candlelight gleamed on her body. Her thick black hair was twisted into a coronet, as Blade had seen it once before, but now she wore painted wooden combs in it. Her nails were as blood red as ever, both fingers and toes, and she wore golden bangles on each ankle.

She moved at last and the gold bangles chimed like muted clocks in the silence.

"You still do not kneel to me, Blade?"

He was prepared. There had been enough of kneeling and groveling. It was another risk, but his life of late had been nothing but risks.

Blade crossed his arms on his massive chest, the muscles rippling, and smiled at her. "I do not kneel, my lady Sadda. I do not think that you really want me to kneel. I think you seek a man and not a cringing animal. That is what I think. If I am wrong I must pay for it."

She considered him gravely, the brown eyes lucent and yet fathomless over the veil. He saw a flash of white beneath the gauzy stuff as she smiled at last.

"So that is what you think, Blade? You dare greatly, *I* think. But you are right. This time you are right. I have watched you closely, closer than you know, and it may be that you *are* a man of all men. We will see as to that. But first be warned. There will be no second warning."

She clapped her hands once, suddenly and sharply, and

111

somewhere in the shadows curtains parted and two of her personal bodyguards appeared, the young and handsome Mongs who laughed so much. They were unsmiling now as they approached and bowed, choosing not to see Blade.

Sadda said, "They are always near me, Blade, always. A change in my tone of voice will bring them. Remember that."

He would remember. He saw something now that had not occurred to him before. This woman was a little afraid of him! It might be in that fear that part of his fascination for her lay.

Sadda made a sign, and the guards left.

When they were once more alone Blade stood waiting. That she was puzzled was obvious. At last she stirred in the chair, the bangles chiming, and said: "I have not been able to think of a slave name for you, Blade. Maybe it is because you are so strange. So I shall call you Blade. Not *Sir* Blade. I do not think a slave should have a title."

"Nor I," agreed Blade. "Anyway I have given up my title while I am a captive."

It was the first time he had heard her laugh. To his amazement it was a pleasant sound, a full deep contralto full of genuine merriment. Her teeth glistened beneath the veil.

Blade smiled and bowed slightly. "I am glad you find me amusing, my lady."

She laughed again, then said, "Of course you must amuse me, Blade. That is why you are here. To amuse me in any way I choose, as long as I choose. When you *cease* to amuse me will be time enough to worry."

She was serious again, staring at him with her chin cupped in one hand. "I saw you kill the warrior Cossa, with my own eyes. My brother thought me under guard in the tent, but I dressed as a common kitchen slave and mingled with the crowd. It was I who had the snares laid in the earth. I saw you kill Cossa, our champion, and I saw no mercy in you then. Now I detect a softness. How is this?"

112

"No softness," he said gruffly. "But why do we speak of these things, my lady Sadda? You have sent for me. I am here. I am your slave. Why do we waste time?"

She threw back her head and laughed at him. "You are impatient, and impertinent, Blade! I decide what we do—talk or other things. That you must understand. You will never touch me unless I command it."

"I do understand it." He pretended to sulk, but was well enough satisfied. He had found the key. Boldness— but not too bold. Be a slave—but not slavish. If he could hold her interest, feed her curiosity, and titillate and dominate her sexually when the time came, he would gain precious time. Like the wizard in Baber's story he had everything to gain and nothing to lose.

Sadda left her chair and approached him. She held up a hand. "You will remain where you are. Do not move."

"As you will." Blade crossed his arms and waited. He was well aroused and more ready for her, but he had always been able to control that. The one exception had been the first time with Lali in the Temple of Death.

Sadda stopped and preened before him. She struck a pose with her arms high and her fingers pointed at him. The motion pulled her small round breasts up tight and taut and he saw she had painted her nipples red. She did a slow pirouette, standing on tiptoe, watching him over the veil.

Her skin glistened like dark golden honey. She had oiled herself and her belly was a flat mirror that caught the candle flame and flung it back. Shadows half concealed a triangle of dark hair. Her haunches flared wide from an incredibly small waist into slim thighs and delicate well-turned ankles. He guessed her at an inch or two over five feet.

"Do you like me, Blade? Do you desire me?"

Here was something he could answer truthfully. He was finding it hard to breathe and the tension in him was unbearable. It took all his self-discipline to keep from taking her and to hell with the consequences.

He nodded curtly and restrained himself. "I am a man, my lady. I desire you. How much longer will you tease me?"

She laughed deep in her throat. "As long as it pleases me, Blade. Pleasure prolonged is all the better—and I take my pleasure in many ways."

She smiled at Blade, then took his hand and tugged him toward the rug, unspeaking, knowing perfectly well how she was affecting him.

She went slowly to her knees, then rolled over on the rug on her back and extended her arms to Blade.

"Now show me, Blade!" There was an undercurrent of suppressed excitement in Sadda's voice. "Take me, Blade. Show me what a man you are, Blade!"

As Blade sank to his knees, her arms clamped around him like a vise.

"Show me, Blade!" she cried.

Chapter 10

Blade slept on a rug before the golden cloth that shielded the entrance to Sadda's apartment. As her personal body and bed slave he was now allowed to carry a blunted wooden dagger and a whip. The toy dagger greatly amused the Mong warriors, who now showed as much contempt for Blade as they had for Aplonius. Had he chosen to die instead of entering Sadda's bed they would have admired him, as they had once, and made up songs about him. Now he was just another slave put out to stud until the royal mare was tired of him. Blade encouraged this. They were underestimating him. Good.

It was the fourth night of his new bed slavery and he was pleasantly exhausted. Sadda had at last taken him to bed and he had given the performance of his life. She had been in a good mood, for her, and he left her depleted and wrung dry, caressing him and muttering: "Ah, Blade—ah, Blade—" She pushed him away from her, turned over and fell into a deep sleep.

Blade was drifting into sleep when he heard the sibilant whisper. "Sir Blade? Sir Blade?"

Blade half roused, fighting sleep, cocked an ear but did not stir on his rug. Had he been dreaming?

"Sir Blade? Do you hear me? It is Morpho the dwarf."

Blade sat up, yawning, rubbing his eyes. Down the carpeted corridor a single torch guttered near the entrance. A shadow moved as the Mong guard there shifted his position. There was no other movement. The women's quarters had long been darkened and Sadda would not stir until late morning.

Blade whispered, "Where are you?"

"To your left, in the apartment of Trina. She sleeps and does not know I am here. I came beneath the tent. Listen well, Sir Blade, as I have little time."

It was strangely comforting to hear himself addressed as Sir again. He had lost much of man's natural human dignity, just to stay alive, and it galled him.

Blade turned on his rug so that he faced the black cloth separating the girl's apartment from the corridor. "I hear you, Morpho." He could visualize the little man squatting in the dark, dressed in his fool's costume, wearing his eternal grin.

Morpho whispered on. "Can you contrive to visit the stockade tomorrow to see Baber? He will tell you what I cannot now say, for lack of time. It is about the things of which you and Baber have spoken. You understand me?"

He was fully awake now. Through narrowed eyes he watched the guard move back and forth across the tent entrance.

"Baber and I spoke of changes."

"Yes. Of changes. Make some excuse, and visit Baber tomorrow. He will tell you more."

Silence. After a moment Blade whispered again. "Morpho?"

No answer. The dwarf had gone as stealthily as he had come. And now Blade found it hard to sleep. He seethed with excitement. Morpho had risked his life by entering the women's quarters without permission. Why? Had the time come at last?

The next day he was in luck. Sadda was summoned by the Khad and left with her retinue of servants. She looked worried and had no time for Blade, though she smiled and petted him as she would a favorite hound. She rode off with a sullen frown. There were whispers that the Khad was slipping into madness again and nobody, not even Sadda, was safe. At such times, Blade had heard, the

116

Khad would once more desire his sister carnally and would rage and cry because his ravaged body would not respond. Then the Mongs would try to hide their young daughters.

Blade was bold about it. He took his whip and rode the pony he had been given to the stockade with a sneer on his face that would have done credit to the dead Aplonius. The guards, watching his approach, snickered and nudged each other.

Just as he dismounted, Blade had an inspiration. Maybe he could kill two birds with one stone.

"I come to see that old fool Baber," Blade announced. "He who loafs and sleeps, spoiling good straw and eating food which he does not earn. The Lady Sadda has said that *I* might have a slave of my own. I have chosen Baber, and I come to teach him what a whip is like."

The Mong guard smiled in mockery. "Yes, your greatness. As you wish. Baber has not been whipped in a long time. But how can you make a slave of a legless man?"

Blade gave him an insolent stare. "You are a fool and would not know that. But you will help me and so find out. Go to the place of wagons and bring me wood of this certain size and measurement." Blade, using his hands, indicated exactly what he wanted.

The Mong guard was doubtful. "Wood is precious, your greatness. Not to be wasted on slaves." It was true. The Mongs must cut their wood in distant forests and haul it in wagons.

There was nothing for it but more boldness. Blade slashed the man across the face with his whip. "Do as I say! Or would you have me tell the lady Sadda that you disobeyed her personal slave?"

The Mong retreated a step, rubbing his cheek. The slant eyes glared at Blade. But the guard could wait. He made a mock bow and muttered sullenly, "It shall be done, *Greatness*. I am on duty now, but I will send another."

117

"See that you do." Blade snapped his whip and sauntered into the stockade.

There were three other prisoners now, their carrels in an opposite row to Baber. They watched Blade's progress across the clearing and made obscene comments. He ignored them. They were all thieves waiting to have their right hands cut off.

Baber, seeing him approach, pulled himself to the entrance of his hole on muscular arms. He squinted at Blade, who read doubt and suspicion in the look. Baber was old, a veteran of many terrors and disappointments, and he sought now to see if Blade had changed.

Without a word Blade struck him across the face. "They are all watching," he said in a low voice. "I will have to beat you."

Baber winced and dropped his head. "Of course. But not too hard, my friend. Did the dwarf come to you?"

Blade struck him again. "He came. And I come to you at his urging. You will tell me the reason?"

The older man regarded Blade with his steely gray eyes. "What there is to tell I will tell. I see you have not changed, even though you are clean and dressed like a peacock."

Blade rained a frenzy of blows on him, then stood back and said in a loud voice: "Do not talk to me so, you filth. I say you will serve me! I can make a useful slave of even such legless trash as you."

Baber concealed a grin. "In my time, in my country, there were those called actors who could simulate a thing they did not feel. You would have made a good one."

"Get on with it," Blade urged. "I cannot stay too long. Sadda does not know I am here. If she finds out I will have to lie for my life."

"The dwarf came last night and whispered to me also." Baber glanced about furtively. "Beat me a little more to make it look honest."

Blade struck him, swearing loudly.

"Rahstum is ready," said Baber. "Three days hence is

118

the Khad's birth time and there will be a great feast and celebration. Then Rahstum will strike. If you are with him there will be weapons and armor for you."

"I am with him," Blade grated, striking the man again. "Can you doubt it?"

"Not I. But Rahstum must see you and speak with you first. He will judge for himself. That is like Rahstum, as I know him. His thoughts, and his will are his own."

"How is it to be contrived that I meet Rahstum? He is Chief Captain. I am a slave. *I* cannot arrange it."

"Fortune has contrived it. They have taken a Cath spy. Under torture he has confessed that he was sent by the Empress Mei to find you and assist in your escape. The Khad is in a rage, which Rahstum encourages. He tells the Khad that you are as guilty as the spy, that you are dangerous and must be questioned about this matter because there may be other spies who have not been discovered. He urges the Khad to arrest you."

Blade frowned. The thought of torture sent a chill down his spine.

"If this is so why have I not been arrested and taken before the Khad before now?"

"Because the Khad is in a fit of madness and once more desires his sister—or thinks he does, which is the same thing for our purpose. He also has much guilt, and fears the wrath of Obi, and listens to Sadda when she defends you. She would not have you harmed. You must be pleasing her, Blade!"

A thought struck Blade, of such importance that he marveled he had not thought of it before.

"One thing I must know, Baber. Do Rahstum and Sadda conspire together?"

"No! That I swear. Rahstum does not trust her. She courts his favor, as I told you, but he smiles and keeps his thoughts secret. Why, Blade? Has Sadda hinted that Rahstum is *her* man?"

Blade shook his head. "No. She plots, though, I am

119

sure of it. And she means to use me if she can. But she does not yet trust me with any of her secrets."

Baber scowled. "No matter, then. She will not have time to interfere. The Captain will prevail, I think, and the Khad will have you arrested. This gives Rahstum a chance to talk to you and judge you. Be ready."

Suddenly Baber lunged at Blade, striking out with one fist, missing and falling on his face in the straw. "You louse. You swine. You bastard of a horse and an ape. I will not be slave to such as you!"

The guards were coming toward them with the wood Blade had asked for. He began to beat Baber.

"You have made the wheels as I ordered?"

Baber groaned loudly. "Yes. They are hidden in the straw along with the knife."

"Keep them hidden, then. They are bringing wood. Make a platform and axles and pretend to make the wheels last. And make a pair of pointed sticks to propel yourself. I must go now. Forgive these blows, old friend."

Baber grinned through the blood on his battered face. "I will wait, and pray to my own Cauca gods. Goodbye, Blade."

Blade watched as the wood was tossed into Baber's carrel. Then he accompanied the guards back to the gate. "You have done well," he told them haughtily. "But see that you obey more promptly in the future or I will speak to Sadda of it."

The guards, all old Mong warriors, did not trouble to conceal their sneers.

Sadda did not return to her tent that night. Blade lay on his rug and sought to unravel the complexities of this thing he faced. Back in H-Dimension he was expert in all matters of intrigue and espionage. Here he was alone and without facilities and must fend entirely for himself. He lived from minute to minute, and each minute could be his last.

Lali was helping him by sending spies to contact him.

120

It meant that she had not forgotten him and in this bloody desert of the Mongs he welcomed that, but he wished he could send her word to forbear. If she persisted she would only get him killed.

Occasionally the Caths would fire the huge cannon at night, hoping that the flash in the darkness and the whistle of the great jade ball would terrify the Mongs into leaving. He remembered Queko sighing and saying how pleasant it would be to wake up and find the plain before the wall deserted. It had never worked.

It did not work now. Blade heard the cannon boom and listened as the jade ball fell short into a cluster of tents. There was a great screaming and much running and shouting.

There would be children killed, Blade thought sadly. Innocents. In this, X-Dimension was not so different from his own.

He thought of the Khad and his lust for young girls. Hardly more than children. Did Rahstum, the Captain, have a daughter? Blade did not know. He knew nothing about Rahstum except that he was a Cauca and a successful mercenary. Would the Mongs, and Blade, be any better off under Rahstum's rule than under the Khad's?

That was easy to answer. Yes. At least Rahstum was not insane and did not lust after children and his own sister. He was an intelligent man who might listen to reason. Blade hoped so, for he had plans of his own far beyond a mere palace revolution, plans that he hoped would mature before Lord L called him back.

First he must remain alive, and Rahstum might aid in that. But later, Blade thought as he finally drifted into sleep, he and Rahstum might very well be enemies. After each had used the other.

Chapter 11

Blade was arrested the next morning. Six of Rahstum's men came for him. They allowed him to keep his wooden dagger and whip and, amid laughter, poked him along with their lances. There was no sign of Sadda.

Blade was taken to a small watch tent near the Khad's Imperial enclosure. He was pushed inside and told to keep silent and wait. In a few moments Rahstum came in. For a minute he said nothing, standing and surveying Blade with keen gray eyes and fingering his silver chain. His armor was burnished to a higher sheen than ever before. The horsetails of authority on his shoulders swung in unison as Rahstum began to pace. Then he wheeled on Blade.

"You have spoken to Baber? And the dwarf came to you?"

"Yes, to both questions, Captain." Respect without servility, thought Blade. The truth was that he *did* respect this man.

Rahstum stroked his beard and frowned. "I will be brief. I only risk this interview because the Khad is—is busy with other matters at the moment." No mistaking the disgust on Rahstum's face.

Blade nodded. "I have heard of this."

Rahstum's fine teeth glinted in a thin smile. "No doubt you see and hear many things, Blade, and remember them all. I have been watching you. You play the slave well enough, but you do not fool me. But no matter for that—are you with me in this?"

It was time for a little bold bargaining.

Blade lowered his voice. "If you speak of killing the Khad I am with you. That is a good thing. But what of my future? What am I to have of this?"

The Captain's eyes narrowed. "What you most desire in the world, Blade. Your freedom! And you will have position. You will be second in command to me. And, if and when your ransom comes—" here Rahstum smiled slyly—"*if* it comes, you will be permitted to go back to the Caths. I hope you will not do this. I saw you kill Cossa and I need such a warrior as you. There is also mystery about you, Blade, which intrigues me. But none of that now. You are with me?"

"Yes."

"Then listen closely. I must take you before the Khad in a few minutes. I myself insisted on this, for the purpose of this meeting, and I do not think you in any great danger. Anyway Sadda will plead for you. But keep your mouth tight and do not anger the Khad. He is full of madness just now and hard to predict. In his madness he suspects no danger and will see none if we are careful. It is Sadda who must be fooled. In the next two days you must keep her amused as never before. You understand me, Blade?"

Blade nodded. "I understand. But suppose the lady is not in the mood?"

"Get her in the mood. Keep her so. At least until the celebration of the Khad's birth time. After that it will not matter. Now listen well . . ."

They talked for another five minutes. Then Rahstum struck Blade hard across the mouth to draw blood. "That is to explain the delay. You were stubborn and gave me trouble. Come now."

With Rahstum leading the way, Blade was taken to the Khad's great black tent, escorted by the six warriors who had arrested him. They would be the Captain's men, sworn to live or die with him. Blade wondered how many others Rahstum had recruited?

Sensuous music leaked from the tent as they approached. But when he was pushed inside, he was surprised to find it almost empty. Musicians played in one corner. In another corner a squad of the Khad's men guarded a Cath who stood in chains. The Khad and Sadda were on the dais, on their respective thrones. To the right of the Khad, on a miniature throne, sat a pretty girl wearing filmy pantaloons and soft leather shoes and a little jacket that partially concealed small breasts. Mong women matured early, as Blade knew, but he did not think this girl could be more than thirteen. She looked as though she had been crying. As Blade approached the dais, the Khad stroked the girl's shiny hair and whispered something to her. She looked up at him and nodded gravely.

Sadda, her thick hair in a coronet, had shadows beneath her brown eyes, visible even through the veil. Her eyes brightened at the sight of Blade, but then she looked away.

Near the Khad's feet, juggling his four balls in the air, was Morpho the dwarf. He ignored Blade, staring at nothing with his comic-sad smile showing his teeth.

The Khad, his chalky spine twisting him forward at a cruel angle, glared at Blade with his good right eye. He wasted no time.

"That whore Empress Mei is missing you, Blade. She sent one to find you and plot escape." He pointed a finger at the Cath in chains. "Did you know of this, Blade?"

Blade shook his head. "I knew nothing of it, O Scourge of the World." That much was true.

The Khad's single eye glittered. It was rolling and bloodshot and showing a lot of the white, and in the murky depths the shadows of madness moved and coiled.

The Khad showed bad teeth in a grim smile. "So *he* says, also. He does not implicate you. Yet Rahstum does not trust you and coaxed me that I should question you."

The Cath was pushed rudely forward, his chains jangling over the soft music as the musicians played on, paying no heed to the grisly tableau being enacted so near them.

The Khad leered at both Blade and the Cath. "You have seen this man before, Blade?"

"Never." More truth. The Cath was wearing the Mong leather armor, with markings of a subchief. His lemony skin had been darkened, the dye now wearing off, and some shreds of dark beard still clung to his face. They had cut the beard off a dead Mong and pasted it on this man in an effort at disguise.

The Khad turned to the Cath and pointed to Blade. "You have seen *this* man before, Cath?"

The Cath gazed at Blade without expression. "I have seen him. He is the great Sir Blade, Courier-Chief from Pukka. He slew your champion in fair battle and was taken when his horse threw him. Because of treachery, I was sent to speak with him and plan his escape. I have *never* spoken with him."

The Cath had given up. He was plunging to his own destruction, yet he was trying to save Blade—and himself, as Blade found out a moment later.

"I have spoken the truth," the Cath went on, "for which I was promised an easy death."

The Khad's eye rolled and glittered. "I made no such promise."

"Your men did, when I was being tortured." The Cath was standing slim and tall, but he had begun to sweat. Blade's heart went out to him. He would not have an easy death.

Sadda leaned toward the Khad, her eyes on Blade.

"You have seen, brother, and you have heard. Blade has not been plotting to escape, so give him back to me unharmed. I still have use for him."

The Khad went into a roar of manic laughter. He slapped his chest and the tears welled from his eye. "I know, sister. I know! He must please you greatly, by Obi! And so I will not judge him. Not I. I will let my horse judge him. Bring my Thunderer to me. He shall decide."

Blade got it immediately and did not dare look at Morpho. So he was to be judged by a horse!

If the dwarf, who was a fool but no fool, meant to play him false now was the time for it.

Thunderer was led into the tent. The stallion was as shaggy as the other Mong ponies, but much larger. He was docile and the music did not appear to disturb him. Blade guessed that it was not the first time the Khad played such a joke.

A black slave took the reins and led Thunderer to the dais. The Khad, reaching painfully, stroked the animal's velvety muzzle for a moment and his voice softened.

"You will answer my questions, old war friend. First about the Cath. Is he guilty of spying?"

Blade watched carefully. The black made a slight movement and the reins twitched. Thunderer nodded. The dwarf's lips did not move at all.

"The Cath is guilty," said the horse. Blade was amazed and puzzled. Not at the ventriloquism but at the art of it. He had never heard a horse talk, but if a horse *could* talk he would, Blade thought, have spoken exactly as Thunderer did.

The Khad laughed like a child. "I agree with you, Thunderer. And we know the punishment is death—but shall it be swift and easy? Or cruel? On this, Thunderer, I will follow your advice."

Blade, who had great empathy, found himself holding his breath. But what could the little fool do? Only, of course, what the Khad expected and wanted him to do!

Thunderer spoke again. "He must die a cruel death, master. He is a confessed spy and must suffer for it."

Blade risked a sidelong glance at the dwarf. Morpho, spinning his colored balls, stared back with his deathly grin.

The Khad pointed at Blade. "And this one, Thunderer? What of this one? Is he so innocent as he claims, and as my good sister claims?"

The horse was silent. The brightly colored balls twirled

126

in the air. The black did not twitch the reins, waiting for his cue.

"Blade is not a fool," the horse said. "He is innocent of this thing. He waits, though not patiently, for the ransom that will free him. In all this your sister speaks truth, great Khad. Let Blade not be punished for that he did not do."

The Khad turned sideways to leer at Sadda. "My Thunderer agrees with you, little sister. I find that interesting. Have you been feeding him sweets on the sly?"

Sadda joined in the laugh. Her dark eyes glowed at Blade. "You are wise, brother, to listen to Thunderer. The horse may be wiser than both of us."

The Khad raised a hand. "Blade is not guilty. I return him to Sadda to be slave as before. Let the Cath be taken to the execution place at once. Summon all who do not have pressing duties to attend." The doomed Cath was dragged to his feet and led out.

Blade, no longer a prisoner, accompanied Sadda to her apartment, walking a few paces behind her as befitted a slave. She had women with her, but as they drew near the big tent she waved them aside and fell back to speak with him.

"That was too near a thing," she said. She studied him over the veil. "I do not understand why I try so hard to keep you alive, Blade."

He allowed himself a smirk that was in character. "Because I please you, my lady?"

"Perhaps. But you will cease to please me if I find you in more trouble."

"The trouble was not of my making, my lady."

"That is true—this time. And it puzzles me why Rahstum was so insistent that you be questioned. Rahstum himself puzzles me a great deal."

For the moment they were walking alone, out of earshot of any of the Mongs streaming to the gallows ground.

Sadda watched Blade, her eyes fathomless over the veil. "I give you a command now, Blade. You will watch this Rahstum when you can. In a way that will not be noticed.

127

You are sly, as I know. Use that slyness. I would know where Rahstum goes, what he does, who he speaks with. You understand?"

Blade, concealing his elation, looked both eager and slavish and at once began to exploit the situation.

"I understand, my lady. But to do that I must have more freedom to come and go. I cannot watch Rahstum from the women's quarters."

She nodded. "This I know. I will arrange for more freedom. But be you warned, Blade!" She pointed to the execution ground. "Play me false and the death this Cath is going to suffer will seem merciful in comparison to what *you* will suffer."

That night Blade made love to Sadda with a pure cold hatred that left her gasping and enthralled. When Blade was spent at last, and she long since, she did not turn over and fall into sleep as usual. She lay close to him and whispered in his ear.

"No man has ever made me feel like this before, Blade. I do not understand it. I am not sure I like it."

He had released tension enough so he could wear the mask again, a mask that had nearly slipped during their love-making. He said: "Have you ever had a real man before, my lady?"

He felt her nod. He was laying with his back to her, she nuzzling him from behind.

"I *thought* they were men. I had Cossa, whom you killed, and many other famous warriors. I had the Emperor Mei Saka." She dug into his shoulder with her long nails. "Another week and he would have opened the wall to us. He had promised. I cannot understand how he was slain in battle. Our warriors had strict orders that he should not be attacked. For once my brother and I agreed, and it was he who issued the order. Yet the Emperor was killed and all my scheming went for nothing. The wall still stands and the Khad will never get the cannon. I would like to know which of my people killed the Emperor Mei—he would be treated as that Cath was today."

128

Blade kept discreetly silent. Only he and Lali knew who had killed the Emperor. Lali had seen to that. He was curious as to how Sadda, a Mong Princess, and the Cath Emperor Mei Saka could have had a love affair. But he did not want to seem too curious.

But Sadda was full of surprises tonight. She kissed his shoulder where she had clawed him. "Are you not curious, Blade? About the Emperor and myself?"

Blade stifled a grin. "It is not my place to be curious, my lady. I am a slave."

"See that you remember it. But you have made me feel very good and I will tell you. But just because I take you into my confidence does not mean that you can forget your place."

"Never, my lady."

There was, she explained, a postern gate some miles westward along the great wall. Far beyond the battlefield. On occasion Sadda, with a few trusted men and ladies, would ride out after dark and pitch a small tent on the plain near the postern. When he could get away from his captains, and his Counsel, and his wife, the Emperor would leave the wall by the postern and ride to join Sadda in the tent.

Finally he had promised to betray the Caths and open the main gate. The Empress was to be turned over to Sadda.

"Another great disappointment," she said now. "I was looking forward to that, Blade! I had a cage built for her."

He was hard put to restrain his laughter. A cage for Lali. A cage for Sadda. The ladies thought a great deal alike.

She was silent for a long time. Blade thought her asleep and was puzzling over her new behavior, this sudden warmth for him, and wondering how much of it was due to his sexual prowess and how much to her own devious mind and desires. The next moment he found out.

"Blade?"

"Yes, my lady."

"I had thought you asleep. Now listen—I have decided to trust you."

He was instantly alert, all sleep banished. Was she at last going to come out with it? He weighed his words carefully.

"You honor me, my lady. You will find that I am worthy of your trust." He could lie as well as any Mong or Cath.

She was whispering into his ear again. "I plan that the Khad Tambur shall die. Then I alone will rule the Mongs. And you are going to help me."

Blade turned to face her, pretending to be surprised and a little frightened. It was what she would expect. Yet he was careful not to overdo it.

"How can I help you in this, my lady? I am a slave without power or weapons."

Sadda kept a single taper burning in the bed apartment. She did not like total darkness. They lay face to face now and looked into each other's eyes.

When she first removed her veil for him, Blade had not known what to expect. Was she ugly or a beauty? She was neither. She had the slightly flattened nose of most Mong women, but her cheekbones flared higher. This, with her almond dark eyes, gave her an exotic look that the common Mong women did not possess. Her teeth were marvelously even and white and her mouth was large, and, belying what he knew she was, had a sweetness about it. All this with a matte complexion that had the sheen of old gold with a honey patina.

He saw his reflection in her pupils, as she must be seeing hers. "You will have power," she said softly. "If you aid me in this you shall rule beside me. No—I will not lie. *I* will rule! But you will sit beside me."

Blade did not have to pretend now. He really was confused, and more than a little uneasy. Two plots to kill the Khad, developing side by side, along parallel lines, each with no knowledge of the other. It was dangerous. A thousand things could go wrong.

"You say nothing, Blade?"

"I—I must think, my lady. I had not expected this." Not so soon, at any rate, though he had known she was up to something.

"To murder the Khad," he went on, as though the thought was brand-new, "will be very difficult. He is guarded night and day by his personal troops, his bodyguard. They are loyal to him?"

She nodded, frowning. "They are loyal to him. But I also have warriors loyal to me."

And Rahstum had warriors loyal to him. The web was becoming more intricate by the minute.

Sadda tickled his nose with a painted nail. "If my plan works there will be no fighting. I do not want that. I would lose because I do not have enough men. No—I shall kill the Khad by cunning, Blade. Which means that *I* will not kill him at all, nor you. There is another who will do the deed for us, who will take the blame, and who will die for it. No suspicions will attach to us."

"And how is this to be done?"

"You know of Morpho the dwarf? The Khad's fool?"

The fine hairs prickled on Blade's neck. Morpho? The dwarf held both Blade and Rahstum's lives in the palm of his hand. All he need do was denounce them and—

"The dwarf is *my* man," Sadda said. "I know something about him, yet keep it to myself, that ensures his absolute loyalty to me. He only pretends loyalty to the Khad, because I wish it so for now. But in the end he will obey *me!*"

Did Rahstum know of this? Blade thought not. His stomach began to feel a bit queasy. Morpho was playing a many handed game. And yet Baber, whom Blade *did* trust, also trusted the dwarf.

Sadda had been silent for a moment. Now she said, "When the time comes, and it will be two days hence at

131

the celebration of my brother's birth date, the dwarf will slay the Khad. *I can make him do that, Blade!*

"That is when I will need you. I will give you more freedom and allow you to carry a real dagger instead of that wooden toy. You will be at the celebration with me. Now, when the dwarf kills my brother, he must not be allowed to speak. Not one word that can implicate me. You, Blade, will dagger the little man as soon as he has slain the Khad!"

She laughed and caressed Blade's arm. "You see how cunning and simple it is? Morpho is blamed for killing my brother. You gain much, in the eyes of my people, and my officers, by slaying the assassin. I am not involved in any way. I will bury my brother with much pomp and many tears. I cry easily, Blade. Later I will rule alone and you shall sit at my right hand."

But not for long, Blade thought. She would tire of him all the sooner because of what he knew about her.

Cautiously he asked, "How can you be so sure that Morpho will kill the Khad? It is a good plan, my lady, but only if you can be absolutely sure that the dwarf will do his part."

"I am sure. But that I will not tell you. You know enough for what you must do. And keep a sharp eye on Rahstum. I do not know where his loyalties lie, but to himself. I would not have him interfere."

One thing Blade knew. He could no longer put his entire trust in the dwarf. And he must speak to Rahstum of what he had just heard.

Sadda wrapped one smooth arm about his neck and pulled him close to her. "All this talking, Blade, has made me desire you again. You will make love to me, as fiercely as before. Then I can sleep."

In just that moment, Blade thought, she sounded sad and a little lonely. As he obeyed the royal command, he thought that even a pit viper must have its moments of sadness and loneliness.

Chapter 12

Bitter disappointment welled in Blade as he reined in his little horse and glanced back at the endless procession of Mong wagons. There were over a thousand of them. The Mongs were on the trek.

The Khad's madness had left him as suddenly as it came. He had had a vision—the same night in which Sadda confided her plans to Blade—in which the God Obi left his wagon and appeared to the Khad. Victory, said Obi, lay not here before the wall, but far to the east.

On awakening the Khad gave orders and the Mongs began to strike camp.

All plans were off. Sadda, in a fury of disappointment, explained to Blade when they were alone. "We must wait now. There will be no birth celebration and in ordinary times he is too well guarded. His mind is so filled with this vision of Obi that he does not drink too much *bross*. To try to kill him now would be too dangerous. We will bide our time. The madness will come again and there will be other celebrations."

Rahstum was of the same mind. That morning he gave Blade a look and shook his head, muttering as he passed, "Patience."

There was no sign of the dwarf and it occurred to Blade, as it had not before, that Morpho had a habit of dropping out of sight from time to time. Where did the little man go?

Blade prevailed on Sadda to give him Baber as his slave. She also gave him a sharp look, but said nothing.

133

Blade, happy enough with his gains and his increased freedom of movement, knew he still walked a narrow path over quicksand.

Baber had completed his cart and could now propel himself about with two sticks. Blade saw to it that he was bathed and given new clothing, and allowed to ride in one of Sadda's wagons. He even succeeded in commandeering enough precious wood to make a ramp for Baber's cart, so the old man could enter and leave the wagon easily.

Thus far Blade had said nothing of what he knew about Morpho—or did *not* know, which was more important.

Baber, in his turn, made a remark that gave Blade food for thought.

"I have seen how Sadda looks at you," he said. "And perhaps you are in more trouble than you think, my friend, a different kind of trouble than that of which we have been speaking. I had a wife once who looked at me in that fashion, but I was young then, and a fool, and did not value her love. In time she took to other men, which I found out, and so had to strangle her as is the custom. It saddens me now, to think of it."

Sadda in love with him? That would be the final irony. He would rather be loved by one of the carrion apes that dogged the Mong column. Yet it could be turned to his advantage.

It was the fourth day of the trek. Blade moved his mount to a low knoll from which he could see the long dark caravan snaking across the plain. Behind him, glimmering faintly on the horizon, was the great wall. They were gradually angling away from it. The Cath patrols, riding atop the wall, had been dogging them in parallel and Blade knew that behind the wall other Cath cities and villages were alerted in case the Khad turned south again. But Khad Tambur, that Shaker of the Universe and Lord of the World, was telling no one his plans. Obi, he said, had bid him keep them secret.

It was like a gigantic circus train passing before him. To Blade's right, far ahead, were advanced scouting par-

134

ties of horsemen. Beyond the column, out of sight, were outriders to the north.

The Khad, riding Thunderer, led the procession surrounded by his personal guard carrying skulls and horsetails on lances. Behind the Khad came Sadda, sometimes riding a horse, sometimes retiring to her wagon. Her retinue of women in waiting and slaves demanded twenty wagons.

After Sadda was the wagon of Rahstum and those of the men he personally commanded. Then came the lesser chiefs and at last the common soldiers and behind them the prison wagons and those of the camp followers.

Blade, watching now as they passed him, wondered if the dwarf had a wagon of his own. It seemed likely, but Blade had never seen it and did not know where it traveled in the line.

A mile behind the last wagon came the enormous herds of horses and ponies. Blade estimated them at about five thousand head, broken into small herds for convenience of handling and watched over day and night by Mongs who did nothing else but care for, protect, and slaughter the horses when needed. They were aided by scores of fierce lean dogs who kept the horses from straying, nipping and barking and handling them with perfect ease and discipline.

Blade glanced behind him again, toward the just-visible wall, and saw the two Mongs who followed him whenever he rode. They were between him and the wall. Blade smiled grimly and fingered the golden collar. Sadda had eased the leash but it was still there. He ran a finger inside the collar where it galled his neck. So long as he wore the accursed thing, light as it was, he was no free man. He was not allowed to carry a sword, and had been given the leather armor of a warrior, but he was still a slave.

The Mongs trekked on. Each morning, and night, Blade was impressed anew with the skill, efficiency and the amazing speed, with which the Mongs set up and broke camp. Mongs on the march were a vastly different people from Mongs in permanent camp. They were solemn and businesslike and everyone had a task and did it, even children who could barely walk had their small chores.

For the first few nights on the trek Sadda did not summon him to her wagon. Blade was busy supervising the women and the slaves, and found time for an occasional word with Baber. Rahstum ignored him. He caught a glimpse now and then of Morpho, but the dwarf made no effort to contact him. All plots, Blade conceded, must be held in abeyance. This was not exactly a nerve tonic.

On the sixth night Sadda sent for him. Blade, who now had his own wagon, bathed and perfumed himself, and after the evening meal he went to her wagon. The night was cold and stars glittered frostily around a half moon. The fires of the Mongs, scattered widely over a plain that was beginning to turn to desert, outshone the stars in numbers and brilliancy. Somewhere far to the rear, near the herds, a carrion ape gibbered.

Her wagon was large and luxuriously outfitted. A guard stood by movable steps that led up to the entrance in the rear. He gave Blade a sardonic salute but offered no insult. The guards, indeed all of those close to Sadda, had been quick to note Blade's new favor with her. Their manner changed. He knew they still despised him as a slave and a woman's toy, but now they did not gibe openly.

Sadda was waiting for him, naked on her bed. A taper struck highlights from her oiled body, the dark gold honey of her breasts and thighs gleaming softly. She held out her arms to him and Blade knelt to kiss her. At first she had not permitted him to kiss her, because he was a slave, but in a frenzy of passion one night she had kissed him and found it good and thereafter demanded it.

When she had had enough of kissing she toyed with him for a moment, running her fingers through his beard, now thick and luxuriant, and well trimmed by Baber. She tweaked his nose.

"I have missed you, Blade. Take off your clothes and make love to me. Hurry!"

Blade having been deprived for six days and nights, was ready enough for sex, if not for love. The first bout was short and furious and Sadda moaned loudly in her final convulsion. She had never done that before. As they lay resting she began to stroke his face and hair.

"I find myself too much taken with you, Blade. I cannot understand it. But I like it. Perhaps, when we have slain the Khad, I will marry you and let you rule with me after all. Would you like that?" She was whispering, even though they were in private.

Blade thought that he would bloody well hate that, but he smiled and said: "You honor me too much, my lady. I would not know how to rule such a people as the Mongs."

She frowned at him for a moment, then pouted. She had never pouted before, either, and he thought the coyness did not well suit her barbaric beauty.

"You are always evasive, Blade. I note it much. And I do not like it. And another thing—when we are alone you will call me Sadda. Not my lady, or Princess, or anything but Sadda. That is understood?"

"Yes, my—Sadda."

"Then kiss me again. I like kissing with you, though I never did before. *This* kind of kissing."

Blade shrugged inwardly and was glad that her appetites had changed. But she was like a chameleon, changing from minute to minute. So, he thought with resignation, if it was to be a love affair then it would just have to be, or he would be the late Blade. If he must feign love, then he must feign it and not be caught at the feigning. Even in H-Dimension one did not spurn a lady with impunity. He did not like to think of the consequences here in X-Dimension, with a woman like Sadda.

When once again she had enough of kissing she lay back and closed her eyes. "My brother confided in me today—the first time since Obi came to him in the dream that he calls a vision."

137

Blade stroked her hair and kissed her ear. He whispered, "And what had the Khad to say?"

Sadda scowled, looking more like her old self. "He is very pious these days. He goes to consult Obi each morning before we march. Obi bids him march eastward. Always eastward until the wall ends. Then he is to turn behind the wall and march to the west again, so coming in behind the Cath. Obi has promised him victory if he does this."

Very likely, Blade thought. He had seen the Mong cavalry at work. In open fighting the Caths were no match for them. Without their wall they would be quickly defeated. It might be Lali, after all, who ended in the cage.

But he shrugged and said, "This idol only tells your brother what he should know for himself, and commands him to do what he should have done long ago. The Khad, when he is not mad, is no fool. Why has he not done this before?"

She laughed and pulled him down on her again. "You are the one who does not know, Blade! The march will be terrible. Thousands will die before we reach the end of the wall. If we ever do. I have heard there *is* no end, that the wall goes on forever!"

She was ready for love again and would not talk. She whispered as he left the wagon before the sun could shoot up, "Keep a close mouth and watch Rahstum. Our chance will come again. The madness will return, as it always does, and he will grow careless and fall to drinking too much *bross* and lusting after virgin children. Then leave it to me. I will arrange a celebration on some excuse and we will go through with the plan. Go, Blade."

Before many days Blade came to see that she was right about the trek. The days grew colder and the nights bitter. He was given a cape of thickly braided horsehair with a dogskin lining, and a pointed dogskin cap with thick earflaps. All the Mongs now dressed in this manner.

The wall was no longer in sight. The land began to slant upward, barren desert at first where the only moving

138

thing, other than the trekkers, was black sand that blasted them constantly. The wind never stopped blowing. For three days a sandstorm buffeted them, three days of black hell when Blade, in spite of the cloth worn over his mouth and nose, spat out black sand constantly. Still the Mongs marched, on and on. Children began to die, and women, and even some of the older warriors. They were left for the carrion apes that dogged the caravan relentlessly. The apes were growing bolder and sometimes at night would rush the herds and tear at the horses' throats before they could be driven off.

By the time the sandstorm blew itself out, they were into a narrow pass that climbed abruptly toward distant mountains where snow glimmered. It grew increasingly colder. The Khad no longer rode Thunderer, but retreated to his wagon. Sadda sent for Blade nearly every night and they managed to keep each other warm, making love under heaps of horsehair blankets.

They got into a belt of trees, just beneath the snowline, and halted for a week while the Mongs cut precious wood and stacked it in wagons. They never used wood for fuel, it being so rare, but not a bit of pony dung was wasted. The dung gatherers, lowest in the order of Mong society, followed along after the herds and collected each precious dropping. It was flattened and dried on racks in the moving wagons, and used for fuel.

They left the forest behind and climbed above the snowline. The pass narrowed and grew precipitous, only wide enough for one wagon to pass at a time. Glaciers hung over them like mammoth glistening swords and beyond the trail there was only empty space layered with gray wet clouds. And always the wind blew, merciless and interminable. Cold became a way of life.

Each day they lost horses and men, and sometimes wagons, that slipped into the chasm bounding the trail. They went down in a welter of threshing bodies and hooves, screaming away into the silence beneath the clouds. The Mong officers barked harsh orders and the caravan closed up and kept on going.

The bodies of those who died from the cold were tossed into the chasm as well, the carrion apes having turned back at the snowline. When night came each wagon stopped where it was and the occupants fended as best they could. Dung fire smoked in the snow.

Blade, even with his awesome physique and endurance, suffered from the cold. He gulped down warm *bross* and gnawed on half-frozen horsemeat and was thankful that Sadda, far ahead in the column, could not call on his services at the moment. He had not seen his guards for two days, which was sensible of them. No need to worry about Blade. To the right was the chasm, apparently bottomless. To the left monstrous glaciers climbed away into infinity. Now and again, during the day, Blade would glance at the vast sheets of snow and ice poised overhead and shiver. If they ever broke away and started sliding!

Baber's wagon, since the old man was now Blade's slave, was just behind his on the trail. On this night, when the breath froze instantly on his beard, Blade did not fear spies. He was in Baber's wagon, both of them huddled in straw and wearing their heavy capes, when a tapping came on the rear of the wagon.

They looked at each other. Baber put a finger to his mouth and whispered. "Not even *she* would seek you out on a night like this. Who can it be?"

"I know a way," said Blade through his icy beard, "of finding out." He loosened his sword in the scabbard and opened the door. The wind howled like a wolf and tried to invade the little wagon. Blade laughed and reached out to pluck the little figure inside.

Baber said: "You pick a fine night for visiting, Morpho. It must be urgent. Good news? Has the Khad fallen into the chasm in a fit of madness?"

The dwarf, more gnomelike than ever in his heavy coat and peaked cap, brushed snow from himself and looked at

140

Blade with his perpetual grin. He looked weary and there was entreaty in his dark eyes as he touched Blade's arm.

"I went to your wagon and had no answer, Blade, so I thought to try here. I must have your help. I am desperate, Blade. Help me."

Blade, still reserving judgment, had never mentioned his doubts to Baber. There would be time enough for that when he was sure. Now he placed a big hand on Morpho's shoulder. "I will help if I can. What is it? You are in danger?"

Baber, supporting himself on his arms, kept silent.

"I am not in danger," Morpho said. "But another is— someone very dear to me. You will come, Blade, and see what you can do?"

Blade glanced at Baber. The old man hunched his shoulders to indicate ignorance. Blade wondered if it could possibly be a trap of some kind.

Morpho tugged at his sleeve. "Please, Blade. Come with me. There is no time to waste. We have a long way to go."

Blade stared into the dwarf's eyes for a long time. He was a good judge of men and he did not think the little man was feigning his anxiety. Yet he hesitated. He walked in constant peril and could not afford a single slip.

"I will gladly help, Morpho. Anything I can do. But I have a right to know who needs help, and where we go?"

The dwarf retreated to the door, his wretched grin belied by the anguish in his eyes. He glanced from Blade to Baber, then shook his head.

"I cannot tell you that. Not here. I—I do not wish Baber to know this thing, for his own safety."

Baber nodded. "If it is like that, I do not want to know. My head is loose on my shoulders now, for reasons we all know. Go with him, Blade, if you will, and tell me nothing of it."

"We go," said Blade.

They forced their way out against the terrible wind and

closed the door, leaving Baber sipping thoughtfully at a cup of *bross*.

"They huddled for a moment in the shelter of the wagon. "Now," said Blade, "where do we go? Speak out, man, before we freeze to death."

Morpho leaned close to scream against the wind. "We must go far back, to the camp of the dung gatherers. I came from there."

Without another word or sign he turned and trotted back along the icy trail. Blade followed, marveling at the fool's endurance. All the way from the dung gatherers' camp in this cold and wind! It must be at least five miles.

Soon he had no breath for talking and very little time to think, except about survival. The footing was treacherous and the chasm yawned to their left. Once Blade was buffeted nearly to the edge and only saved himself by falling and wedging his body against a boulder. Morpho, who because of his size was not so much bothered by the wind, scurried back to tug at Blade and urge him forward again.

"Hurry—hurry!"

They bowed into the shrieking wind and pushed on. Blade reckoned that in H-Dimension temperatures, it was at least twenty below zero. His feet and hands were lumps of ice. But the cold and the wind were allies, for they were not challenged. Not even the hardy Mongs, when there was no danger of attack, bothered to post guards in this weather.

The wagons were pulled over as close against the glacier-studded cliffs as possible. Most of the wagons were dark, though soft light glowed in a few. The horses had been taken back along the trail to where it widened enough to herd them. The main herds were far behind and would not come over the pass until the wagons had cleared it. They would then be driven over it in single file, a long and tedious task.

It was not snowing now, but the wind, whooping like a demon straight down the glaciers, hurled fine particles of

142

snow and ice at them. Presently they got into high drifts, caught by boulders at the chasm edge and piled back across the track. Here Morpho fell for the first time.

Blade hauled him up and set him on his feet. The little man was gasping painfully. Blade, mindful that the dwarf had made this trip once tonight, said, "Are you all right, little man? Shall I carry you?"

Morpho shook his head, unable to speak. He plunged on, and fell again in the very next drift.

This time Blade did not ask. He picked him up and swung him on his broad shoulders and kept going.

Morpho, when he could speak, shouted into Blade's ear. "A little farther. A mile, not more. There will be a string of dung gatherers' wagons. They came up to bring fuel against the night. The track is too narrow, so they could not turn and go back."

Now came a stretch of track that was deserted. The Mongs, even the camp followers and the commonest of the soldiery, were careful to keep a distance between themselves and the gatherers of dung.

Then more wagons, and higher drifts. Blade was panting now, and staggering from time to time. They passed half a dozen wagons, all dark, then approached one in which a light glowed. Morpho tapped Blade on the shoulder.

"That one. And, Blade, I would have an oath from you."

Blade, frozen and gasping, encompassed by an icy hell, thought it a poor time indeed for oaths. He growled like a wounded bear.

"What oath, man? This is no time for such matters! We will freeze to death while you yammer about oaths. I—"

Morpho was insistent. The carven grin, colder than the Khad's heart, pressed against Blade's ear.

"A simple oath, Blade! I must have it—that you will not speak of what you see in the wagon!"

Blade nodded. Anything to get on with it. "All right,

Morpho. I give my word. Now do we go or does the wind murder us?"

"Let me down."

Morpho slipped from Blade's shoulders and fought his way through the drifts to the wagon. Blade followed, wondering about this new complication and what perils it might hold for him.

The wagon stairs were down. Morpho opened the door and Blade went in, hunching down to avoid striking his head. Morpho followed and slammed the door against the wind.

Blade's first sensation was of enormous relief. His face felt as if it had been flayed. He stared around the dimly lit wagon, trying to adjust his eyes to the shadow-haunted light.

There was a bad smell in the little wagon. By a pallet laid on the floor there crouched an ancient crone, well robed and cowled. She did not turn when they entered, but kept staring down at the face of the girl on the pallet.

Morpho tugged Blade toward the pallet. "My daughter," he said. "Her name is Nantee. She is dying, Blade. I think she *will* die unless you can help her. *I* cannot help her. Nor she." He indicated the crone. "And I dare not ask anyone else for help. Only you, Blade. Only you!"

The dwarf was clutching Blade's sleeve and staring up at him. He grinned his terrible grin. Tears trickled down that broad, ridiculous face.

Pity and anger, frustration, all commingled in Blade. Here was part of a mystery explained, but he was not thinking of that. How was *he* to save the girl? He was no doctor.

He patted Morpho's shoulder. "I will do what I can," he said gruffly. "But do not expect miracles. How long has she been sick?"

"Since five days now. Before we came into the pass. It is a fever. She burns, Blade, like a fire."

Blade knelt by the bed. The crone, who had been wiping the girl's face with a cloth, moved away. Blade,

144

feeling helpless, put a hand on the girl's forehead. It was dry and hot, yet she breathed easily enough. He moved the heavy robe covering her and put his ear to her chest. Her skin was light, nearly as light as the Caths, and her breasts had budded and were well on the way to development, with tiny rose-tinted nipples.

She breathed easily and deeply, yet her flesh was like a stove. There was no rasp of congestion. Blade covered her again and looked at Morpho.

The dwarf spoke first. "It is not the coughing sickness. I thought that at first, but no. It is only fever—but such a fever as I have never seen before. Can you help her, Blade?"

Blade smoothed back glossy dark hair from a high brow that gleamed lemony in the taper. There was Cath in her, no doubt of that. It showed in her face as well as her Mong heritage. Her nose was delicate and straight, her mouth a rosebud still, though the lips were badly fever cracked, and her eyes were oval, neither round nor narrow, and without the deep Mong fold at the outer corners.

At that moment the girl opened her eyes. Blade felt a shiver trace along his spine. Her eyes were green! A darker jade than those of Lali, but as pure, with all the depth and none of the translucence. The girl stared up at Blade, sensing the presence of a stranger, and raised a hand. By then Blade had guessed.

This girl was blind.

The fragile little hand touched his beard. The girl said, "Are you here, my father? Who is it that I touch?"

The dwarf knelt by the pallet and leaned to kiss the girl's cheek. "A friend of mine, Nantee. He is going to make you well."

The fingers, delicate as flowers, traced Blade's face. They touched his lips beneath the beard, his nose, lingered on his eyes and stroked lightly across his forehead. Suddenly the girl smiled.

"I like your friend, my father. He is good."

There was a tightness in Blade's chest and his eyes were

145

hot. Compassion banished his remaining anger and irritation. But what could he do?

She left off touching Blade and searched with her hands for her father. The dwarf, weeping unashamedly now, caught her hands and pressed them to his malformed face.

"Yes, Nantee. Yes, he is good. He will make you well." He stared at Blade across the girl, desperate and pleading through the tears.

Blade nodded curtly and looked away, unable to face such misery. "I said I would do what I can. How old is she?"

The girl had lapsed into coma again. Morpho arranged her hands and said. "Twelve. Old enough for marriage, Blade. And old enough for—"

He did not finish the sentence, nor did he need to. Blade already understood *that*.

Blade stood up abruptly nearly braining himself on a low beam. He rubbed his head and said, "We must get the fever down. Otherwise she will die soon."

"How, Blade? How?"

He stood frowning for a moment. How indeed? Then he knew what he must do. Must do because there was nothing else to do!

He glanced around the gloomy wagon. The crone, squatting in a corner, watched him with beady dark eyes and no expression on her million-wrinkled face. How much of death she must have seen!

"You have something in which we can gather ice and snow?"

"We have earthen bowls. And the dung baskets beneath the wagon. They will do?"

"They will do. Come on, little man. There is no time to lose."

They collected bowls and went out again into the blizzard. The wind leaped at them with a howl of triumph.

Morpho got the dung baskets, hanging beneath the wagon, and they set about collecting ice and snow, scooping it into the receptacles with their bare hands.

146

"I had not thought of such a thing," Morpho said against the scream of the wind. "Your brain is better than mine, Blade."

Blade kept scooping and the dwarf added, "But then I am a fool and that is as it should be." The wind could not obliterate the bitterness in the gnome's voice.

They lugged their burdens into the wagon and Blade sent Morpho back for more snow and ice. He stripped the covering from the unconscious girl until she lay naked.

She was well developed for twelve. That was the Mong in her. The slim legs were Cath. Her feet were small, with high arches and fine bones.

Blade glanced at the crone and jerked his head in command. She came to the bed and began to assist Blade in packing ice and snow around the slim body. Blade began at the shoulders, the crone at the feet, and they mounded the ice and snow against the burning flesh.

The dwarf came back with a dung basket full of snow and Blade dumped it on the girl's flat belly. He tossed the basket back to Morpho. "More!"

In a few minutes she was completely covered but for her face. Morpho sent the crone back to her corner while he and Blade squatted on the floor.

Blade studied the girl's face. It was so lovely, so tranquil, that for a moment a claw hooked at his heart and he thought she was dead. Then he saw the miniscule rise and fall of the snow covering her breast.

"She will not freeze?" asked Morpho.

"If we leave her too long like this, but we won't. And we must have heat in this wagon, Morpho. How can you do that?"

The dwarf snapped his fingers at the crone and gave a command. She brought forth a large bowl of wood into which an earthen sheath had been fitted. A crude brazier.

"When it is time," the dwarf explained, "I will have her start a fire of dung chips. There will be enough heat."

"She must be well wrapped," Blade warned. "As many robes as you can find."

147

"I will find enough." Morpho sat staring at the bed and his eyes were tender now. "She is all I have, Blade. All I care about in the world."

Blade watched him. "You have kept her well hidden."

"Yes. I have lived in fear that the Khad would come to know of her. I know his perversity too well. Her blindness, and her sweetness, would have great appeal to him. And I would be powerless."

"He will never learn from me," Blade promised.

"I believe that, Blade. I, who have never trusted anyone, trust you. I do not understand it myself. But now three people know—you and me and the old woman yonder. To the other dung gatherers I pretend that Nantee is my niece. I have kept her always with the dung gatherers, wearing rags and with her face dirty, and she gathers and cures dung with the others. My Nantee who is as beautiful as any princess! It was the only way."

Blade nearly asked the question then, nearly had the answer, but he let the moment slip away. Nantee moaned and he rose and went to her. She gazed up with sightless jade eyes and mumbled, "My father? I am cold—so cold."

Morpho came to comfort her and Blade pondered how soon to remove the ice and snow and warm her. Not for at least an hour.

While they waited the dwarf explained. "Once, many years ago, we Mongs caught a party of Caths raiding into our territory. Several of them had women with them. We killed the men and took the women captive. The Khad was drinking much *bross* at the time and he thought it a joke to give me, his fool, one of the women. I pretended to be grateful, though at the time I did not want her. I had often seen the way our women looked at me, a stunted man, and I did not like it. But I took her. And I came to love her, as she did me.

"We had a child, Nantee. My wife died of the coughing sickness and I, knowing how lovely Nantee would become, hid the baby with the dung gatherers."

148

"She was born blind?"

The dwarf nodded, "Yes. She has never seen, except with her fingers. But with them she sees well enough. I have never known her to be wrong. She knew *you* were good, Blade!"

Richard Blade was, after all, an Englishman. Now he was embarrassed. He waved it away with a gesture and said bluntly, "I do what I can, Morpho. It is not much. And I am as concerned as any of you to keep my head on my shoulders. And, now that we are together, this is a good time to talk of—"

Morpho leaned toward him, a finger to his lips, and nodded at the crone. "Nothing of that, Blade." He lowered his voice to a whisper. "I trust her, but if she were tortured she would tell anything she has heard. I would not blame her. So nothing of that. The time will come."

And yet Sadda has said that the dwarf was *her* man! That she could *make* Morpho do her bidding. How was that? Again Blade very nearly had it, and again he was distracted.

The girl called out loudly. "My father! I am freezing. My father—my father!"

Both men went to the bedside. Blade felt her brow. It was as cold as marble. He nodded at the dwarf. "Quickly now! Start your fire." He began to scoop the ice and snow away from the slender body.

By the time he and Morpho had removed all the ice, the crone had a dung fire glowing in the brazier. Stinking sworls of blue smoke filled the little wagon and Blade fell to coughing. Morpho, more accustomed to it, sat waving the smoke away from Nantee's face. Slowly the wagon grew warm as the crone fed the fire more and more pony chips.

Blade heaped robes on the girl until she was nothing but a mound of horsehair, with only her face showing. She was sleeping again.

Time passed. Blade had not dreamed that a brazier could throw out such heat. He and the dwarf sat and

149

waited, Morpho very quiet now, occasionally reaching to pat the pile of robes as if he were patting the child beneath them.

Blade saw it first. A trickle of sweat running down her forehead. He wiped it away and it came back immediately. He pushed a hand beneath the robes. She was soaked in sweat. He had broken the fever.

He stood up. "She sweats," he said. "That means the fever has gone. Now keep her warm and feed her well. A little hot *bross* would do no harm. But just a little. And I must be gone."

Morpho went with him to the door of the wagon. "I thank you, Blade. I am your man from this hour. Ask what you will. I have your promise, and I know you will keep it, but I ask that you do not tell even Baber of this. He also good, in his way, which is not yours, but he is a man and will speak under torture."

"Not even Baber," Blade assured him. "Let me know how it is with Nantee, but do not approach me too boldly. We have not been friends. It would look odd now if we talk too much together."

For a moment the old cunning sparked in the dwarf's eyes. "I know, Blade. I will be careful. As for other things—bide your time."

Chapter 13

Blade had little time to think of Nantee during the next week. The track narrowed and new storms broke on them. The cold increased. Mongs died of it, or of the coughing sickness, and the corpses were flung into the chasm. He went only once that week to Sadda and she was sullen and demanding in love, but would not speak of the plot against the Khad. When he had satisfied her, she clung to him with a hint of tenderness, then dismissed him.

Food and dung chips ran low. Horses had to be brought up and slaughtered in the snow, in a narrow space between wagons. One poor beast, sensing the knife, went into a panic of rearing and kicking and took three Mongs with it into the chasm.

At last they reached the summit. Beyond this point the pass began to slant downward. Blade, leading his pony at the moment, looked out over the roof of this strange world. It was utterly dreary, a lifeless waste that stretched to every horizon, and it was utterly grand.

Blade stood at the center of a gigantic bowl of mountains. As far as he could see, in every direction, they thrust jagged peaks into the sky. Range after range after range of shale and snow and basalt and granite, glinting all dark and gray in the twilight air. No Jade Mountains here. He began to understand the harshness of the Mongs a little better. They were as their land was—cruel and hard.

The Mongs never halted. The van of the column crested the summit and began to spill down the far pass, slithering like a slow dark avalanche. Horses moved faster and men breathed easier of the thin dry air. Blade, who had been sickened and weakened by the altitude at first, now was as oblivious of it as any Mong.

He tugged his pony onto an outcropping and watched them pass. To his left there was no end to the dark straggle of horses and men, and the herds must still be brought over the summit. To his right the line was lengthening as the caravan picked up speed and moved toward a widening of the track.

Blade looked up to see Morpho passing on a horse, jogging at a faster pace than the others and passing when he could. The dwarf, who normally rode close to the Khad's party, must have been back to see Nantee.

Morpho gave no sign of recognition when he saw Blade. But his head moved in a nod, once, slightly up and down. Nantee lived.

Another three days and they were out of the pass and into desert again where the sands blew yellow instead of black. They halted on the desert to rest and reorganize, and for the herds to catch up with them. The black tents were hauled from the wagons and pitched, like sable mushrooms on the desert, and once more there was singing and laughter and quarreling around the fires.

Blade was called to service the lady Sadda regularly, in his role of first stud, and she was at times affectionate and nearly tender, and teased him about a secret concerning him which she would not tell.

"When it is time," she whispered. Then she bit his ear. "Come, Blade. Again—again!"

He carefully avoided the dwarf. Rahstum, he thought, carefully avoided *him*. The Khad remained aloof, sober and serious, with no hint of madness. He was still pursuing the vision of Obi, though he no longer spoke of it. None of the Mongs had ever been in this country before and while there was superstitious murmuring, there was no fear of the unknown.

Blade and the legless cripple, Baber, had long talks from time to time. When they camped Baber left the wagon on his little cart and propelled himself about with his pointed sticks. He was now Blade's personal slave and attended to his needs with loving care. It gave him something to do, as Baber said, and it accustomed the Mongs to seeing them together.

And so Blade waited, watching for a sign from Rahstum, for a sign from the dwarf, for a sign from lady Sadda. Everything was in midair, suspended in doubt and uncertainty. He was a man walking a tightrope over an abyss. A free man now, in all but name. But he still wore the golden collar. Each day it galled him more.

It took a week for the Mongs to recoup from that terrible journey over the mountains. An official tally was taken, in which Blade was called on to help, and they found they had lost over a thousand dead, men, women and children, and nearly four hundred horses.

Baber, with his cynical laugh, said the loss in population would more than be replaced during the halt. The married warriors were hard at it in the tents and the bachelors visited the camp followers in a steady stream.

"Making little bastards," said Baber, "who will have to spend their lives gathering dung. It was not our way among the Cauca. A man had to acknowledge his child."

That very night Sadda told Blade that she was carrying his child. She rubbed his nose with her own and for the first time he thought her near to tears. He had not thought her capable of tears.

"Not a word of this to anyone," she commanded him. "Until our plans are carried out and I give you leave."

Blade, who was stunned at the news, managed to gulp weakly and say, "This, then, is the secret of which you spoke?"

"Only part of it, Blade. Only half of it. The best part you will hear later."

He did not even tell Baber. He did not like to think about it, and tried not to, yet it began to haunt him. A child by Sadda! A tiny half Mong, half Englishman

153

brought into this cruel barbaric world. He found himself wishing that Sadda was wrong.

As soon as they camped the Khad sent scouting parties out to the east, north and south. The parties sent to north and south came back in three days and reported to the Khad in private. The group that had gone east did not return for a week and then a long secret conference was held in the Khad's big tent. The next morning they struck camp and headed east.

Gradually they moved into steppe country, vast undulating savannas, sparsely treed, where the grass grew tall and sweet and the Mong horses and ponies fell into an ecstasy of eating and rolling. They found wild hay, which was cut and baled by slaves. Tons of it was loaded into empty wagons and they were again on the trek. The steppe, as vast and empty as ever, began to slant downward, and one day when the wind blew from the east, Blade caught a scent that riffled his nerves with odd pleasure. Salt water! They were nearing the sea.

None of the Mongs had smelled salt water before and it amused him to watch them sniffing and frowning. Then the wind changed and the salt smell was gone.

One day a scouting party came in from the east with a prisoner. Blade, supervising a slave work group, stared as curiously as the others as they rode past. The prisoner rode a horse, his hands tied behind him and his feet held with rawhide under the animal's belly. He was a Cath, but not like the Caths Blade had known. His skin was light yellow, and he was beardless, but he was much sturdier with arms and legs well muscled and nearly as large as Blade's own. The prisoner, who held his head high and stared straight ahead, wore wooden armor with the moon symbol emblazoned on the chest. On his left shoulder he wore an epaulet. He was a Cath officer of fairly high rank.

That night, after they made love, Sadda told him about the prisoner.

"He calls himself a Sea Cath. He speaks freely, without threat of torture, yet he tells nothing that we could not

154

find out ourselves. He is a subcaptain and thinks he is very grand." She frowned and added, "As do all the Caths!"

Blade, who was eaten with curiosity, managed to appear bored.

"Where was he taken?"

"There is a pass three days march to the east that leads into a valley. A small fort guards it. Our warriors took the fort and slew all the Caths except this one, who was in command."

Blade yawned. "What will happen to him? To this Sea Cath?"

Sadda shrugged her slim shoulders. "Who knows? Who cares? And do not yawn when you are with me, Blade! I do not like it. If I bore you I will find another way of amusing you, and myself."

In that tense moment she was the old Sadda, her eyes narrowed and dangerous, and Blade cursed himself for his laxness. The new Sadda, the princess of tenderness and love for him, and the mother of his child, was only a mask, a thin veneer that need only be scratched to reveal the reality beneath.

He sought to repair matters as best he could.

"I could never be bored with you, my lady."

She frowned. Another mistake.

Blade smile and kissed her averted face. "Sadda. I am tired. Sleepy. I admit it. These nights with you are paradise, but they are also long. And I have my duties during the day."

He bent to put his ear against her belly, flat and taut as ever, and again smiled as he said, "I could not sleep anyway. I keep thinking of this miracle—of being a father to a new prince or princess."

For a moment he thought he had overdone it, troweling on such obvious flattery, for she still frowned and regarded him coldly. Then she smiled back, for she was a woman after all and Blade spoke what she wanted to hear. She moved into his arms and began loveplay. Blade,

155

sweating a little, vowed never to grow careless again. She was a kitten that could turn into a tigress in a second.

The Sea Cath was eventually tortured, and he babbled like a child. When his tormentors deemed him bled of information he was put to death.

The steppe, funneling downward now, led them to the pass guarding the valley. They were greeted by a few Mongs who had been left to hold the captured fort. They reported no sign of hostile action in the valley. Blade, contriving to see and hear as much as possible, wondered at that. Were these Sea Caths as proud, as haughty, and as stupid, as the wall Caths back in Serendip? It appeared so, otherwise the fort would have been retaken and reinforcements brought up.

The smell of the sea grew stronger as the Mongs wound their way through the valley, ever downward into a belt of thick vegetation where trees clustered in dense copses and huge orchid-like plants bloomed and gay-plumaged birds sang and traced lines of color in the sky. The Mongs marveled at such country, and did not like it. It was too soft, too efflorescent, too tender, for these hardy sons of the black sands. Sweet bird song grated on their ears.

A last gradual rise and the sea lay before them, sapphire and unruffled, edged by golden crescents of beach where wavelets creamed in and out.

On this day Blade was riding with Sadda, not far behind the Khad and his guard of honor. From the top of the rise the party surveyed the downward slope and what lay beyond it.

The Khad Tambur held up a hand. The order was repeated and carried back and the marching column of Mongs came to a gradual halt. Twenty miles of horses, men, and wagons stretched far back into the pass.

Blade and Sadda moved their ponies up to the crest, off to one side of the Khad. No one paid them any attention. The Khad, slumped in his saddle, his malformed back bent half over in constant pain, stared at the scene with his good eye.

156

Blade, with two excellent eyes, was seeing it differently. This, he knew immediately, would not be easy. He understood why the Sea Caths had not reinforced the fort at the mouth of the pass. They thought themselves secure enough in their city.

Below them the land sloped away to level into a great green plain. Perfect terrain for the Mong horsemen—if the Sea Caths would come out and fight.

They would not be such fools. Blade was sure of it. The city below was perfectly situated for defense. It stood at the mouth of a harbor shaped like an hourglass. An enormous chain, glistening now in the sun, stretched across the narrow waist. The inner harbor was crowded with craft of every description from tiny fishing boats to tall clumsy-looking men of war. They floated placidly at anchor, with no sign of bustle or alarm. As well they might. The Sea Caths had nothing to fear from that direction.

High cliffs ran around the inner harbor, right up to the waterfront of the city. There was no approach that way. The cliffs were effective flank guards. The only feasible line of attack was the direct frontal, across the broad green plain which lay below them. It was inviting—until you got to within two hundred yards of the low city wall.

First there was a wide ditch that sloped gradually down until it met the perpendicular back wall. Blade guessed the wall at twenty feet. From the lip of the ditch to the wall, the slope was covered with sharp-pointed stakes set firmly into the earth and pointing at the lip. Men could move among those stakes. Not horses.

Beyond the ditch—Blade saw immediately and understood, and knew the Mongs would not comprehend—was the trap. The real defensive trickery. A wide moat. Dry now.

Blade traced the moat around the city and his lips twitched in a dry smile. Those were sluice gates where the moat ended in the harbor, and those long poles and levers would open them and let in the sea. A quick glance and rapid calculation convinced him. The sea wall fronting the city was keeping the harbor in its place. Open the sluice gates and gravity would do the rest.

For an hour the Khad and his Captains studied the town and the terrain. Blade saw Rahstum and the Khad in deep debate. Meantime he and Sadda had ridden even more to one side and were safely out of earshot.

Sadda, her knee touching his as the horses stood patiently, said, "We must make ready now, Blade. The time is coming again. I know my brother as few do, and I see signs of the madness returning. Not yet, but soon. And when he takes this city there will be a great feast and celebration. Greater, and wilder than would have been on his birth date. That will be our chance. Be ready."

He masked his eyes and nodded. "I will be ready. I have forgotten nothing and I know what I have to do."

Kill the dwarf after Morpho had killed the Khad! Blade knew it was not going to work out that way, but he still puzzled about *how* Sadda expected to force the dwarf into killing her brother?

She laid a hand on his, whispering. "I will tell you the other half of my secret now. You will see how clever I have been, and how perfectly everything fits."

A child bragging and wanting praise.

"Before this battle, Blade, I am going to ask the Khad for your freedom, that he let you break the golden collar. He will ask me why, in that sly way of his, and I will tell him truth—up to a point.

"I will say that I have love for you, which *is* true, and that I mean to marry you. He will shake with rage and scream at me, but in the end I think he will permit it. It has been done before, as I shall remind him. Not often, but royal women have married their slaves before."

Blade was watching her face. She was veiled, as always when they rode abroad, but he had come to read her beneath the veil. Her coronet of black hair glistened in the sun as she leaned to tap his knee with her whip. Her eyes were narrowed in speculation.

"There must be no mention of the child I carry. No one

158

must know of that yet. But you see it, Blade? If my brother permits the marriage, and it is done according to Mong law, then our child is a legal prince or princess. Our marriage is legal. And when he is dead you will sit by me as legal Consort. We will have many children, Blade, and so found a new line of great warriors and conquerors the like of which has never been seen before."

Blade had not thought her so ambitious, and had deemed her much too selfish to be concerned with her posterity. It was another facet of this diamond-hard lady.

The Khad wasted no time in sending a courier to demand the immediate and abject surrender of the Sea Caths. Unconditional surrender! He promised them nothing but their lives, which would then belong to the Mongs.

Meantime the Mongs were on the march again, moving from the pass out onto the broad green plain before the city. They debouched and spread in their thousands, covering the plain like a dark tidal wave. Tents were pitched and fires built and horses slaughtered for food. There was a great furbishing of weapons and much laughter and song. After the bitter defeats at the wall, and the horrible trek over the mountains, the warriors were primed for blood and booty. For killing until they were surfeited with killing. To none, save Blade and possibly Rahstum, did it occur that the attack might be beaten back.

While they waited for the courier's return, the Khad entertained a small party in his tent. Blade was included.

He kept well in the background and watched. The Khad was in high good humor, drinking often of *bross,* and though Blade could discern no sign of the madness yet he judged that Sadda was right. It was on the way. Now and again the Khad's voice would reach a high pitch, nearly a scream, and his laughter was shrill. He demanded constant entertainment. Belly dancers were summoned, and acrobats and eaters of fire, and Morpho had to run through his entire gamut of tricks. The Khad's beloved melons, packed in snow, had been kept in supply at great expense of time and men, and now the dwarf must throw his voice into a melon and beg, in a whimper, to be eaten by the Scourge of the World.

Morpho performed skillfully, without a glance at Blade, who wondered at the little man's thoughts. As the madness grew the Khad would once again be casting about for little girls. But surely Nantee, in her rags and dung gatherer's filth, would be safe enough.

Seeing the Khad in such high good humor, Sadda leaned and spoke to him from her throne. Blade, noting this, felt himself tense. He knew, even before the Khad crooked a finger at him, that Sadda was beginning to carry out the first part of her plan.

Blade went to the throne and bowed with dignity. His nerves were jumping but he kept his face impassive. He was not, as he well knew, an unimpressive sight. He towered over them all, but Rahstum, and his leather armor was as well fitted and burnished as any. His beard, though kept well trimmed by Baber, bristled fiercely and he wore a sword as though he had been born with it.

After his bow Blade met the Khad's eye without flinching, matching that single orb stare for stare.

"You summon me, Lord of the World? I am at your command."

The single eye narrowed and something fanatic gleamed for a moment, then it widened and the Khad struck his knee and laughed harshly.

"Are you now, Blade? Hah. I had thought you only at the command of my sister—and Obi knows she commands enough of you, eh? How do you fare, Blade? How is it to bed my sister?"

Hate and jealousy in that eye now. The Khad was impotent, except with small girls, and he was remembering.

Blade, walking on eggs, felt them cracking beneath his tread.

He bowed again. "I have no complaint, Khad Tambur. No complaint at all."

There was a moment of silence. Rahstum crossed his arms and stared stonily at Blade. Morpho juggled. The

160

Khad inched his tortured spine forward to peer at Blade. Then he went into a gale of laughter.

"No complaints, eh? No complaints! I think not, Blade, and I know! Or once I knew. But it is most generous of you to acknowledge that you have no complaints."

The company, taking their cue, joined in the laughter. They ceased abruptly as the Khad raised a hand.

"Be still, all. I want you to hear this. Hear my sister's request—and hear my answer. She would have me free Blade. Strike the golden collar from his neck! What think you of that?"

Murmurs of puzzlement. None of them knew what to think—the Khad not having yet told them.

The Khad raised his hand again. "But wait. My sister tells me more, makes another request of me, her beloved brother. Would you hear it?"

Assent from the crowd. They knew what was expected.

The Khad, Blade admitted, was not a bad showman. He waited until the murmurs and whispering died away, then went on: "Sadda wishes to marry this man Blade! After he is freed, of course, for no Mong princess can marry a slave. And what think you of *that*?"

Blade, watching for reaction from Rahstum and the dwarf, saw them glance swiftly at each other, then at him. Their blank faces told him nothing.

The tent was buzzing like a beehive. Everyone was darting glances at Blade and Sadda. He got the impression that some of the company were not too much surprised.

And now madness did flare in the Khad's eye. It glittered at Blade and the Khad's grin was that of a carrion ape.

"I will permit this marriage," the Khad said. "I will free you, Blade, of your collar. After the town of the Sea Caths has been taken, and *after* you play a part in taking it. An important part, my friend, for I would have you in the formost rank!"

Blade bowed and nodded. "That is most generous of you, great Khad. I will try not to disappoint you."

161

The Khad snarled and pointed to his sister. "Just be sure that you do not disappoint her! I know you are a great warrior, Blade, or so I am constantly told. And I saw you defeat Cossa, so there may be some truth to it. But tomorrow we will see if your victory over my champion was a freak of luck."

Rahstum, without looking at Blade, spoke up. "A wise decision, great Lord. But I would have a favor also. I would have this Blade fight with me and my men, and in the foremost rank as you say. I will give him such a testing as he has never had."

The Khad nodded shortly. "So it shall be. And if the city surrenders, as I do not think they will do without a fight, then we will find yet another test for Blade. He who aspires to marry my dear sister must prove himself more than any ordinary man."

The Khad meant that he should die. Blade was sure of it.

Sadda, taken by surprise, had been battling to restrain her anger. She leaned to the Khad and in a silky voice said, "You forget something, my brother."

The Khad glared. The madness was coming on fast.

He mimicked her tone. "And what do I forget, my sister?"

"The ransom, my Lord. Surely it will come one day, for the Caths think Blade a great man, and how shall you have the ransom if he is killed in battle?"

The Khad smashed his fist on his knee. "Bah, sister! For one thing I do not think the ransom will ever catch up with us. For another, when I take this city, the way around the wall will be clear. I will scourge Cath, and plunder it, and leave nothing alive. Who needs ransom then? I will rule Cath! And a third thing, which your woman's brain has not enough of, is that ransom is for a slave, not a warrior and husband of my sister. If he marries you, I will be his brother-in-law, will I not? And who can sell his own brother-in-law!"

His logic, by Mong custom, was impeccable.

162

A warrior came hurriedly into the tent. He carried something in his hands. To Blade it looked like crumpled folds of parchment, dark parchment. Blood dripped from it into the richly hued rugs.

The Khad looked up and stared at the man. "What now, man? And where is my courier? I had expected him back long before now."

The warrior held out his hands and let the parchment unroll and dangle before him.

"The courier *has* returned, your greatness. This is he— what the Sea Caths sent back of him."

It was the skin of a man, dripping blood still. The Sea Caths had sent their answer.

Khad Tambur stared for a long time at the remains of his courier. Blade, so fascinated that he forgot his own danger, watched the man who ruled all the Mongs.

The eye began to roll and show white. The bad teeth were bared in a soundless snarl. The Khad's face twitched, contorted, and a froth of spittle appeared at the corners of his mouth. He twisted his decaying spine and clawed at his chest with both hands.

Blade knew, even before the Khad fell silently forward from his throne, that he was seeing the falling sickness. It was epilepsy. He had forgotten that the Khad was subject to fits.

Only Blade was surprised by the sudden convulsion. The others watched in silence as the Khad lay on the rug, foaming at the mouth, kicking and twitching and making horrible sounds. He picked up a corner of the rug and thrust it into his mouth and began chewing savagely.

Morpho gave Blade the tiniest wink as he hurried past to the Khad's aid. The dwarf carried a small round cylinder of wood, and passed so close to Blade that he could see the teeth marks in the wood.

Morpho deftly inserted the piece of wood into the Khad's foaming mouth. Four huge blacks came forward with a litter and the twitching figure was lifted on it and carried out.

Blade, thinking of the Sea Caths, hoped their sea moat was efficient. There would be no mercy for them now. Then he remembered that he would be in the foremost rank of attackers. He could not afford to waste sympathy on the Sea Caths. He had to think about himself.

Chapter 14

The Mong armies were arrayed in the plain before the city. When the sun shot over the horizon they would attack. All night the horsemen and foot soldiers had been moving into position and, once there, sleeping on the ground.

Rahstum, who commanded the center, kept Blade close to him. His manner was curt, near to insulting at times, but he had designated Blade to fight at his right hand. It was nearly dawn before they found a chance to speak alone.

Rahstum said: "What of this marriage, Blade? Do you and Sadda plot against me?"

They were riding along the line of battle, well forward, near the lip of a huge ditch. There was no moon and the city was dark but for an occasional vagrant light, but the star sheen was sufficient for Blade to see the Captain's face. It was grim. The gray eyes glinted hard at him.

Blade had foreseen this moment and thought it out. He could not go on forever picking his way through plots. He must choose. He had chosen. He told Rahstum as much as was needed to indicate Blade's loyalty. They reined the horses and Rahstum listened without comment. A sea breeze sprang up and moved salt air across the plain. Horses nickered softly.

When he had finished Rahstum fingered his beard and said, "She is clever. I never doubted that. And it is a good plan. But how is she going to force Morpho to slay the Khad? What hold can she have over him?"

Blade knew of one possible hold, one lever, and yet he did not see how it could be. And he dare not mention it. He had given his word.

He said: "I do not know. Yet she seems positive. Perhaps she deludes herself. It is all a fantasy, or a lie. I cannot say."

"Waste no time thinking about it," Rahstum said harshly. "I will strike first and that will settle the matter. My men are ready. I am more than ready, for this waiting has been agony."

Blade watched a torch moving in the city. "The plan is the same, then?"

"The same. It should be easier now. He is going fast into madness, and when we sack the city he will grow worse. He has told me of his plans for the Sea Caths. No quarter. And afterwards a great feast to celebrate his triumph. Be you ready when the time comes."

Blade said: "What of Sadda?"

Rahstum snarled like a wolf, showing his white teeth. "What of her? She dies also, man! Surely you see that? What good to kill the big viper and leave the small one? She has men loyal to her and would raise a revolt against me. She is also a princess of the blood and has law and tradition on her side. I could not rule with her alive. She dies!"

He was right. Blade said: "As you say. I only ask that I not be the one to kill her. After all I have made love to her, shared something of her life, and do not want to be her murderer."

The Captain laughed curtly. "You *are* a strange man, Blade. But no more of this now. You saw those gates holding back the sea? Do you think they will open them?"

Blade was surprised. He had not thought the Mong command astute enough to notice the sluice gates, or guess at their use. But Rahstum was not a Mong.

"They will let in the sea," he said, "if they are losing the battle—which they may not do, Captain. This will not be an easy victory."

166

Rahstum agreed. "I know. And they *will* let in the sea. I am counting on it. I intend to use most of the Khad's men, as many as I can, to storm into the dry moat. I will hold back my own as long as possible. The more of *his* men drowned the better!"

At this Blade was *not* surprised. He nodded and said, "I have gauged the depth of that moat. When full it will rise to ten feet, well over the heads of our men and, as you say, many will drown. But there is a way over it if the men can be protected while a bridge is laid down."

Rahstum looked at him in puzzlement. "How know you how deep it is? You have not been close to it, or in it."

Trigonometry would have meant nothing to the Captain.

"A thing I learned in my own land. Suffice that I know. And the bridging will not be hard if the men are protected."

"I know of bridges. We Caucas built them. But in our country there were many trees, enough timber. Here we have nothing."

Blade told him how it could be done.

The sun shot up then, an instant red ball of flame, and the Mongs scrambled from sleep and into formation, rubbing their eyes and gnawing on chunks of cold horsemeat. Trumpets brayed and officers ran to and fro, dressing the ranks and cursing, prodding and slapping with the flats of their swords.

Sea Caths lined the ramparts of the town, waiting. No huge cannon here, or they would have fired it before now. But they had catapults of a sort, like massive crossbows on wheels, mounted at intervals along the ramparts and firing twelve arrows at a time.

Chunkkk—whanggg! The first catapult was fired and a dozen long thick arrows screamed over Blade and Rahstum and did bloody work in the first rank of Mongs. Two men, transfixed by the same arrow, flopped and scrabbled like fish on a single hook.

Rahstum gentled his nervous horse and cast an expert

eye at the Cath ramparts. "A good weapon," he told Blade, "but they cannot depress. When we move forward they will be firing over our heads. That is all to the good."

His teeth flashed beneath the beard. "They will be firing into the Khad's men then. Now, Blade, heed well! We will lead the first attack in and move the obstacles and plant scaling ladders against the far wall of that ditch. We will lose men, but not too many, and the Khad will think nothing but that we are valorous to go first. While he sits in safety and drinks *bross* and caresses some poor child!"

Blade followed the Captain's contemptuous glance. On the crest of the rise behind them the Khad's throne had been set up. He was on the throne now, Sadda standing beside him, the sun brave on his honor guard and the lances flaunting horsetails and skulls. As they looked the Khad shielded his good eye with a hand and peered toward them. He raised a hand in command. The order to attack.

"He was never a coward," grunted Rahstum. "I give him that. But now that he is old, and has the madness, he is not so fond of battle. And *will not* die. So be it!"

Arrows *planged* just over their heads. Blade could not help but wince a little. Rahstum did not move a muscle but to calm his prancing horse.

"When we have made a ramp to the moat," he said, "it will be fair that we fall back for rest. Then I will send in the Khad's best troops. He will suspect nothing and if the Caths open the sea gates he will lose a great many men."

Rahstum leaned to Blade and spoke a final word. "Watch your back today."

He brought his steed about and raised his sword high over his head. Blade moved his horse into position on the right. Sunlight glittered on their polished leather armor, flung sparks from the upraised steel.

Rahstum uttered a stentorian cry that echoed up and down the line of battle, heard clearly over the *hiss-hiss-hiss-hiss* of arrows.

"To me, Mongs! To me!"

The lines surged forward. High time. The crossbows had found their range and were chewing up the first ranks. Every volley brought down a score or more of the Mongs. The dead and wounded were ignored. When a man fell, another stepped forward to take his place.

Rahstum led them to the lip of the first sloping ditch. There his lieutenants dismounted the horsemen and set them to answering the fire from the city. They knelt, each beside his horse, and the short crooked bows began a nasty *ssstt—sssstt—sssstt*. This fire was not particularly effective, for the bows had no great range, and Blade, now beginning to be caught up in the battle fever, found himself wishing for an English long bow.

Yet the fire gave some cover. Under it the foot soldiers came storming up and into the ditch. They carried scaling ladders and some had large baskets of withe and digging utensils. This puzzled Blade at first.

He and Rahstum remained mounted, riding up and down the lip of the ditch, commanding and urging, and were fair targets for the Caths on the ramparts. As Rahstum had predicted they were in defilade now, beneath the fire of the crossbows, and the Sea Caths began to line their ramparts with bowmen who could aim better. Dark flurries of arrows came down, but the Cath bows were no longer-ranged than the Mong's, and only the first ranks, now deep in the ditch, suffered much.

The Mongs were tearing the obstacles out of the earth, clearing a way for horsemen, but they did not content themselves with loosening the pointed stakes and tossing them aside. They were passed rapidly down the line to the base of the slope, where the wall stopped progress. They were wedged into the ground and Blade, still puzzling, saw that a platform was being built. First one, then another. They were building stairs!

Mongs with baskets and tools were shoveling dirt frantically and filling in the narrow platforms as they rose. Blade nodded. He knew how agile the Mong ponies were.

They would easily climb the stairs when they were finished, and the footmen behind them.

But the arrow fire began to intensify. The Caths had stronger bows and were bringing them into action. An arrow grazed Rahstum's horse and another, nearly spent, bounced off Blade's breast armor. Rahstum sent a rider off to order diversionary attacks on both flanks. Sadda's men, on the right, moved into action and immediately began to suffer from the big crossbows. Blade saw the Captain's lips move in a faint smile.

Blade was nearly caught unawares. But for his fine peripheral vision he would have been murdered. He caught a flicker of movement from the right and saw the bowman aiming. In the last second the bowman turned slightly and loosed his arrow at Blade. Blade got his shield up just in time. It was a Mong shield, round and of leather, and the arrow pierced it and hung dangling an inch from his throat. Blade pulled his horse around and rode at the man. The Mong ducked, eluding him, and tried to run. He ran straight into Rahstum, who slashed down with his sword and cleft the man from shoulder to belly.

Rahstum shouted. "Coward. Deserter! Run toward the enemy, not away."

He winked at Blade as he rode past. "You see? On guard! They will try again."

Blade peered down at the dead man. He wore the insignia of the Khad, not that of Rahstum. He had mingled, then, with the clear purpose of killing Blade.

His spine cold, Blade glanced about him. The incident had gone unnoticed in the din and clangor and rise and fall of the battle. From that moment on Blade guarded his back as well as his front.

The stairs were rising up the wall now. Another long line of warriors had moved up into position near the lip of the ditch. The Khad's own troops.

The Mongs had thrown another attack in on the left as a further diversion. These were also the Khad's men. Farther back, on the green slope, the second line of reserves moved into position.

It was still in essence a frontal attack, and brutal. The high cliffs guarding the moat at either end served as a funnel to divert the Mongs against the ramparts where the sea Caths were strongest. No real flank attack could be mounted, and as the Mongs pressed forward, urged by the pressure of their own troops behind them, they began to converge and the separate companies to lose identity.

The ditch was now filled with thousands of screaming, working, fighting, blood-crazed Mongs. The sound was one long anguished scream of battle. Men died beneath the arrows and were stepped on and trodden into soft earth. Some who were merely wounded were trampled to death.

The Sea Caths, all this while, had been quietly warping their tall clumsy ships in toward the sea wall which held back the ocean. Blade had wondered about those tall ships, more like towers on a raft than ships, and now he saw their use. The sides of the towers fell away and revealed long slender poles with cup-shaped devices at the top end. Blade could see this because Rahstum had now given the order for his own men to fall back, and Blade rode back up the slope as the Khad's troops poured into the ditch and toward the completed stairs up the wall.

Blade, from this new vantage, saw a crew winching back one of the slender poles. It bent like a resilient whip and something was loaded into the cup. It glittered in the sun and even at that distance Blade recognized it. Jade. Not cannon balls, but jade just the same.

He saw a Cath officer pull a rope trigger. He could imagine the nasty *spanggg* as the slender catapult whipped up and over, though he could not hear it over the battle. A huge shard of jade, flattish and sharp edged, soared high over the city and came down in the ditch. Nearly a vertical fall, a mortar effect. The jade missile smashed twenty men to pulp. There was no way to miss the target in that fighting, dinning mass.

171

Rahstum was riding furiously up and down, extricating his men from the ditch so that Khad's men could rush in. He turned and rode toward Blade as another shard of jade smashed down and squashed the attackers like bugs. The Caths were warping more of the tower ships in. Blade counted a dozen of them.

Rahstum, after sending his officers scurrying to reform and rearm his men, joined Blade. Together they watched the carnage grow as more and more of the ships began to hurl the deadly chunks of jade over the city.

Rahstum tugged at his beard in puzzlement. "Are they wizards, then? Every one finds its mark. I would expect a miss now and then."

Blade did not try to explain. The Sea Caths had tested and fired and planted sighting stakes, all against this emergency. Those tall catapults were perfectly adjusted for range.

"Anyway," Rahstum said with a grin, "those are the Khad's men. Not mine."

He turned to shout at a lieutenant. "Form up again, Lusta. They will be in the moat in a few minutes."

It was true. The Mongs in the ditch had completed a series of shallow steps up the wall. They bounded up and over into the moat, waving their swords and bows and screaming defiance at the Caths on the rampart beyond the moat. A wave of horsemen went charging down the ditch and put their ponies at the moat. A wave of horsemen went charging down the ditch and put their ponies at the stairs. The shaggy little beasts plunged up, as agile as mountain goats.

Now came another wave of foot, carrying ladders. The rank and file of the Mongs thought it was almost over. Soon they would be in the town and cutting throats and raping to their hearts' content.

The actual rampart of the city offered no serious obstacle. It was barely ten feet high, of earth and stone and braced by timbers. A broad way ran atop it, where the crossbows were still at work. The wall was thronged with

172

Caths who screamed insults and every type of obscenity meant to lure the Mongs into the moat.

Blade tapped Rahstum's arm. "Soon now. If they mean to flood it at all."

He glanced up the hill behind him. The Khad had left his throne and ventured down the slope a few feet, staring and shielding his eye with both hands. He also was thinking that victory was within his grasp. Nothing could stand against the Mongs in hand-to-hand combat.

The Sea Caths waited, cunningly, until the dry moat was a raging mass of attackers from sea gate to sea gate. Some ladders were already up and being thrown back. Great cauldrons of boiling oil were tipped on the Mongs as they swarmed up, uttering blood-curdling yells, swords in hand and knives in teeth.

Slowly, paying a terrible price, the Mongs began to gain a foothold on the wall. A line of Mong archers came into the ditch, at a proper distance from the wall, and poured in a murderous covering fire. More and more of the ladders went up and stayed. There was hand-to-hand fighting on the wall now, and the archers began to kill Mongs as well as Caths. Rahstum could have sent an order to the archers, but he did not. The arrow fire ceased, after minutes, when some sublieutenant gave the order.

A low, growing, rushing thunder sound began to fill the air. Rahstum pointed. The Caths had opened the sea gates.

From both ends the sea rushed into the moat, foaming and churning, a roaring green monster flecked with muddy white, a manmade tidal wave that was twenty feet high and scoured everything before it. It overflowed the moat and spilled into the ditch below like an avalanche. There it turned muddy and churned in frenetic whirlpools and killed everything in its path.

Blade thought it unlikely that any of the Mongs could swim.

There was a tremendous clashing hiss as the two streams of hot water met. Horses and men were tossed high in the air, to be immediately sucked down and under. The Caths, screaming in triumph, and having finished off the Mongs on the rampart, began running up and down and making pincushions out of the few that could keep their heads above water.

Blade looked back at the Khad again. The Scourge of the Universe was beating his breast.

Rahstum nodded at Blade. "Now, man! Your wagons. We will see how well your plan works."

Chapter 15

The wagons were ready on the slope. Fifty of them with a thousand men assigned to handle them. The felt tops and wooden sides had been removed, and the sides mounted on the front to serve as arrow shields. The tall wooden wheels were locked straight ahead. All this under Blade's supervision.

Blade spurred back, shouting commands. Rahstum cleared his men from the center, leaving an aisle down which the wagons thundered. Some of the Mongs pushed, others guided and braked by means of long rawhide lines.

Blade sent twenty wagons into the ditch first, ten to a side, leaving a reserve of thirty. By now the sea had found its level and the water was not quite waist high. Bodies of drowned Mongs and horses were brushed aside as the wagons were run down to the steps. Then, fifty men to a wagon, they were hoisted up to the moat level.

The Sea Càths, who a moment before had been screaming in triumph, fell silent as they watched this strange new maneuver. Not for long. A signal was passed back and the catapult ships began to cast their deadly missiles again. One slab of jade, weighing tons, missed Blade by inches and smashed two wagons and thirty men. Muddy water splashed fifty feet into the air and Blade was drenched. He went immediately to direct removal of the crushed wagons lest they slow the line.

The Caths brought their archers into play again and directed a heavy fire on the wagons. Still they went up, one after the other. Men fell and horses died and the Cath

175

trumpets screamed high defiance as Blade began to fashion a crude pontoon bridge across the moat.

He rode up and down the rim of the moat, his horse
belly deep in the surging water. Some of the Cath archers
spotted him and began trying to bring him down. Arrows
hailed about him but none touched him. Blade, caught up
in battle fever now, forgot about guarding his back.

When he had two wagons in place, end to end, he saw
that his plan was in trouble. He had meant to string a line
of wagons across the moat, then bring up another line and
manhandle them atop the submerged wagons. The tops
would be replaced and the Mongs could cross, with the
water only slightly above their knees. It was slow work,
and the price in men was murderous, but he had thought
it would work. Now he saw that it wouldn't.

The first wagons, sloping down the bank of the moat,
held easily enough. But when the Mongs sought to get the
third wagon into position it was swept out of their hands
and away. One Mong forgot to let go and was taken with
the wagon. He clambered to the driving seat, out of the
water, and yelled back at them as the wagon went spinning away down the moat. A moment later the Cath archers put twenty arrows into him.

Blade, frowning, watched the wagon drift away toward
the sea gate to his right. The tide was coming in, that was
obvious enough, and there was a strong current through
the moat. Blade leaped atop his saddle, as agilely as any
Mong, and peered after the wagon. He had thought the
tide, rushing in from both ends, would cancel itself. Not
so. He soon understood why. The Caths had dug a drain
channel near one of the sea gates to direct the flow and so
create a current. And drain the moat when the sea gates
were closed.

Blade saw Rahstum spurring toward him, making slow
progress in the corpse-cluttered water.

Blade waved his sword at a sublieutenant assigned to
him. The man moved in close. Blade had to cup his hands
and yell over the clamor of battle.

176

"Forget the bridge! Get poles. Hurry! Take a hundred men."

The Mong stared at him. "Poles? I do not know where—"

"The wagon poles, man! Bring them."

He had ordered the wagon poles detached as useless and liable to impede movement. Now he saw how he could use them. They were slim, only about three inches in diameter and sixteen feet long.

Rahstum reached him at last. An arrow dangled in his chest armor. He broke it off and glowered at Blade. "Your plan is not working!"

Blade grinned. "Not my first plan. I have another. It will work."

When he explained the Captain nodded. "Yes. It is a better plan than the other. We had boats in Cauca."

Blade snapped an order to a young Mong officer. "Bring the rest of the wagons into the ditch. All of them."

To Rahstum he said, "The Khad's men are pretty well used up. They'll break and run any time now."

It was true enough. The Khad's men had been doing the extremely dirty work, and the punishment had been terrible. They had lost over half their number, and the survivors were rapidly losing heart. They were terrified of the deep water in the moat and moved sluggishly along the banks and in the ditch where the water was waist deep or more. All of the catapult ships were in action now and monstrous hunks of jade fell from the sky in a steady rain. Blade, counting, judged that a ton of jade was slapping into the disordered ranks every twenty seconds. A direct hit left nothing recognizable.

A missile struck near them and drenched them with muddy water. Rahstum wiped his face and beard and said, "You are right. They have taken enough punishment. They will blame the Khad for it, and will not be much good to him when the time comes. Signal me, Blade, when you want my men in again. We will lead the attack in your wagon boats!" He gave Blade a wolfish

177

smile and spurred away back up the slope. An arrow glanced off his helmet and hummed away. Rahstum did not turn around.

When he had all his wagons in the ditch, and the poles, Blade put a horsetail on a lance and waved it at Rahstum. The Captain gestured acknowledgment and barked orders to his officers.

Five hundred of the dung gatherers were driven down into the ditch, miserably clad men without arms. Blade thought briefly of Nantee, but there was no time for thought or pity. The Mongs sacrificed dung people as they stepped on beetles.

Behind the dung gatherers Rahstum sent a wave of his best men. Five thousand of them, rested now and eager for battle again. They left their mounts at the rim of the ditch and ran screaming down into the water. The Khad's men, battered and decimated, began to fall back.

Rahstum joined Blade again. "You will have to lead," he said. "Show them it can be done. My men are no boatmen."

Blade nodded and spurred down into the water. Rahstum shouted after him, "Remember your back!"

Blade leaped from his horse and waded up to the bank of the moat. The arrow fire from the ramparts over the water was not as heavy as before, and he guessed the Caths were running low on arrows.

He brought twenty of the wagons, lifted by the straining dung people, into line along the bank of the moat. Another twenty to be lifted into position when the first rank left the shore.

Judging that ten men to a wagon would be enough, he selected his first ten and leaped into the wagon with them. He shouted instructions and orders with a throat that had gone raw. Four of his Mongs were given poles and told how to use them.

Blade leaped to the driving seat, brandishing his sword, and shouted at the top of his voice.

"Hear me, Mongs! Watch me. And do as I do. There is no return from this journey."

He pointed with his sword to where the Caths waited on the rampart. A ton of jade sliced down from the sky. An arrow nicked his arm. It broke flesh but drew no blood.

"Once on that rampart," Blade told them, "we stay or we die. Now follow me, Mongs!"

He turned to the pole men. "Push off."

The wagon tops, removed and bound into place as shields, afforded some cover. Even so he lost three of his men before the wagon butted into the rampart.

Now the fury! And the Caths made a fatal mistake. In their eagerness to dispatch the invaders, they rushed howling to the water's edge. Too many of them. They jammed into a crowd and none could use their weapons effectively. Blade gave an order and his remaining men, but for two poling, sent a deadly hail of arrows into the packed crowd of Caths. They emptied their quivers and the carnage was such that the Caths broke and fell back. Blade leaped onto the rampart. He had breathing room. Fighting room. Barely, but enough.

He had but seven men. They formed a semicircle and linked shields and fought for their lives. Arrows fluttered at them with a steady *pstt-pstt-pstt*.

Blate shouted and they closed in, fighting on top of the bodies of the dead men. Lances now, and spears and hurled axes. Blade lost another man. He was fighting like an automaton, streaming with sweat and other men's blood, parched with thirst and his voice almost gone. A dozen Caths charged, yelling taunts, and it became hand-to-hand as the circle broke and the fight swirled up and down the rampart. Blade found himself beset by three Caths at once.

He slashed at one, daggered another, and took a nasty blow on his helmet from an axe. The world spun and he felt sick and his knees nearly betrayed him. He staggered back, retreating to the water's edge, fending off the blows that rained on him. He got his wind back and parried and dodged and at last ran the Cath through.

Sudden respite. Never had it been more welcome. He was dizzy and spent, on the verge of vomiting, drenched in sweat and blood and barely able to stand.

Suddenly Rahstum was at his side, bellowing and laying about him with his sword to deadly effect. The Caths about them began to fall back.

Rahstum turned to Blade with his white grin. An arrow had nicked his forehead and blood trickled down into his eyes. He pointed with his sword.

"You see, Blade. It works. Your plan works! We have them now."

A score of wagons had landed and spilled their Mong cargo onto the ramparts. A dozen small battles were being waged to the death. More wagons were crossing in a steady stream, ferrying far more men than Blade's original ten. The Mongs clung to the sides, the top spars, the front and the wheels, everywhere. Many drowned. All were anxious to get across and share in the booty and the killing.

Back across the moat, on the slope beyond the ditch, more of the Khad's men were getting ready to come in. Trumpets brayed and horsetails fluttered, skulls glistened in the sun as the reserves moved forward and down the slope. The Khad was still standing in front of his throne, grotesquely hunched, staring across the distance with his good eye.

Blade, having recovered his breath and his strength, could smile at Rahstum and offer advice.

"Send a party to both ends of the moat, Captain. Close those sea gates and the water here will soon drain through their outlet ditch. We cannot have the Scourge of the Universe getting his feet wet."

A smile twitched at Rahstum's mouth. "Well said, Blade. We cannot have that. It will be done."

He sent parties to close the sea gates. By this time the Mongs had cleared the rampart of Caths and were following them down and into the city itself. Behind them the Mong reserves came into the battle in a never-ending stream, cursing, eager and hurried, each man afraid he would be cheated of the spoils of war.

Blade and Rahstum, as befitted the dignity of commanders, found a stair leading down from the rampart into a small square. There had been fierce struggle here before the fighting swirled on, and the square was littered with corpses. A dozen houses were already burning. The screaming of women was a constant high note of terror in the murky air, now so besmudged by smoke as to blot out the sun.

They rested for a moment. The real fighting was over and Blade had no wish to engage in senseless slaughter. He was calmer now, the battle haze leaving his brain. He could think clearly again, and he deemed it time to tell Rahstum that he did not want Sadda killed. Not while she carried his child. Blade had said nothing before, had seemed to agree with the Captain, but even then he had known. That he was being illogical he admitted. That it was dangerous was certain. He would jeopardize his new and hard-won camaraderie with the Captain. But so it must be. The child was his, no matter what the mother was, and he would not have it murdered in her belly.

Rahstum had taken off his helmet, badly dented and pierced in several places, and was wiping blood and sweat from his face with a cloth.

"These Caths fight like fiends," he said. "I had not thought them such warriors, Blade. But it is over now. Look!"

Horsemen were streaming down the ramparts and galloping past them into the city warrens. The horses were coated above the fetlocks with thick black mud.

"The moat has been drained," Blade said. He turned back to the Captain. He was determined to seize the moment and tell him that Sadda must be spared.

He never spoke the words. An arrow hissed between

181

them, closer to Blade than the Captain. They wheeled in time to see a Mong wearing the Khad's insignia shooting at them from a corner of the square. He loosed another and Rahstum bellowed curses as it grazed him.

"After him, Blade! Get the son of a she carrion ape!"

Rahstum was running toward the Mong, who was fitting another arrow to his short bow. As Blade pounded after the Captain he wondered what price the Khad had placed on his head. A high one, he guessed, because this Mong was making a determined effort to earn it.

The Mong got off one more arrow that missed them both, then turned and fled down the narrow street. Still bellowing curses Rahstum went after him. A second later he was back around the corner, yelling a warning at Blade.

"Cath horsemen! Get your back against a wall."

The little party of Caths had been harried and beaten from place to place. They knew now that there would be no quarter. There were ten of them left and they came galloping into the square in a clatter of hooves on stones, half of them wounded, some dying, looking for Mongs to kill before their turn came. They spotted Blade and Rahstum and came at them with cries of rage.

The skirmish was short and brutal. Blade and Rahstum, their backs against the wall of a house, fought like two fiends. Blade ducked in to hamstring two horses and dodge back before he could be lanced. He pulled a Cath down and cut his throat. A lance point slid along his ribs and left a trail of fire.

The Caths were weary and frightened and disorganized, else they would have made quicker work of it. As it was they drew off for an instant of parley and Blade and Rahstum separated and each found a doorway to defend.

The Caths, seeing this, split into two groups and charged them again.

Blade, using his shield and sword, and fighting like a maniac, beat off the first charge. There was no second. A large party of Mong horsemen swept into the square and finished the work in a minute.

Blade walked to where Rahstum still stood in his doorway. The Captain was clutching his right arm and staring down at something on the ground. Blood was spurting from the arm to crimson Rahstum's hand and his armor-clad legs. Blade ran toward him.

Rahstum's hand lay on the pavement, the fingers still twitching in reflex action. He looked up as Blade approached. He had gone steadily pale, but his teeth flashed white in a grin.

"My luck is bad, Blade. As bad as his." He nodded to a dead Cath nearby. "Curse his ancestors! It was the only blow he struck—and now see. I am finished."

Blade wasted no time. The Captain was bleeding to death. Blade whipped off his sword belt and twisted it high on the arm as a tourniquet, using his dagger for leverage. The spurting blood dribbled to a halt.

Rahstum swayed and clutched at Blade. "I am as weak as a woman. Let me sit down here."

Blade supported him as he sank to the doorstep. Then he beckoned to the lieutenant in charge of the horsemen who, seeing their High Captain, had lingered.

"Bring a fire pan and an iron," Blade commanded. "Make haste, man. This wound must be cauterized and the bleeding stopped. Ride!"

Rahstum's forehead was beaded with sweat. He gave Blade a strange look and spoke almost in a whisper. "I will tell you what I have never told any man, Blade. I dread the flame. I fear no man or devil but I dread the flame. I do not think I can bear it."

Blade clapped him gently the shoulder. "You will bear it, Captain. I will see to that. I will hold you myself. You have lost a hand but there is still much to do—or has the pain made you forget?"

Rahstum shook his head. "I do not forget. It will be this night. But now you will have to do it, Blade. You must act in my stead. When the dwarf has poisoned the Khad you must kill Sadda. And quickly. I will do all I can, I will be there, but I cannot slay even a woman with this thing."

Chapter 16

The rape of the Cath city had taken a little over four hours. By noon it was a smoking ruin and the corpses had been collected and dumped on the green plain near the Mong encampment. All had been slain according to the Khad's orders.

By those same orders only the Governor of the city had been spared. He had been taken before he could commit suicide by falling on his sword. His name was Ozmandi, and he was a man of great dignity. He appeared in chains before the Khad, wearing a richly colored cloak of messaline and a yellow headdress. He was tortured for an hour, to deliver him of his secrets, and then he was killed and his body placed with the rest of the dead.

All this came later, by hearsay, to Blade who was in his wagon resting and being ministered to by Baber. Blade's rib wound was superficial, painful and bloody, but nothing to bother him. Baber cleansed it, muttering that he did not think the fire necessary. Blade was happy to hear this. He having watched them put the hot iron to Rahstum's arm. He could still see the Captain's contorted face as he fought to keep from crying out.

Khad Tambur was building a monument of bodies that he hoped would ensure his lasting fame. A great slab of jade was brought from the city and an artisan found who could engrave it with the primitive Mong characters.

Read and tremble, all ye who view this stone. Khad Tambur, Lord of The World, Scourge of the Universe, passed this way. These are the bones of those who resisted him. Take heed.

The Khad, who was directing matters in person, found this an occasion for a great deal of mad laughter. He was well into the madness now, and drinking heavily of *bross*.

Sadda sent a message to Blade by one of her mute and deaf black slaves. On a piece of flat wood she scribbled in black tallow: *Do not come near me until tonight. He rages because you still live. Do as you must tonight, quickly, instantly, and all will be well.*

Blade fingered the golden collar as he read the note over again. Baber had gone.

Do as you must. He was to kill Morpho the instant the dwarf killed the Khad. Blade pondered for a long time. He had no intention of killing the dwarf and he could not kill Sadda because of the child. It amounted to this: Sadda *thought* he was going to kill Morpho. Rahstum *thought* he was going to kill Sadda.

He was still puzzling when the note came from Rahstum. It was short. *Come to me after dark.*

By the time the sun fell out of the sky, the Mong camp was one great convulsive orgy. The *bross* was flowing freely. Men quarreled and fought and laughed and sang. Children and women kept out of the way. Horsemen, so drunk they could hardly stay in the saddle, galloped madly around the camp, whooping and screaming and at times riding through and over tents. At first the provost, a cadre of the Khad's own men, tried to cope with the disorders, but presently gave up and joined in the *bross* drinking. It was going to be a wild night.

Blade, by taking back ways and avoiding the fires, reached Rahstum's tent without being noticed. Though he wore the golden collar he was now a personage. He had gained much prestige that day. The Mongs had seen him fight and seen him lead, along with the Captain, while the Khad sat on his throne. None of this, Blade knew, would endear him to the Khad.

Matters would have to be settled tonight, one way or

186

the other. He had walked the tightrope as long as he could. He must put his luck to the final test before it ran out.

One of Rahstum's lieutenants stood guard outside the tent, along with half a dozen warriors. They were all heavily armed and all sober.

The lieutenant touched his helmet. "The Captain awaits you, Sir Blade."

Blade grinned as he ducked into the tent. His title had been returned.

Morpho was sitting beside a raised pallet on which Rahstum lay. His eternal grin swiveled toward Blade as the big man entered. He nodded, but said nothing.

Rahstum's stub had been heavily bandaged and was held up and against his chest by a sling of rawhide. He was livid in the torchlight and his eyes bespoke his pain. He had refused to drink *bross* as the surgeons of the Khad had urged. He wore dress armor of light leather and near the pallet was his helmet and sword. He raised his left hand in greeting.

"Sir Blade! We talk at last. No more sly looks and mincing of words and slinking about like carrion apes. This night we strike!"

Bold words. Blade must have shown his surprise, for Rahstum laughed harshly. "We are safe here for this hour at least. Only my men are sober, on pain of death and—"

The dwarf interrupted. "Sadda's men will be sober also. She is no fool. She will also choose tonight."

Blade nodded. "He is right, Captain."

Rahstum closed his eyes and winced as a spasm of pain clawed him. Then: "He may be. It matters not, for we will strike first. My men will be more heavily armed than hers, and will be in such position as to watch them closely. Now, Morpho, tell Blade how it is to be done."

The dwarf fingered his clean-shaven chin and squinted at Blade. "I will poison him. A deadly poison, with no antidote, but it will take several minutes to act. But it *will* act! When it does you will rush in and kill Sadda with your sword."

"Then defend yourself as best you can," broke in Rahstum. "It will not be for long. I will be there, on my pallet, but in the background because I will plead my pain. The moment Sadda is dead I will raise my voice and take command and my men will do the rest. It is risky, Blade but if we are determined enough and carry it through without delay, with no hesitation, we will bring it off. It only takes resolve!"

It was time to tell them.

"I cannot murder Sadda," Blade said. "She is with child. My child."

Both men looked at him in shocked silence. The silence grew. Blade heard the shift and stomp of feet and lances outside the tent. Somewhere a troup of horsemen went shrilling past.

Blade had not expected difficulty with the dwarf. He, because of Nantee, was sure to understand. And so it was. The dwarf studied him in the silence and if he could have smiled, instead of that etched grin, Blade knew he would have.

Rahstum raised his left hand, clenched, the muscles knotting along his forearm. His gray eyes flashed cold at Blade.

"You have known this? And you wait until now to tell me!"

"I meant to tell you before, Captain. There were always interruptions, and our plans not yet so firm. But I tell you now. I cannot kill Sadda."

He hastened on before Rahstum could speak. "What need to kill her? Take her prisoner. I will do that gladly enough, and collect some of my debt in the doing. I care nothing of what happens to Sadda, only the child. After it is born and taken from her you can do with her as you choose."

The Captain's lips twisted in derision. "You are a fool, Blade! You are a man, and I saw how you fought today, and I acknowledge you warrior and a man I would have by my side. But you are a fool nonetheless. As long as that whore is alive our heads are not safe and we shall have no peace."

He looked at the dwarf for confirmation. "Tell him how truly I speak, little man. Put some sense into his thick head."

The question trembled on Blade's lips. The question that had bothered and puzzled him for days. How was it that Sadda was so positive that the dwarf would slay the Khad for *her*? She had called Morpho her man! Why?

He did not speak. It was not the time, and complicating matters further was not the answer to his problem. But he resolved to watch Morpho as closely as he watched the Khad and Sadda.

The dwarf paced a few steps, frowning, his short arms crossed over his brawny chest. He was dressed in preparation for the celebration, and the bell on his peaked cap chimed as he moved.

"I think," he said at last, "that we must let Blade have his way in this, Captain. I—I can understand his feelings. It will be a little more dangerous to let Sadda live, this I admit, but surely when you are leader of all the Mongs you will be able to watch and control one small woman? Anyway, the plan is set and firmed and we cannot change it now."

Pain came to Blade's aid. The Captain lay with his eyes closed, his face twitching and sweat beading on his high forehead. Yet when he opened his eyes it was to glare at Blade.

"So be it, then. But be warned, Sir Blade. I make her your responsibility. If we succeed tonight I mean to make you my second in command. There will be heavy burdens and now you add to them. If Sadda causes trouble, plots, escapes, or in any way seeks to disrupt my rule I will have *your* head for it. I warn you in good time. Mark it well!"

Blade bowed slightly. "I mark it, Captain. I accept the responsibility for Sadda. Until the child is born. Then I will gladly turn her back to you."

Some of the old wolfishness was in Rahstum's grimace. "You do that, Sir Blade."

They talked for another half-hour. Outside, the camp grew ever more riotous. Now and again a woman screamed and the drunken laughter never ceased.

The dwarf would not tell Blade how he intended to poison the Khad.

Blade said: "You are taster to him, Morpho. You must taste of everything he eats. How will you poison him?"

The dwarf shook his head. "I will. But I cannot tell you. I have not told the Captain. If things should go wrong and you are taken and tortured I would not have you know this secret. Then it will be good for another day."

Blade had to let it go at that. They made final plans and, at the last moment of parting, pledged themselves one to the other. Blade went back to his wagon and put on his best finery.

The great black tent of the Khad was heavily guarded by warriors. They were a mixed group, half the Khad's men and half Rahstum's. That was all right. At a signal from Rahstum each of his men was to put a sword to the throat of one of Khad's men and demand surrender.

The Khad's men were drinking *bross*. The Captain's men were not. Blade saluted the subcaptain on duty and entered the tent, to be immediately caught up in the wild swirl of music and dancing and drunken laughter. The tent sweltered with the heat of closely packed bodies and the heady fumes of *bross* made him gasp and hold his breath for a moment. A man could get drunk just by breathing!

Torches, garish and smoking, cast a smudged yellow light over the scene. Blacks passed in the crowd with bowls of *bross*. Scattered about were platters of fruits and fine foods taken from the ruined city. In one corner the musicians, their number augmented tonight, brayed and drummed and plucked and chimed in a frenzy of wanton music.

Six women were dancing before the thrones of the Khad and his sister. Their oiled bodies glinted and writhed in the light. They wore only skimps of cloth around and between their legs. They waited for a cue from the music, then faced each other, pairing off, and began to make symbolic love, woman to woman, dark burnished skin to dark burnished skin. Twelve well-formed breasts wiggled and bounced and trembled. The audience roared drunken approval.

Blade waited near the entrance. Against his better judgment he had promised Baber that he might be here tonight. The old man had pleaded hard and Blade had at last given in. Baber was his slave, after all, and so had some right there if the master permitted. Blade shrugged. Small matter. The die was cast now. Baber could not affect the outcome one way or the other.

Sadda had not yet seen him. He watched her peering around, glancing at the entrance from time to time. Blade made himself small and moved behind a group of drunken officers. Khad's men.

Soon there was altercation outside and he heard Baber's voice raised in profane demand. A moment later the old fellow came wheeling in on his cart, propelling himself with the sticks. He spotted Blade immediately and rolled to him. Blade grinned down at the legless man.

"You are finely turned out, old man. But you do not smell much like a warrior. What did you do—tub yourself in perfume?"

Baber was trimmed and clipped and arrayed in his best. He smoothed hair over his bald spot and winked up at Blade. "For an occasion like this a man must look his best. Even a slave. How soon, Blade?"

"Sir Blade, you rascal. Have you not heard?"

"I had not. But I am glad. Could it be that I will not be a slave much longer?"

"That could be. Now quiet—and keep your eyes and ears open."

Morpho entered the tent, carrying a small box of mel-

191

ons packed in snow that had been brought in that afternoon. The dwarf did not glance at them. He went to the dais and took his usual place to the Khad's right. After a moment he took his colored balls from a pocket and began to twirl them absently. The dancers were just finishing their simulated orgy in a sensuous blare of music.

The music soared to a great clashing finale. The dancers ran off through a side entrance in the tent.

Blade waited. Fretting a bit now. He was not to move until Rahstum was carried in. He peered through the crowd. Sadda was watching the door now with no attempt to hide her annoyance. She moved impatiently and clamped white teeth over her scarlet nether lip.

Rahstum was carried in. The crowd parted and four of his men carried the pallet through an aisle to a prominent place near the cleared space before the dais.

Khad Tambur stood up, painfully, swaying, his inclined back thrusting him forward nearly parallel with the floor. Blade doubted that he felt pain now. He was swimming in *bross*.

The Khad made a sign and trumpets called from the orchestra. Silence now, but for whispering and coughing and drunken chuckles. The Khad pointed to Rahstum.

"I give you greetings, my Captain. And I give you all my thanks. And your men, and mine, I also thank. This day you taught the Caths a lesson they will never forget. I regret your grave wound. What say the surgeons?"

The Captain, raising himself a trifle on the pallet, held his bandaged stub aloft for all to see.

"The surgeons, great Khad, are angry because they could not cut it off themselves. They curse the Cath that did it, thus robbing them of practice—which they sorely need."

A great roar of laughter went up. The Khad smiled, his eyes glittering and rolling.

When the laughter died Rahstum said: "It was only a hand, gracious One. A small thing to offer my Khad."

That was Blade's cue. Rahstum had judged perfectly

192

how the scene would fall out, even to the Khad's words and his own reply. Blade moved toward the dais. The people stepped aside for him and the whispering began.

Blade came into the open space, floored with rugs, and approached the two thrones. The music had stopped. Sadda's eyes were soft as she watched him draw near. She raised a hand in greeting.

Blade bowed first to the Khad, then to Sadda, then straightened and faced the Scourge of the Universe.

"My thanks, great One, for allowing me to be here. It is splendid, but not as great as your splendor, gracious Lord. I respected the Caths before as soldiers, but no more. Today I learned. You *are* the Scourge of the Universe!"

The Khad leaned toward him. His face twitched and his eye seemed to spin and flash. Blade sensed that he had not even heard the cloying flattery. The Khad was fighting for self-control.

But when the great one spoke his voice was low, harsh, with a neutrality that must have cost him dear. At first he spoke for Blade's ear alone.

"You were fortunate today, Sir Blade. Most fortunate. Twice. Or was it three times?"

Blade gave him back stare for stare. "Twice, Lord. Only twice." He saw it now. The Khad was going to bide his time. Play out the farce and settle with Blade at a better time.

The Khad gnawed at his lip with bad teeth. "I thank you as I thank the others, Sir Blade. But I will do more than thank in mere words—you are Sir Blade once more, so cast off that golden collar."

At last. Blade unfastened the collar and flung it away from him. One of the black eunuchs pounced on it.

The Khad held up a hand for silence. This time he waited until the crowd obeyed. Then: "We have seen how Sir Blade fought today. We have seen his valor in our cause. We have also noted his luck." The eye glinted at Blade and the thin mouth smiled.

"We Mongs know the value of luck, of good fortune.

This man has it. So I permit his marriage to my sister, in due time and with great ceremony, and I make him an officer of mine. Of *mine*! Responsible solely to me. As *my* officer he shall have whatever he desires—of my treasure, anything. And he shall sit on this dais, beside my sister, and be consort to her even before they are married. You have heard me."

Two blacks came running forward with another throne. It was put down beside Sadda and the Khad motioned to Blade.

"You see, Sir Blade, how I keep my word."

There was a roar of approval from the gathering. For the first time Blade knew just how popular he was at the moment. It would not last, but for the moment he had status. He had displayed that day the two things that Mongs worshiped above all else—courage and fighting ability.

Blade took his seat beside Sadda to a buzz of excited approval. She thanked her brother, then leaned to put a hand on Blade's. Her eyes were bright with excitement and anticipation.

"Soon now. Remember what you must do," she whispered.

The Khad waved a hand at the dwarf. "A melon, fool. All this ceremony dries my throat and makes me hungry." He took a huge quaff of *bross* from a bowl beside him.

Blade watched the dwarf. How? How was it going to be done?

A black slave came and whispered something into the Khad's ear. He nodded and waved the slave away.

Morpho selected a plump melon from the snow-filled box. He whipped a knife from his belt and carefully sliced it. With a little bow he extended half of it to the Khad.

In the past Blade had noted that the Khad did not always question his food. At times, especially when he was drinking heavily, he would forget, or did not bother, so secure did he deem himself.

194

Blade was so tense his muscles ached. Sadda was look-ing at him rather strangely.

The Khad raised the melon to his mouth, then hesi-tated. A sly look flitted over his ravaged face and he rolled his eye at the little man. He half laughed as he said, "You taste first, fool. Do I not pay you to taste? So taste!"

Morpho held up the half melon in his hand. The crowd was watching now, once more silent.

The half melon in Morpho's hand spoke in a tiny voice: "Eat me, fool. Eat me. So the Khad can eat my brother. Such nonsense!"

The melon laughed squeakily. "I was whole when I came. My skin was not broken. Everyone saw you cut me. Does the Khad fear a wizard, then, who can poison a mel-on without breaking the skin? What nonsense. Eat me. Eat me!"

The dwarf took a huge bite out of the melon. The crowd roared with laughter in which the Khad joined. He sank his teeth into his slice of melon, chewed and swal-lowed.

Blade felt the sweat creeping out on his forehead. Mor-pho had said it would take a little time.

Sadda leaned to him, her hand on his knee. "What is it, my Blade? You look so strange."

The Khad took another bite of melon, swallowed it, and stood up. He raised a hand and the gathering fell silent once more.

"I have more news," said the Khad. "Concerning my-self. I, your ruler, am also to be married soon. I have at last found the moon of my desire. My heart is smitten af-ter all these years."

He clapped his hands sharply. "Bring in the bride of Khad Tambur. Bring her who will soon share the throne of the Ruler of the World."

The crowd sighed and hushed. The Khad smiled in triumph at having so surprised and caught them off guard. He raised his bowl of *bross* and drank, his eyes feral over

195

the rim. Of all things in the world they had not expected this.

Only Sadda was not surprised. Blade saw that and also saw the flutter of malice and hate and anticipation in her eyes. Her gaze eluded his and followed the blacks. She formed the words with her red lips. "Soon now. Be ready."

The blacks came back. Between them, led by one of them, was a slim little figure, a girl A child-girl. She was richly arrayed, her dark hair piled and caught on her head with scarlet combs. She was beautiful. Blade's heart stopped beating. Too late now, but he understood.

The girl stumbled and one of the black slaves caught her. She peered around, her eyes blank, and she raised a hand and said, her voice chiming in the dread silence:

"My father? Are you here, my father? I do not like this place. I am afraid, my father."

Nantee.

Chapter 17

The dwarf uttered a cry of rage and anguish and rushed at Sadda.

Blade was frozen and moved too late. Sadda half turned on the throne, wide-eyed in shock and surprise, as Morpho buried his knife under her left breast. She screamed once then, and stared down in disbelief at the hilt protruding from that golden flesh.

She fell slowly forward onto the rugs before the dais.

The next moment, while shock and horror held the crowd, the Khad fell beside his sister. He gasped and clawed at his throat as terrible convulsions racked his body.

Blade came to life. The blacks were the first to leap at Morpho. Blade flung the throne at them and they went down in a heap. Blade drew his sword as he bellowed at the dwarf.

"Behind me—behind me!"

Rahstum had whipped a sword from under the covers of his pallet and was brandishing it and roaring at the top of his voice.

"To me! To Rahstum! Obey your orders—to me, to me!"

It was whirling, sweating, screaming, fighting pandemonium. Some of the Khad's men tried to fight and were cut down. Two of them rushed at the dwarf, sheltering behind Blade, and he killed one and badly wounded another.

Blade moved quickly back to guard the little man,

seeing that it was not going to be much of a fight after all. Rahstum had planned too well.

There was a flurry of action near the entrance as some of the Khad's men sought to break out of the tent. Baber, a wide grin on his face, rolled his cart into the melee and began to slash at legs. He had had a sword in a sling beneath his cart.

In five minutes the worst was over. Some few of the Khad's men escaped by slitting the tent cloth with their swords and bursting out. Rahstum sent men after them.

Rahstum had himself carried to the throne and placed on it. He smiled at Blade and waved his arm.

"Too weak to walk. I must be carried to my throne. A fine beginning for the new Khad, eh?"

"At least a beginning," Blade replied. "But what now, Captain? Or shall I already call you Khad?"

Their glances locked and held for an instant. Rahstum smiled faintly. "You will call me Captain—at least in private. But there is no time for that nonsense now. We must get on with it. You, Sir Blade, and Morpho, will remain here with me. My men have their orders."

It was a long night and a bloody one. Rahstum had planned so well that most of the Khad's men and officers were caught completely unaware. With the common soldiers there was no difficulty. It was all one to them who paid them, they had not cared much for the Khad anyway, and they came over to Rahstum in droves and without demur.

Rahstum's troops rounded up all the Khad's officers, those who had not been in the tent, and brought them before the Captain. It moved rapidly. They were given a minute to swear fealty to Rahstum or lose their heads. The headsman waited just outside with his block. A good three quarters of the officers took the oath.

They finished as the sun came bounding up. Rahstum was fatigued and in great pain, and greatly in need of sleep. He dozed on his pallet and a rug was thrown over him.

The bodies of the Khad and Sadda had been taken away. Not before Blade asked, and received, a promise that Sadda at least should have a decent burial. His child was dead now, which could not be helped, but he would not have Sadda, with whom he had shared a bed, if not love, treated as the corpse of the Khad was to be treated.

The dwarf spent most of the night in a corner of the tent with Nantee, cozening and petting her, and allaying her fears. At last she went to sleep, her cheeks tearstained, and Morpho holding one small hand.

Blade, seeking explanations now that it was over, smiled down at the sleeping girl.

"She will be all right, Morpho. He had no chance to harm her. And it is unlikely that she understood what it was about. She will not be haunted by it. And now she has Rahstum's protection. You heard him promise it."

Morpho nodded. His own rugged cheeks were tear-stained. "I owe you much, Sir Blade. More than before, which was my life."

Blade, who was also weary, found a seat and regarded the little man with a touch of sternness.

"Commence repayment, then, by telling me something of the truth. How came Sadda to know about Nantee?"

Morpho's eyes were sad over the fixed grin. "She was a devil. She had known for many years. Since Nantee was a baby. I do not know how she found out, but she did. She had spies everywhere."

Sadda had been right, Blade thought, when she told him she could make the dwarf do anything. He *had* been her man. He had no choice.

"You lied," he said now. "You told me that only three people knew about Nantee. You, me, and your old crone. I half guessed, and would have known the truth, but you lied. Why, Morpho?"

The dward nodded slowly. "Yes. I lied, Sir Blade. I had to lie. She made me promise that I would never tell anyone that *she* knew about Nantee. I did not understand then. I do not understand now. But I had to promise and

I dared not break it. She also promised *me* something—that if ever I told anyone that she *knew* about my child—Nantee would be killed at once. What could I do but obey, Blade. I dared not tell even you or Rahstum. If you were tortured and spoke, my daughter would die."

Nantee stirred and mumbled in her sleep. Morpho soothed her and stroked her hair.

Blade thought he understood. Sadda had been subtle beyond all knowing. But what had she been protecting herself against? Her brother—who might have taken it amiss if she knew of such a lovely child as Nantee and concealed it from him?

Blade shrugged and gave up. She was dead and that was the end of it.

By noon the camp was nearly back to normal. Rahstum awakened, refreshed and hungry, and began issuing orders and making plans as he gulped his breakfast. Nantee was given to the charge of a trusted woman and taken to special quarters. Morpho went back to his tent to sleep. Baber, drunk on joy and *bross,* had to be carried to his wagon by four men. Rahstum, remembering the way Baber had fought on his cart, promised to make him a sublieutenant.

Blade and Rahstum went to look on the final humiliation of the Khad Tambur, Ruler of the World and Shaker of the Universe. It was a last degrading, but that was not the only end. Long lines of men and women and children, even the dung gatherers, waited to pass the body.

"There is no time for oaths of loyalty from all these," Rahstum explained. "This will do just as well. These people do not really care who rules them, and they know that I cannot be worse than the Khad. See how eager they are!"

The Khad's naked body had been tossed on a great pile of human dung. He lay on his back, his sightless eye staring at the sky. One by one the Mongs filed past, each one spitting on the corpse.

Blade looked at the Captain. "How did the little man do it? I meant to ask, but we got to talking of other things. Did he tell you?"

Rahstum eased his stub in the sling and grimaced. Blade thought his powers of recuperation far beyond the mere human.

"He did not *tell* me," Rahstum said a bit dourly. "I questioned him and made him talk. Lest I turn out to be a bad Khad and he use the same method on me one day."

"I doubt that," Blade said.

Rahstum shrugged, then laughed. "He is a clever little fiend. You saw the melon he took from the snow. It was whole? Uncut?"

"I thought so. But how could it have been—or had he a way of placing the poison without breaking the skin of the melon?"

The Captain shook his head. "Not so. He put the poison in the melon before the Khad's very eyes. It was on his knife. One side of the knife he had smeared with honey. On this he placed the poison so that it would stick—it was a powder."

Blade grinned. "I see it now. When he cut the melon the poison was left on one half only—the half he gave the Khad. So he could bite into the other half without harm to himself. He is a little fiend, Captain. I agree."

Rahstum laughed again. "It was a near thing at that, when the Khad challenged him. But that trick with his voice got him out of it. The Khad laughed and forgot and his laugh killed him."

They went back to the big tent. As they entered Blade said, "Suppose Morpho had failed. What then, Captain?"

"I would have killed the Khad myself. With my one remaining hand."

In the tent Rahstum swung on Blade. "I have much to do. As I am sure you do also. But you wanted a word in private, Sir Blade. You have it. What is the affair?"

It was more than a word. It was a long hour of talk, of question and answer, of anger and impatience and some little bellowing and shouting. But when Blade left the tent to sleep at last he felt that he had won—for the time being. His instincts had been right about Rahstum. He was a Cauca, not a Mong, and he was a reasonable man.

Chapter 18

The Mongs were trekking again. A week had seen vast re-organization in the warrior class and the several tribes, and under Rahstum's firm and relatively merciful guidance the various factions achieved at least the appearance of unity. The Captain made a swift recovery; after the first two days he ignored his pain and was in the saddle constantly. Some days he snatched but two or three hours sleep. Even so he had to delegate many tasks to Blade, who in turn had Baber and the dwarf as his aides.

Gradually, as time wore on, the four of them came to constitute an unofficial, shadowy, but authentic quadruplex of authority that was not questioned. Rahstum commanded, Blade implemented. Baber, who now had a gentle old mare to draw him about on his cart, was learning to ride again and wielded power far greater than his rank, Rahstum being too cunning to immediately elevate another Cauca and so cause jealousy.

Morpho, with skill and determination, set about organizing a new provost and a secret spy network so that Rahstum might know all that was whispered or plotted. Business was very slack. The Mongs seemed satisfied.

They moved to the south, following the line of the seashore, and after twenty miles they topped a rise and saw the great yellow wall glimmering along the horizon. Blade and the Captain were riding at the head of the column. Scouts had been sent ahead, but had not returned or sent any word.

Rahstum signaled a stop and looked at Blade. "So there

is our wall again, Sir Blade. What say you now? We come in peace, for I will keep the promise you extracted from me, but who can parley with a wall?"

Blade studied the wall for a long time, shielding his eyes against the blazing sun. There was no sign of movement, no life, and the wall did not reach the sea. As best he could make out it tapered off, unfinished, some five hundred yards from the ocean.

"I think nothing has changed," he told Rahstum. "We can pass between the end of the wall and sea and then turn back west again, just as we had planned. Just so your outriders do not disobey orders and provoke fighting. Make sure of that, Captain! The Caths must understand that this time we come in peace."

"I have made sure," grunted the Captain. "The officers know they will pay with their heads if they provoke a fight."

The column moved on. They skirted the end of the wall and swung back to the west. The wall snaked away, deserted and desolate, to the far faint beginnings of mountains. That night, just before the sun dropped out of sight, it hovered over those mountains and a wondrous green light lay shimmering along the edge of the world, like a jade mist that moved and swirled and formed fantastic pictures of itself.

Blade watched it with a feeling of awe. It could not but mean that the range ahead was another mass of the Jade Mountains he had seen in Serendip. This was raw stone, uncut and unpolished, yet of such purity that it dyed the heavens with its color.

Remembrance of his last night with Lali came. What of Lali now? Who had replaced him?

The long column of Mongs, a fat disjointed serpent, crawled over to the west. The land began to revert to steppe, though fertile and with many trees, and one day Blade caught the scent of *banyo* trees. After that the air was increasingly soft and sweet. They were getting into the heartland of the Caths. Still they met no opposing forces, saw no towns or villages, and nothing moved along the wall.

It was some little time before Blade noted that the dwarf seemed to be avoiding him. One day he taxed the little man with it.

Morpho, sitting his pony, nodded. "That is truth, Sir Blade. It is not of my own wish, but I thought it best. Time will heal, but until it does I thought it best to stay away."

Blade understood and smiled and patted the little fellow's shoulder. "It could not be helped, Morpho. In your place I would have done the same. You were in a rage and thought only to protect your child."

"And slew yours, Sir Blade." Morpho did not look at him. His eyes were on the horizon.

Blade was silent for a moment. He had put the matter from his mind. No good came of thinking too much in the past, or grieving over what might have been. In his case especially. For the last two days now he had been having dull headaches, and now and then a stroke of real pain. Lord L was groping for him with the computer.

"Avoid me no more," he told the dwarf. "We are friends. I tell you I *would* have done the same—only I would have killed the Khad, not Sadda."

Morpho flexed his grin. "As I would have, had I not known him already dying of my poison. Sadda counted on that because she did not know about the poison. We were fortunate in the way things fell out, Sir Blade."

Blade nodded in agreement. "We were lucky. She reckoned that the shock of seeing Nantee would drive you to slay the Khad. Then I was to kill you, and Sadda would reign. It was a good plan. Had there been no counterplot it might well have worked."

Their eyes met. "Would you have slain me, Sir Blade, to save yourself?"

"I cannot answer that," answered Blade. "Forget, Morpho. Let it blow with the wind. She sleeps now, in a decent grave, and the matter is best forgot."

"So it shall be." The dwarf pointed to the horizon. "See yonder. Dust. I think our scouting party returns."

Blade had duties back along the column and it was an hour before he rode back to the vanguard. The Mong scouts, fatigued and dirty, their ponies drooping, were still being questioned by Rahstum. When Blade rode up, the Captain beckoned to him with an odd smile on his face. He held up a small object that glittered in the sun.

"Come and see yourself, Sir Blade. You are now become a house god to the Caths."

Puzzled, Blade rode into the group. The Mong scouts eyed him curiously. Rahstum handed him the little object with a thin smile. His tone was sardonic.

"I had not known you so famous, Sir Blade. I think we waste time in this long march to treat with the Caths. You and I might settle matters between us, since you are so great in Cath."

Blade, staring at the little statuette, was dumfounded. He reached to take it in his hand. It was a foot high, of faultless jade, and carven in the exact image of himself as he had been in Cath. He wore the wooden armor and carried a sword, standing erect and calm with one foot slightly advanced. The artisan had caught his features exactly.

Blade looked at the Captain and shrugged. "You speak in riddles, Captain. How came you by this? What does it mean?"

Rahstum signed to the lieutenant of the scouts, a little man with a fierce beard and dusty armor. "Tell him, man."

The Mong lieutenant spurred closer, his eyes glassy with fatigue.

"We came on a Cath village, Sir Blade. As ordered, I sent in a man to parley and promise peace. When this was agreed they let us ride into their town. In the center was a great statue of you, Sir Blade, like this one but much larger." The man raised a hand over his head to indicate size.

206

"And in every house—for we remained a time and became friendly, especially with the unwed Cath girls—in every house there is a small statue of you such as this one. The Caths have many gods, as we knew, and now you are added to them. When we left I begged this statue of the head man, saying that I thought it would please you."

Blade was still slightly in shock. He held the little statuette to the sun and watched the sun strike through the pure jade.

"Did they give you explanation of this, lieutenant? How these came to be?"

The Mong nodded. "They did, Sir Blade. By order of the Empress Mei. Every Cath village and town in her domain has a big statue of you, and every house a small one. All this is your memory."

Lali thought him dead.

The Mongs trekked on. They passed the first Cath village and Blade rode in to see for himself. The villagers saw him and fell on their faces. The children screamed and ran and Blade wondered if mothers were using his image to threaten the children into obedience.

"Mind now, or Sir Blade will get you!"

He sat his horse before the statue and gazed at it a long time. It was ten feet tall, on a pedestal, and of the same immaculate jade. Blade thought he looked noble enough and was not displeased. But why? He had not thought Lali capable of such love and devotion.

As he rode back to join the column the pain smote his brain again and he gasped and fell forward in the saddle, clinging to the horse's mane to keep from falling.

They marched on. Still no movement on the wall, but now signal fires blazed ahead of them night and day. At last they reached the first of a long series of signal towers. Each tower had three wooden arms atop it, each painted a different color, and operated by ropes from the base. The towers all stood on high land and within sight of another farther to the west. Never did they find a Cath, or a party,

207

operating the signals, but occasionally there was a faint cloud of retreating dust on the western horizon.

Rahstum was growing impatient. "How can we make peace with these wall Caths if they will not parley? They are like ghosts, or carrion apes, always scampering out of sight."

"Be patient," advised Blade, "and send out more parties, weak ones, only a few men, with our message of peace. One day we will have an answer."

Rahstum grumbled, but he followed the advice. Small parties, not more than ten men in each, and lightly armed, were sent ahead with the white horsetails of peace on their lances.

Far ahead of them the semaphore arms wigged and wagged and the fires blazed incessantly. And still the wall loomed barren and no Caths came to meet them.

Rahstum forgot his impatience and became uneasy— and wary. He scowled at Blade and muttered of traps.

Baber was riding again now, having learned to grip the saddle without his thighs. He was armored in leather and carried sword and lance and made as fierce a warrior as any. As the days passed he became increasingly worried. He was a personal dilemma.

He rode beside Blade one day and voiced his anxiety. As usual he spoke bluntly and to the point, and with his poet's fluency.

"I am torn," he admitted. "If Rahstum is right and we are riding into a trap I know not how to turn. I am your man, Sir Blade, and I am also Rahstum's man. A fickle fettle, I think, and most serious. We are deep in Cath land now, at your bidding. If we are ambushed, fallen upon, I will have to kill Caths, Sir Blade. But *you* have brought us here. Will you kill these Caths you came to see?"

Blade regarded him unsmiling. "Did I not kill Sea Caths? Did I not lead across the moat when no one else could? Answer that, Baber, and you have answered your own question."

The old man pushed his helmet back on his bald brow

and gave Blade a knowing look. "You were slave then, Sir Blade. You had to fight. Now you are a free man and a leader. You are a Cath god! All this could make a difference."

"It will not. If the Caths attack us first, I will fight with the Mongs. I have promised the Captain that. I promise you now. But there must be no fighting—and if I have a chance to parley first with the Caths there will be none. Tell me in truth, old man. Are you not sick of war?"

Baber squinted and tugged at a hair in his nose. Then he nodded vigorously. "That I am, Sir Blade. For a long time now. I am old and I would like to enjoy my last years. But you dream if you think there is an end to war! There has always been war and there will always be war." He shrugged. "How else can a young man earn a living? And yet I wish as you, that there was another way."

Pain lanced at Blade then and he closed his eyes and held tight. For a few seconds the pain was almost unendurable and he trembled and sweated. Then it passed. Lord L was getting closer to him. Blade shook his head and wiped his face with a cloth. He was ready, but not before he had finished his task.

Baber said: "You do not feel well, Sir Blade?"

"It is nothing. I am tired, as we all are, and worried, Baber. I admit it. I wish the Caths would come to meet us and talk of peace. I do not like this running game of theirs any more than you."

Early next morning, after having marched but two hours, they climbed a long rise that overlooked a deep bowl-shaped valley. In the center of the valley was a neat Cath town. The moon flag of Cath fluttered from a pole in a center square and, even at the distance, Blade saw the iridescent glitter of his statue. The town was busily going about its business, the people hurrying here and there and paying no attention to the Mong host on its doorstep.

Rahstum, scowling, signaled a halt. He eased his stub in its sling and turned to Blade, indicating the easy pass that led down into the valley.

"I do not like this, Sir Blade. It is too easy." He gestured to a ring of low hills surrounding the valley on every side.

"There could be a million Caths in those hills. And we, as who knows better than you, are not strong. The march over the mountains, the fight at the sea, and now this long march, has left us weak. You took census, Sir Blade. How many able warriors?"

It was true that Blade had just made a head count.

"Some forty thousand who can fight," he said now. "But I see no Cath armies. No one threatens us, Captain."

Rahstum, still staring around at the hills, frowned. Then he spat decisively. "No! We halt here. Your Caths must come to us, if they come at all. I will not lead my people into that." He motioned to the valley lying placid and fertile below them and for a moment his face lightened.

"It is a fine valley, for all that. It would make a fine home for the Mongs, did we but own it. We could live well here, and find other ways than war, and grow strong again."

Blade had been watching his face. "You are no Mong," he said. "Yet I think you are, Captain, in a way no Mong would understand."

Rahstum nodded. "I am no Mong, as you say. I am a Cauca and proud of it. But they are my people now. I killed their leader and I am responsible for them. I would do my best."

"Blade, who had been watching the hills, tapped the Captain's arm and said, "Then control your temper now. Do nothing in haste. And send me to parley. Me alone."

He pointed to the hills. "You were right."

On three sides of the valley the Cath host was moving into position. They left concealment and rode to the crest of the first line of hills and began to take formation. Pennons waved and the thin call of trumpets came across the distance.

Rahstum fingered his beard and muttered. "I told you,

Sir Blade. See how many! If we fight now we are finished."

From the left, around to the center and back to the right, the Cath hordes were wheeling into line. Cavalry by the thousands. Foot soldiers by the hundreds of thousands. Blade, counting rapidly by rank and depth of files, estimating, put them at over half a million. There was planning here. That he knew instantly. This place and time had been deliberately chosen by the Caths. Had he, after all, led the Mongs into a trap?

All about them the Mongs, Rahstum's chosen men and guard of honor, were muttering in consternation. One of them, a grizzled veteran with a dozen scars, began to hum the Death Song.

Rahstrum glared and rebuked the man sharply. "Time enough for that. We are not dead yet!"

But when he turned back to Blade his smile was arid. "I wish now that I had proclaimed myself Khad before this—for it looks as though I have left it too late."

A rider left the Cath town and came toward them, riding hard, a single rider, spurring, the dust rising behind him in a saffron cloud. They watched his approach in silence. As the horseman grew gradually closer, Blade thought he detected something familiar about him.

Blade leaned close to Rahstum, a hand on his arm, and whispered, "Do nothing yet, Captain. Pass the word back that every Mong remain calm and in his place. I think I know this Cath and I alone will talk with him. It is possible that we will not fight after all."

Rahstum agreed moodily and passed back his signal.

The Cath rider reined in at the mouth of the pass, below them, and waved a pennon. He removed his helmet.

It was Queko.

"I do know the man," said Blade quickly. "Queko, the Empress Mei's chief captain. He is to her as I am to you."

"He is signaling parley," said Rahstum. "Go and talk to him. And come back, Blade. You have given me your word of honor and I hold you to it."

Blade smiled. "I will come back."

He spurred down the pass to meet Queko. As he approached, Queko raised a hand in greeting and friendship. He was fine in respendent wooden armor, the moon symbol brave on his breastplate. For the first time in months Blade heard the sweet singsong of Cath speech, so like to music.

"Greeting, Sir Blade. It has been a long time. We thought you dead until a few days since, when one of our spies brought word that the man of the statue was riding with the Caths."

Blade grinned at him. "I have seen the things, Queko. It was the doing of the Empress?"

"Yes. She has been desolate since your capture. Nothing pleases her and nothing can console her. Not even my fine plan to annihilate the Mongs forever."

He waved a hand around the valley, at the serried ranks of the waiting Cath host. "You came well into the trap. Too easily, and I have been wondering. This had been your doing, Sir Blade? You had our message, then? One of the spies got through? We have sent a score or more."

Blade frowned. "I had no message. Saw no spy. We come in peace, Queko. *That* is my doing. Listen well to me."

He explained much of what had happened since the Mongs left off attacking the wall and begān their trek, omitting only personal matters and that which was not to the point.

Queko said, when Blade had finished, "You believe this Rahstum truly wants peace?"

"I do. As you must believe also, and the Empress."

Queko stroked the soft down on his chin. "You undo me, Blade. I have planned long and hard for this moment, as has the Empress. Together we plotted the whole thing. We let a Mong prisoner 'escape' after letting him overhear what he thought was a high conference. We spoke of a lack of troops to man the wall this far to the east. We spoke of the wall being unfinished and defenseless. We spoke of the Sea Caths being cowards and poor fighters—"

"You spoke a lie," Blade said grimly.

"I know. It was all part of our game. I knew that the trek over the northern mountains would kill many Mongs. The Sea Caths would kill more. The trek back west would be long and hard and more would die. I summoned help from Pukka and many other provinces and arranged that we should meet you in this valley, where we hold the high ground. And now, Sir Blade, you come to me and cry for peace!"

So that was it. So much for the counsels of Obi, the dark God in the wagon. The Khad had listened to the "escaped" Mong and made his decision and given the credit to Obi.

Blade fixed Queko with a stare that contained all the arrogance and the authority he could muster.

"It was a good plan. But now it is not needed. There will be peace. I have pledged my head on it. If there is not peace, and we must fight, I fight with the Mongs! Understand that well, Queko."

After a moment the Chief Captain of the Caths looked away. "As you say, Sir Blade. But I cannot make this peace, only the Empress can do that."

"Where is she now?"

Queko pointed to the little village in the center of the valley. "There. Where else? As soon as she heard you were alive she came. She is waiting for you now. Come. I will take you to her."

"A moment. I will be straight back."

Blade pulled his mount around and went galloping back up the pass. Lali so near! He was conscious of excitement. Even knowing what she was, very little better than Sadda had been, still he was excited. It was only physical, of course, but there it was. Those green eyes. Those marvelous green eyes into which a man could fall

213

forever. The body that was perfection and the color of ancient ivory. Lali!

Fool, he told himself. You have a job to do before the computer makes final adjustment and finds you and snatches you back to H-Dimension. Attend to it. He would not take back any treasure this time, nor any great knowledge. Or was peace a treasure? A moral treasure?

Blade spoke briefly with Rahstum and they came to agreement. They rode off to one side and were alone for the moment.

"Make fair terms if you can," Rahstum said. "But do not surrender our honor. If we must fight and die here we will die well, as warriors should."

"I will do my best, Captain. And if there is to be no peace I will return to die with you. Farewell for now."

"Farewell, Blade. For now."

As Blade spurred away he waved at Baber sitting his horse nearby. The old warrior waved back and shouted, "Bring us peace, Sir Blade. I like this place. I will get married again and raise little Mongs."

Someone scoffed and there was laughter. Blade saw the dwarf alone, dismounted, sitting on a rock and peering down into the valley. He rode to him.

Morpho spoke first. "Goodbye, Sir Blade. It is as it must be. I am only sorry for Nantee, who spoke of you last night. She is fond of you and would see you again. Remember her, and me, in this place you go."

Blade smiled at the little man. "How do you guess at these things, little man?"

The dwarf's frozen grin did not change, but his eyes were eloquent.

"I am a fool, Sir Blade, or was until you came. I know. And I know not how I know, any more than I know how it came to me that I should warn you before the fight with Cossa."

"That was wasted." Blade laughed and leaned down to clap the little man on a shoulder. "Goodbye, Morpho."

"Goodbye, Sir Blade. Nothing is wasted."

214

Blade pondered that remark as he rode into the Cath village with Queko. He could make nothing of it.

They jogged past the statue of himself in the square. Blade now thought that the jade man looked a little smug. The thought was torn away by new pain in his head. Not yet, Lord L! Not quite yet.

They halted before the finest house in the village. Queko pointed to the door where Cath sentries stood guard. "She is in there, Sir Blade."

Blade entered and stalked down a corridor, conscious of eyes watching him. Tall, brawny, in his dusty Mong armor, he knew he inspired awe in these slim Cath soldiers. How would Lali greet this great hulk of a soiled apparition? A thousand miles had separated them. Many weeks and bloody events. Would she be the same Lali? His smile was wry. Must he be on guard again so soon, and begin the playing of a new role?

A Cath sentry indicated a door with his lance. Blade threw it open and stalked in without knocking. He slammed it behind him. Lali must know, now and for once and all who was master.

Pain struck at his head.

"Blade. Ah, Blade. You come back to me at last."

She was lying on a round bed in the center of the room. She wore the silken body sheath, nothing more. For a long moment they gazed at each other and he felt himself devoured by those green eyes.

By the bed was a small block of wood. On it was one of the small statuettes of Blade. He picked it up and looked down at her.

"You have made me a God, Lali?"

"I thought you dead, Blade, yet could not bear to lose you. But put it down. A statue is no comfort now! You are here at last. Come, my Blade. Here beside me."

"Soon," he promised. "First there is a matter of which we must speak."

"Speak, Blade? This is not a time for talking."

"I'll keep it brief, then. Listen." He told her what he wanted.

For Lali she was immensely patient. She had paper and brushes brought, and summoned Queko. In his sight and witness she signed a pact of peace with the Mongs. She handed it to Queko.

"Take it to this Rahstum. Arrange a council at once. Twelve of the chiefs from each side. You have all my powers behind you, Queko. If the Mongs desire this valley, to dwell in peace, they are to have it. Now go, Queko, and do as you are bid, and do not disturb me until you are called or I will have Sir Blade cut off your head. Go!"

She raised her arms to Blade. "Now, my love. Come to me. I have ached and dreamed of this too long and will not be denied another moment. Put down that likeness and let me feel your body against mine."

He still held the statuette of himself, so delicately wrought, so clear that his fingers were limned through the stone.

"I am filthy," said Blade. "I have been long on the march."

"I will cleanse you. Come now."

Blade fell to his knees beside her on the bed, still clutching the jade statue, and leaned to kiss her. Her eyes were narrowed, cloaking the green depths, her mouth half open and quivering and she put her hands on his face and gently drew him down.

The pain clawed him like a tiger. Blade gasped and fell forward and felt her soft breasts on his face, her fingers entwined in his thick hair.

"Blade! What, Blade? What is it?"

He heard himself uttering strange sounds, senseless noises. She was raising his head now, coddling him and crying and peering into his eyes.

Blade fell through the jade curtain. He was very tiny now, a Tom Thumb, a midget of a midget, and he fell into her eyes. She snatched at him, with an enormous hand, but too late and he was gone. Down and down, fall-

216

ing and falling, into greenness that shouted at him and shocked and hurt him and was so green that it could not be true. He fell into a green splashing fountain and was shunted into a drain and was gaining speed and more speed and at last was shot out into a green sky where he knew he would be forever and eternally lost. He went curving around a green orb that had Blade printed on it in green letters.

He was in an echo chamber and the sound waves kept thrumming at him and would not cease: *Blade—Blade—Blade—Blade—blade—blad-bla-bl-b*.

Nothing.

Chapter 19

J, listening to the tapes in the audio and projection room far beneath the Tower, frowned now and again at the jade statuette. Exquisite workmanship. No jade like it in the modern world, so said the lab report. The statuette contained a new element, a mineral unknown today. A famous mineralogist was on his way from the States. J shrugged. No great treasure there. Lord L had already admitted that this second venture into Dimension-X had been another failure from the material standpoint.

Lord Leighton was not at all discouraged. He was jubilant. The memory molecule had worked to perfection and he had, to use his former expression, tapped Blade's memory tank and poured the stuff out of him like wine from a barrel. It was all on the tapes.

Blade, under deep hypnosis, spoke in a low, but perfectly audible, monotone. In nine hours he had filled tape after tape.

". . . the Mongs are born horsemen, nomads, and what we would call barbarians. They are short, swarthy of skin, with powerful legs and arms and big chests. Some of the women are beautiful, all are as savage as the men . . ."

J reached to switch off the tape. It was his third hearing. He yawned and rubbed his eyes and was beginning to stuff a pipe when Lord Leighton came in.

His Lordship, J conceded, looked full of beans today. He must have been sleeping better of late. The yellow eyes were clear and even the polio-stricken legs had a new energy. Today Lord L was wearing a discreetly chalk-striped gray lounge suit that somewhat mitigated his hump. His tie was a horror, of course, but then it always was. J, who was prissy in the matter of dress, tried not to look at the red and yellow monstrosity as he held a match to his pipe and asked about Blade.

Lord L clapped his withered hands together and rubbed them. "Fine, fine. Still sleeping it off. Should be ready to leave in a few hours. We'll give the lad a nice long spot of leave. About six months. I should say. Then we can start tuning him up for the next venture."

J was silent. No use voicing his doubts and fears. No use in this world. That particular die was cast.

Lord L was hobbling around the audio room, chuckling to himself and clapping his hands now and then. It was a nervous habit and it *did* get on J's nerves.

After a few moments he said, "Something is amusing you, Leighton? Top secret? Or do you want to share it?"

"My dear fellow! I'm sorry. Nothing, really, but I can't help chuckling when I think of Blade knighting himself. Sir Blade! Heh-heh-heh-heh."

Lord Leighton's laugh reminded J of a file in a lock.

J saw nothing amusing about it. "He needed a title to impress those people. He took it."

Lord L held up a hand. "Do you know, J, a thought has just occurred to me. Why not get the boy on the next Honors list? I am sure I can arrange it. I can swing a bit of weight, you know."

Sir Richard Blade! J pondered. Why not? They were handing them out to actors and jockeys and brewers and soon, God save us all, there would be a rock and roll singer dubbed Knight. He smiled then.

He shook his head. "No. I think not. Call too much attention to Blade, for one thing, and we don't want that. Another, and I am sure about this because I know Dick rather well, is that he wouldn't have any part of it. Dick Blade is a very *real* person, Leighton. He doesn't need a title to shore up his ego. He'd just laugh at us and think we were bonkers."

Lord L chuckled again and shuffled crawfishlike to a chair and eased his old body into it. "All right, man. No need to get testy about it. It was only a passing thought." He took a sheaf of yellow paper from his pocket and began to cover it with cabalistics in a tiny hand.

J supposed that he had sounded testy. His relief at having Blade back safely was so great that he didn't quite know what to do with himself, laugh or cry or go out and get horribly drunk—a thing he hadn't done since Boat Race night in 1928.

Lord L looked at J with his lion eyes. He tapped paper with pencil.

"This second trip into Dimension-X has pretty well proved out my theory, J. God! I wish I could publish it. Heh-heh-heh-heh. Shock half of them into asylums and have the other half on me like vultures. A brand-new and contra-theory of the nature of the universe! There is not *one* universe, there are many. Dozens, hundreds, thousands! Each in its own dimension and perceivable only by brains attuned to it. God, J! When I think of it!"

Lord Leighton swung his arm about violently, cutting a swathe in empty air. "There! You see that. I just swept my arm through an entire world, containing what, and peopled by whom? We cannot know, J, because our brains are incapable of seeing it. It cannot exist for us. But for Blade, ah! For the lad—"

J's pipe had gone out. He ignored it. Very quietly he said, "We'll lose Blade one day, you know. Bound to. Law of averages. He just can't keep going out into Dimension-X time after time and expect to—"

Lord Leighton was paying no attention. He was making marks on paper again and mumbling. "The thing was that the others were content to stop with the space-time continuum, the fourth, and call it quits. Donkeys! The next logical step was inevitable, clear as bumf in the living room, but nothing is ever clear to fools and—"

"Leighton!"

The old man looked up, "Sorry, J. What is it?"

"When can I see Blade? When are you going to release him?"

Lord L pulled out a ponderous old-fashioned watch. "Soon now. He's all yours. Had all his tests, been cleared, fit as a fiddle except for those minor wounds in his leg and side. Hmmm, I've had him four days now, eh? Good. Fine. That's enough. Soon as he comes out of hypnosis and has a final check he's all yours, J. Give him a bonus, a whopping big one, mind you, and tell him to have fun. I won't need him for another six months or so."

As J left the Tower he suddenly thought of Blade's girl, Zoe. Saucy little wench! Sticking her nose into things that didn't concern her. He had to smile as he tried to hail a taxi. The lass had pretty well blown the Whitehall cover thing, nosing about and asking questions and using her relatives and friends. J nodded reprovingly to himself as he stepped into a taxi. The Whitehall bit *had* been a little ramshackle and hastily set up. Have to change it.

2

Blade parked the MG off the lane and vaulted the stile leading to the cottage, thinking of the last time he had cleared it with Zoe in his arms. Zoe!

He had been trying to get in touch with her for two days now. Her family didn't know, or wouldn't tell, where she was. Everywhere he tried he was greeted by the same vague answers:

"Sorry, old man, haven't seen her lately."

"No, Mr. Blade, I do *not* know where Zoe is."

"Seems to me she said something about popping over to Paris for a week or so."

"I heard she had a spot of work to do in Wales."

"No, sir. Miss Cornwall hasn't been in her flat these past four days . . . Thank *you*, sir."

He unlocked the cottage, went around raising windows, then got out because the scent of her was everywhere. His heart ached with a dull ache that both pained and angered him.

He wandered down to the cliff, to the Snuggery, as she called it, and stood looking out over the Channel. It was a day of mist and intermittent sun, and a mild swell was running in to break foaming on the shingle. Gulls circled in boredom and puffins investigated the wet black rocks far beneath him. Blade lit a cigarette and let the wind carry the match away.

They had been playing the quote game that evening. She had not responded, not at all.

Blade was in love and miserable. He admitted it. He was feeling sorry for himself, which was a crime to a man like himself. Okay. He was a criminal. Goddamn it, Zoe! Come back to me. I need you. I want you.

He had never cared for Wordsworth. He did not, especially, care for Wordsworth now. The line just popped into his head.

I wandered lonely as a cloud.

Which line would Zoe quote back to him? There was nothing of love in the poem.

Perhaps—*And then my heart with pleasure fills?*

Something dark caught his eye. It lay in the tall grass where they had been making love that last night.

He took half a dozen steps and picked up the black panties, wispy and crumpled and damp now with rain and dew. Blade smiled ruefully. They *had* been in a hurry that night, when the phone began to ring in the cottage.

He stuffed the damp panties in his jacket pocket and started back up the lane to the cottage. Halfway there he heard it. She had never gotten around to having that sticky valve repaired. Click-click-click—click-click. She was turning off the blacktop now, into the lane.

Blade began to run.